Praise for the Base Branch Series

"Megan Mitcham's books are well-paced, well-plotted suspense novels edged with stunning sensual intensity. Her lovers are cold and deadly--except when they are skin-to-skin. I can't wait for the next book in the series!"

- DELILAH DEVLIN
New York Times and USA Today bestselling author

"Nail-biter all the way to the end."

- Michelle, MsRomanticReads
Adult Romance & Erotic Book Reviews

"This is a fresh and exciting story with lots of great characters."

- 5 Star Amazon Review, Enemy Mine

"Megan now joins my elite team of must read authors. I fell in love with her work in *Enemy Mine*, and it just gets better the more I read."

- TNT Reviews

BOOKS BY MEGAN MITCHAM

BASE BRANCH NOVELS
ENEMY MINE
JUSTICE MINE
STRANGER MINE
WARRIOR MINE
DANGER MINE
PRISONER MINE
SURVIVOR MINE - 2017

BASE BRANCH SUBSERIES
VERSIONS - updated 2016
VIRTUES - 2016
VARIATIONS - 2016

BUREAU NOVELS
FOR ALL TO SEE
PAINTED WALLS

ANTHOLOGIES
ANTICIPATION
CONQUESTS
COWBOY HEAT
ROGUE HEARTS - 2016
SEX OBJECTS - 2016
HIGH OCTANE HEROES
WILD AT HEART VOLUME II
benefiting Turpentine Creek Wildlife Refuge

BOX SET
HEARTS IN DANGER - June 2015
benefiting The American Heart Association

For All to See

See

Bureau Novel #1

Megan Mitcham

Copyright Warning

Published by MM Publishing LLC

Edited by Lacey Thacker

Cover Design by Deranged Doctor Designs

For All to See
All Rights Are Reserved. Copyright 2015 by Megan Mitcham

First electronic publication: April 2015
First print publication: April 2015

Digital ISBN: 978-1-941899-10-6

Print ISBN: 978-1-941899-11-3

To dreams. To the sweat, the tears, and the perseverance it takes to make them a reality. To the people who encourage us along the rocky road. To my grandmother, who led with her heart and followed it with a spunk all her own. Thank you for encouraging my dream. You are loved and missed.

Chapter One

Madelyn heaved the sturdy door to Paradise Bar. The sun-bleached wood worked double-time as a drunk-o-meter. Those only a little tipsy added a Herculean flare to their efforts, grunting and shoving the door into submission. Pass the line into too-intoxicated-to-drive and their wrestle with the door typically ended with a face-plant in the gravel parking lot. The real lushes usually gave up after a few tries and passed out under a nearby table.

Success greeted her as the tinny beat of a scratch band on center stage and the spice of a sizzling mango salmon filet. A waiter held the bubbling dish high in the air along with several peach-colored slushy drinks that frosted the glass mugs. Her mouth watered while her shoulders relaxed into the easy rhythm of the island. In front of her three bartenders manned the square mahogany bar with its faux thatched roof, working their smiles, skills, and tropical shirts.

"Maddy!" The feminine voice cut through the crowd and the music. Not a wonder. On a daily basis the woman's pipes trenched the boisterous noise only elementary school-aged kids could maintain for hours on end.

She turned away from the band and dance floor to the left and skirted through the sea of tables toward her best friend—second best friend, since

Deacon slept in her bed at least two nights out of any given week. Nichole held up a half-syphoned coconut mango-rita in one hand and hurried her over with frantic flaps of the other.

"You're a half a drink behind. Sit and sip." Nichole sat forward and gestured at the untouched beverage complete with a salt halo and cherry on top.

Madelyn shrugged her purse, hung it on the back of her chair, and leaned across the table. Their lips met in a smacking kiss. "Please, tell me that's your first."

"It is, but it won't be my last." Nichole held up a hand. "Not another word until you down it."

Before she finished the last sip the waitress presented another round. Good thing it was hotter than hell outside. Otherwise, the frosty drink would have chilled her brain.

"We still have to get through tomorrow," Madelyn reminded.

"I'm testing in almost every subject. And a dab of concealer will cover up the dark circles."

"Pfh, you haven't ever had dark circles under your eyes." Madelyn scoffed.

Open mouth. Insert foot.

The sole of her sandal tasted bitter. On a blink the memory of Nichole bloody and bruised stained the back of her lids. Her friend had indeed had a black circle under one eye. An eye that had been swollen shut.

Nichole's gaze hit the floor. Her long lashes nearly caressed her cheeks.

"Hey, I'm sorry." Madelyn groaned.

Inky, arrow-straight hair slipped off Nichole's shoulder and curtained a high cheek bone. The waist-long mane grabbed the light, reflecting an ebony gleam. Madelyn reached across the table and covered her friend's hand with her own. Her sun-kissed skin literally paled in comparison to Nichole's toasted almond complexion.

"Hey, are things okay...at home?" She hated to ask, but she refused to shy away from the important things just to soothe her friend's feelings.

Nichole's amber gaze lifted and a wide smile spread across her face. Though, tension remained in the crease of her brow. "Things between Jim and I have been really great."

"Then why the look?"

"Because..." Nichole gnawed her lower lip. "You'll never forget that night."

"You're damn right I won't. And you shouldn't either." Madelyn squeezed the cold hand beneath hers.

"It was one time. I'll never forget. Of course I won't. But I chose to stay. I chose to believe in him. And I won't drive a wedge between us by holding on to the past, to a mistake he knows he made. Things are so good between us. He's not drinking like he used to. He hasn't missed a day of work this season."

Madelyn bit her tongue so hard she expected the tang of copper to fill her mouth. The peak season for mahi-mahi had just begun. And she knew by the end of last season, Jim had missed more hours of work than the impressive number of fish he'd caught in the first half of the harvest.

"I have this look because," Nichole lowered her voice to a whisper, "no matter what I say you'll only see the bad in him. And that sucks because Jim and I have real love, Maddy. It's messy sometimes and our disagreements are heated, but our passion is stronger."

Madelyn released Nichole's hand and grabbed the frosted glass. She pulled a long drink of the fresh glass of bitter-sweet nectar, needing fortification for this conversation.

"When he holds my hand my heart races. When he kisses me it steals my breath."

"I feel the same way before I ride a roller coaster." Madelyn's words sounded as sharp in her ear as the salt tasted on her tongue, but she couldn't stop them. "And it usually ends with me puking. It's called fear."

Nichole's palms flew up as if she were calling on the Lord or summoning his angels to deal with her. "Oh, you're an expert on fear. You use it like a force field to push people away. You keep everyone at a distance. Even me."

Wow. Truth packed a punch. Madelyn folded her arms around her middle to ease the pain of the blow.

Nichole splayed her hands on the lacquer table and leaned forward. Her lips thinned and her eyes softened. "I understand you've been hurt, Maddie. But you shouldn't give up on people because one wronged you. I refuse to give up on Jim because he made a mistake. Just like I won't give up on you."

"You always see the good in things. And people. I can't decide whether it's your gift or curse."

"We're human. Fallible. Completely imperfect. But the beauty of that is we can learn from our mistakes. We can change and grow, if someone loves us enough to put in the effort. To show us we're not a lost cause."

Madelyn gave a weak smile and then pulled her gaze from Nichole's intense stare. She longed to be a lost cause, had moved to the middle of nowhere to be one. Darn her gorgeous, glass-half-full friend. Madelyn's gaze danced across the far wall of glass that opened to the deck. Strands of bare bulbs illuminated the exterior. Beyond it the forest of lounge umbrellas stabbed into the sand and the last whips of color drained from the sky.

Paradise Bar and Grill hopped with locals from lunch through breakfast every day of the week, but tonight it boasted its fair share of tourists. A group of college kids, their Greek letter emblazoned like a Superman symbol on their T-shirts, lined the exterior bar mirroring the row of shots in front of them. She only had a handful of years on some of the collegiates, but their inhibitions subtracted time from their worldly ages.

Two of the students showed more interest in choking each other with their tongues than drinking. The guy's wide hand plowed into the woman's dark corkscrew curls. The coed's greedy hands roved the man's lean pecs, and then slipped south toward his crotch.

Madelyn's gaze leaped back inside. Her cheeks flamed. Not yet ready to deal with her friend, she thought to study the band, but the headline on the flatscreen caught her attention. Inman Trial Begins on Anniversary of Field-Dresser Killings.

She nodded to the television. "You have to admit, some people are lost causes."

Herself included.

Four pictures filled the screen. Each candid shot displayed a brunette beauty with a bright smile.

"You're not a lost cause," Nichole admonished while turning. Her breath caught. The tip of her pointed nose scrunched. A sneer curled her upper lip. "Why don't they just slit his wrists, toss him overboard, and let those girls' families watch the sharks tear him apart?"

"Brutal."

"No, that monster is brutal."

Madelyn blinked wide eyes and struggled to lift her jaw from the floor. "I've never heard you talk like that."

"I don't know how in the world a person could kill another, much less..." Nichole's strong jaw jerked from the report and her gaze flew heavenward. "Much less do what he did to those poor women."

And yet she defended Jim.

Love. What a damn fool thing.

"So," Madelyn cleared her throat. "You admit not all people can be saved?"

"Of course." Nichole's honey gaze prodded Madelyn's. "But you and Jim can. Despite your sketchy track records. I know you can." Nichole grabbed her own drink and pushed the orange concoction toward Madelyn. "Now pick it up. We're here to have a good time."

She didn't know which was more likely to give first—Jim's drinking or her pledge to steer clear of men for the rest of her life. Her poor friend had her work cut out for her.

"To what are we toasting?" Madelyn asked.

A smile gradually stretched Nichole's mouth. Her eyes skittered this way and rolled that, and then settled. "Okay."

Madelyn lifted her glass.

"To the future. To living one little step at a time."

"I can handle that."

Their glasses *clinked.*

"Can you?" Nichole shimmied in her seat. "Because I was thinking Harvey Thompson would look so dashing on your arm."

Madelyn cupped her mouth to keep the chilled liquor from spewing across the table. She swallowed and choked a laugh. "Yeah, right."

"What could you possibly find wrong with him?" Nichole fanned herself. "He's hot."

"Yeah, in that been-around-the-island, knows-every-woman-intimately kind of way."

"Just think how great he'd be in bed." Nichole waggled her brows.

"Wish I could, but I'm too busy thinking about how quickly he could screw me over to think about how well he'd just plain screw me. Besides, the first time I met him didn't go so well."

Nichole's whooping laugh drew several glances. "I almost forgot about that. Tell me again."

"No. You laughed at me for a week after. It's all your fault anyway."

Her friend steeled her face. "I've matured since then."

"It was three months ago."

Nichole drained the last of her 'rita and flagged the waitress for another round. "It's not like you threw the drink in *his* face."

"No. But I threw it in his fancy restaurant." She tipped the last of her drink down her throat and winced at the sharp pain gathering behind her eyes.

"I can't believe you chunked your wine in Evan Whitman's face," Nichole howled.

Her fingers pressed against her forehead. "Brain freeze?"

She grunted and rubbed her tongue onto the roof of her mouth. When the stabbing ceased, she eyed Nichole. "I can't believe I let you talk me into going out with him. What a pompous ass."

"He's the most eligible bachelor in all the Virgin Islands."

"And I'm sure some bimbo with more fashion than common sense would be happy to land him."

"He just wanted to get you naked," Nichole shrugged. "I don't know a man in this place who wouldn't want to do the same."

"Wanting to get my clothes off is one thing. Lack of tact is another. Telling me I'm a prude because I refused to go back to his yacht before we'd even finished appetizers earned him a thousand drinks in the face, if you ask me."

"Sad thing is…" Nichole clutched her side and panted between giggles. "That wasn't the worst date you've let me talk you into."

Yep, Tommy Templeton had been the grandest of dating disasters.

Whether it was the liquor warming her from the inside or her friend's gleeful expression at her failed matchmaking, Madelyn cracked a smile. Then the bottom dropped out. They hooted and howled in a free-for-all of delight.

"It was so bad," Madelyn cackled.

She shouldn't laugh at Nichole's attempts to set her up. The last thing on earth she wanted was another man. In the bedroom B.O.B. worked just fine. Out of the bedroom, Deacon and Nichole filled her need for companionship.

That Nichole tried so tenaciously showed her friend's love. Post-date reports also provided hours of entertainment and an abdominal workout. Madelyn clutched her side. "Stop. You have to stop. You're making my guts hurt."

Tears slipped from Nichole's eyes and ran down her rose-hued cheeks.

"Blot," she ordered, handing her friend a napkin.

"No. You have to stop. He's here." Nichole blotted the mascara running below her eyes. She dragged in a steadying breath.

Madelyn's body flash-fired with a shot of adrenaline. Fight or flight were the only options and she'd trained in both. The smile died on her lips. Her head snapped toward the door. Relief calmed the erratic beat of her heart.

"Relax," Nichole snickered. "It's just Tommy. Not the devil himself. The date wasn't that bad."

She laughed at her overreaction. "You try getting yelled at by Jeannie Lou in front of a crowd of people because I," she added air quotes, "stole her man. I didn't want him. And certainly didn't after he tried to explain that there was more than enough of him to go around."

"A bald-faced lie," Nichole shook her head. "Senior year a bunch of us went to the beach to skinny-dip. He'd be hard pressed to have enough for one."

"And you set me up with him?"

"Hey, it'd be more penis than you've had in the last two years. I figured some was better than none." She shrugged.

Madelyn's shoulders shook in uproarious laughter, dissipating the tension knotting her nape. Nichole's hair pooled on the table as she rested her forehead on the lacquered top and heaved her laughs.

"Oh," Madelyn gasped, "I needed this."

"What's so funny?" a male voice asked.

"Tommy," Nichole snickered her greeting.

Hi, Tiny.

Madelyn bit her lower lip between her teeth to keep from embarrassing them all.

"Glad to see you ladies having such a good time." He planted his hands on the table and leaned over them. His fingers hardly competed with their drinks' straws for width. The white Panama-Jack style button-down he wore billowed around his narrow frame.

"We're just having a girls' night," Nichole explained.

"No boys allowed?" A smirk pulled one side of his cute face.

"Two more," the waitress said in creole. She shooed Tommy Templeton to the side with a string of words Madelyn didn't understand and deposited the drinks.

Nichole laughed silently, picking up the native language since she'd lived in the West Indies all her life. Her ancestors had come to the islands from Spain in the late 1700's. So, her roots ran down to the bedrock.

The official language was English, but most of the island also spoke a unique form of creole. Madelyn had picked up on curse words immediately, thanks to her students. And she was working on the rest. They just had to speak as though they communicated with an infant or toddler.

"No boys allowed," Nichole agreed after thanking the waitress.

"Good thing I'm a man." Tommy dragged over a chair from a nearby table and sat.

Irritation prodded her temper. What was it with men on this island? It was as though women's wishes were suggestions a man could choose to heed or ignore all together. Instead of getting angry, she decided to have some fun. After all, it was girls' night.

"Like I said before," she smiled at Nichole, "sorry I'm late. My feet are just so bloated right now. I could hardly get my shoes on my feet."

A twinkle lit Nichole's dark eyes. "Oh my God, are you on your period too?"

Tommy's hands slid from the table.

"Yeah, the cramps are so bad the first day. And the bleeding. Gah." Madelyn wrinkled her nose for effect.

"A massacre," Nichole nodded, pouting her lips.

Tommy leaned back in his seat, his mouth half-gaped in horror.

"And by day three..." Madelyn added.

"The bloating," she and Nichole said in unison.

"I...ah...I'm gonna go get a drink," Tommy said without moving. "Yeah, yeah. You ladies have —"

A concussive, all-too-familiar roar chilled the blood in Madelyn's veins and silenced the crowded bar. Jim Gallow, the boozer and part-time fisherman, stood at the entrance. Towered, really. On the far side of six feet and two hundred pounds, he had a body made for towing eighteen-wheelers and tossing boulders.

"Get the fuck away from my wife."

Chapter Two

"Oh no," Nichole breathed the words. The joy in her expression mutated into pure dread. At Jim's forceful words her shoulders drew and her head ducked. The glimmer in her eyes shadowed and her murky gaze met Madelyn's. "I'm so sorry. Please," she whispered, "just let me deal with him."

Blood churned in Madelyn's ears like a violent sea.

Breath by steady breath she settled into calm as her body prepared for the confrontation. She refused to answer Nichole one way or the other. What she did depended on Jim.

Tommy stood. When he should've scampered away he spread his feet and puffed his chest.

"Just go, Tommy," Madelyn insisted. "You'll only make things worse." Damn, now she sounded like Nichole.

Behind Jim a bartender flagged his arms toward the back offices. Help was on the way. All they had to do was hold the line. The bouncers would make him leave. They'd had enough practice to perfect the task.

"We've been friends since before you were around, Jimmy Boy," Tommy boasted. "I can talk to your wife if I want. It's not like I'm trying to get in her pants."

Idiot.

Jim stomped forward. In his hand a bottle of Johnny Walker sloshed its meager contents. His thigh grazed a table and sent it careening. The table thudded. Glasses shattered. The couple who'd been enjoying barbecue ribs and draft beers shrieked their displeasure. Jim's bright blue eyes remained locked on Tommy.

The closer Jim stalked the quieter Tommy's sermon grew, but he didn't stop. That took bravery or stupidity. Maybe both.

"It's not the dark ages, man. You can't say who she talks to just because you married her. She's not going to cheat on you. I don't know why, but she loves you. Even though you're a total—"

Madelyn knew it was coming and still she didn't see it until Jim's knuckles connected with Tommy's jaw. The poor guy's head snapped back. A crack pierced the air. Her stomach gave at the sound just as Tommy's slack body descended.

She lunged forward. Ice-cold liquid froze her skin and soaked the front of her pants. Madelyn ignored the tilting table and falling 'ritas. Her arms wrapped Tommy's waist. His height pitched her forward, but she shot a foot out. Straining every muscle, she controlled the man's fall.

"Jim, please stop this right now," Nichole begged. "If you keep it up, Chief will lock you up for the night."

Madelyn straightened in time to see Jim wrench Nichole's wrist from the back of the chair and yank her from the only remaining seat at the capsized table. Her friend used the wooden chair as an anchor, tugging against her husband's insistent tug. It was as effective as holding on to a blade of grass in a typhoon.

One jerk of Jim's thigh-sized arm and Nichole lurched forward, dragging the chair with her.

"Please, Jim. Baby," Nichole sniffled.

The bouncers still hadn't made their grand appearance from the back rooms. What were they waiting for, special music and a spotlight?

"Hey, Jim?" Madelyn shouted over the din.

His sloshy gait slowed. He turned and pulled Nichole tight to his side. She released the chair. Her gaze pleaded with Madelyn. If only she could tell whether it begged her to help or stop. She didn't want to make Nichole's situation worse, but by damn if she'd let this man beat on her friend again.

The dregs of his whiskey swirled as he used the bottle to gesture toward him and Nichole. "We're good." He stabbed the spout toward her. Several drops of amber liquid spilled onto the floor. "You're the trouble maker. You mind your own business."

Shoulder length locks framed Jim's face. Not the slightly greasy roots, the sweated-through T-shirt, nor even the sneer he centered on her detracted from the beautifully sculpted lines of his cover-worthy face.

Gorgeous or not, muscled or not, hung like a rhino or not, Madelyn couldn't fathom why her friend would stay with a man who treated her like a possession.

"You made it my business. The only question is...do you remember what I told you?" Madelyn asked in a voice so low he'd have to strain to hear.

Nichole grimaced.

Jim shoved his wife to the side. He threw the bottle on the ground next to his feet. The shards skittered across the floor. One jagged fragment hit her sandal and bounced in the opposite direction.

His shoulders dropped. Legs the width of old oaks powered forward. All Jim's mass and drunken rage barreled toward Madelyn.

Chapter Three

Madelyn's eyes opened to the blackness in her bedroom. The harsh snores of her companion rumbled from the other side of the bed.

Sneaky, sneaky.

His bed was sufficient enough, but on occasion he took liberties with hers. The hair and dingy smell wasn't appreciated on her linens, but the comfort of his presence was nice. Instead of evicting him, she gently patted the pillow next to hers.

Deacon sleepily wiggled his way up to oblige. The weight of his cinderblock head puffed the air out of the pillow.

"You big smelly lug. How about a bath today?"

He shuddered a breath and then settled into a rhythm of deep, even breathing.

"Faker," she prodded.

Deacon groaned.

Over the loud and lulling breathing of her furry friend, the gulls and terns outside her window thrilled and keened, taunting their early morning feast. The smooth stitching of her sheets and cool weight of the comforter invited her to stay a while longer. With a rolling stretch she moved farther into them, not yet ready to welcome the day.

She reeled.

Her brain sloshed back and forth. It pinched and tweeted the nerves behind her eyes. Placing a hand on either side of her skull, Madelyn tried to steady her thoughts.

It was Friday. She struggled to think through the tequila haze. If she could make it through the day, she would have the weekend to recover.

One drink was her usual check, but she and Nichole had been in rare form last night. They'd whooped it up something big until Jim had shown up and instantly darkened the mood.

What a bastard.

Though...seeing him trip over her well-timed evasion and slide across the floor on his face had been the highlight of her night. Second best came watching the bouncers drag his sorry keister out the front door.

Madelyn grinned, suddenly ready to tackle the day.

She gingerly sat, which immediately sent Deacon into playful fits. He bounded off the bed and danced. His nails tapped on the wood floor. And though she could only make out his silhouette, it was enough to make her laugh out loud. He wagged so forcefully it towed his behind from side to side, allowing the tip of his tail to whack into each side of his ribs.

"You can't talk and still I can hear it— 'Come on, lazy, get a move on it.'" In submission Madelyn slung the covers back and obeyed.

She placed both feet on the floor and held the edge of the nightstand, just in case. Her equilibrium withstood the test. Her stomach, on the other hand, was questionable, to say the least.

Stagnant liquor coated her mouth. She shuffled to the bathroom, scrubbed her teeth, splashed water on her face, and pulled her long hair into a pony tail, all without turning on a light. In the kitchen she slowly ate a banana, and then she sipped some water. Feeling slightly better she dressed in her workout gear. If she could stomach it, she'd grab a better breakfast before work.

Deacon tap-danced at the front door. When she stepped toward the door he yipped.

"Sure you're excited. Because you're going to win."

He barked at that. The vociferous noise bounded back and forth in her skull.

"You know the rules. No barking before sunrise. I'm sticking firm to that today. So don't give me any droopy-faced looks and think you'll get away with it."

Dutifully, he chuffed.

"I swear you're brilliant."

He rubbed his head into her open palm. She opened the door, and then held tight to the doorframe. "Okay," she whispered. Ninety-five pounds of bone and muscle rocketed out the door with more enthusiasm than was humanly possible.

Madelyn stepped from the tiled floor and her athletic shoes settled into the sand. Her lungs filled with salty air. A sigh lifted some of the fog of her mild hangover. Deacon barked.

"Deacon Garrett, the rules," she chided.

She flipped the bottom lock and turned to glare at him. His stocky frame faced the lush vegetation at the back of her small house. The black brindle pattern that made him look like a panther with multi-colored tiger stripes stood out against the white beach backdrop. Her gaze rose over the steep mountain to their back. The first rays of sunshine lightened the sky over the low peak.

Deacon tilted his head, sniffed, and barked again. This time the noise had an irritated edge to it.

"Come on, boy. Leave the monkeys alone. We're late."

With no time for a warm up or easy pace, Madelyn hurried down to the shore where the wet-packed sand held against the force of her churning legs and took off. Or so she thought. Deacon's incessant circling told her she'd eased off instead. His mocking didn't faze her like it normally would have. Most of her effort went to finding a rhythm, keeping it, and holding on to her stomach's contents.

Her calves burned. A sting settled in her chest. The mild morning waves burbled to her right. That sound, and knowing Nichole would be waiting for her, and probably worrying by now, kept her legs moving.

Finally the diamond-white sand met pitted and broken asphalt. Madelyn eyed her destination a quarter mile past the beach's edge. The ramshackle metal building had outlived its better days. Still it remained useful, like an old man past his prime who worked his garden daily. It refused to be resigned. Its light-cream paint was chipped in places and the wooden stairs of its entrance were warped by the moist air and unrelenting sun.

The gleam of its interior lights reassured her. A neon blue sign, jutted out above the entrance, professed *Adisa Gym*. The sign beckoned like a light house's beam. The solid surface under her feet improved the resistance and allowed her a strong final effort. A burst of speed propelled her legs to stretch and pull faster and faster. She ate the road beneath her and smiled when Deacon pulled alongside her, lowered his head, and pushed too.

Madelyn dragged herself inside the gym door. Deacon pranced in front of her and scooted off to make his rounds. Investigating every smell and greeting every patron was hard work.

Dried sweat mixed with the musk of new in the humid air. The stench had become a comfort. She filled her lungs with it as she worked the tremors out of her leg, resting her foot high on the base of the fighting ring and stretching. Several regulars were scattered across the gym. Some wailed on heavy bags while others pounded weights up into the air with animalistic grunts and groans, their strained muscles binding with tension.

At least I'm not the only one moving slowly this morning.

"How's my best girl?" a booming voice asked.

"Don't let Nichole hear you say that," Madelyn warned.

Amadi Chiduben, the owner and Madelyn's mentor, strode his monumental frame from the hallway that housed lockers, bathrooms, and his personal quarters. Muscles wrapped muscles forming a sloping topography of potent ability beneath his midnight-sky complexion.

"She's not here yet. Else, I'd never have said it." His dark lips parted, revealing a brilliant smile. "Nichole is a lover. You're a fighter."

She was now. Thanks to him and years of training.

"There's a tournament in Miami in two months. Let me take you."

"You never give up, do you?"

"Never. So?"

His Nigerian accent and perennially positive attitude always lifted her spirits. She shook her head.

"If I don't bring my best fighters to the match it isn't a true test of my skill as an instructor."

"Pff, if there isn't a first and a *really* first-place trophy, I don't think you have to worry." She pointed to the bloated trophy cabinets framing the entryway. "You've got first covered and have for the last... How many years?"

"The last ten years. Don't let him razz you." Ekene snaked an arm around Madelyn's neck. His thick bicep bore pressure on her windpipe. Her foot slipped off the edge of the ring. The young man's fit body snugged against her backside and he lifted slightly. She fought the instinctual panic, slacking her muscles. "Besides, cousin, she'd have to beat me in the tournament. And we all know that'd never happen."

Using the last bit of wind in her lungs, she laughed. He paused in surprise. Madelyn bent at the waist, pushed with her hips, and tucked into a ball. Amadi's smug relative flipped over her back, landing on his own in front of her. His ready feet braced his landing.

Madelyn stood wary, despite the grin on her face. This kid was tricky.

"Well, you look hung over, but you don't act like it," he groaned from the floor.

"I should have whacked you in the nuts and called it good." She shook her head. "Kids these days. No respect."

"Tell me about it." Amadi folded his arms. His tank-top displayed the kind of chiseled muscle men half his age would kill for. "You two kids, in the ring." He inclined his head toward the eighteen-by-eighteen square of canvas, ropes, and a little bit of padding.

"How old are you, anyway?" Madelyn asked.

"Stalling I see," Ekene boasted. He flipped up from the concrete floor and puffed out his chest.

"I don't think that'll help," she said.

"No it won't. I'll still take you eight points to your one," his brow furrowed. "Wait...what are you talking about?"

"Puffing out your chest won't help. I'll just knock the air right out of it," Madelyn explained with a smile.

Instead of rolling onto the mat like normal, she hiked one knee and her palms onto the edge and pulled herself up. A hand wrapped around her ankle and yanked. She caught her weight on her hands.

Ekene's snicker echoed behind her.

"I'm almost older than both of you put together. Now, let's get some work done. I'm amazed either of you has learned anything at all," Amadi explained.

"He's twelve," she pointed at Ekene. "And I've been twenty-one for several years now."

"Ha-ha," the young man scoffed. "I'll be eighteen in two weeks."

"So you're seventeen. That would put you near forty," she said swinging a look at Amadi. "No way."

The man was a top-ranked warrior in Dambe —Nigerian boxing—and wrestling. He'd unseated the reigning champion in Mayolet stick-fighting two years ago. And he was the reigning champion for five years running in the Shotokan discipline, knife work being his specialty. He looked maybe thirty, but he was nearly as old as her dad.

Just wow!

"Way," he said without inflection. "Face your partner."

She faced the younger—severely more immature— version of Amadi. They bowed.

Twenty minutes passed in a fury of flying fists, knees, and feet.

Their sweat slicked the mat by the time Amadi called for a break. Both she and Ekene hung on the top rope of their respective sides.

"Nice work. Both of you. Once you started working," Amadi said from the floor.

"I think it's Nichole's turn," Madelyn sighed between pants.

"She's not here." Her mentor's voice came from far away.

Madelyn was instantly in her head reliving the nightmare less than a year ago when Nichole had last missed a scheduled workout. She blinked the dread away and hopped out of the ring. "Can I use your phone? I need to make a call."

"Why else would you want to use the phone?" Ekene taunted.

She rushed for the office.

"Sure," Amadi called out.

Madelyn wiped perspiration onto her pant leg, snatched the phone from its cradle, and punched in Nichole's number. The line rang for what seemed like a thousand years. Then the message picked up.

Nichole's bright voice filled the line. "I can't get the phone right now. Leave a message and I'll get to you just as soon as I can. I hope you have a great day."

"Nichole, call me at the gym or at the school as soon as you get this. I won't judge. I'll try not to anyway. I just need to know you're okay. Call me."

Damn, if only Madelyn had her own phone. But she'd left it behind and stubbornly refused to get a new one. Most of the time it didn't matter. But now...

What if Nichole had gotten sick last night or had a car accident on the way home? What if Jim had hurt her again? He had been pretty irate when he crashed their party. But she'd felt certain he would have found a quiet place to pass out before Nichole arrived home last night.

If she had a phone, Nichole could have called her and told her she would not be able to make it to the gym this morning. Madelyn reconsidered the notion and decided not all conventional things were bad. Maybe she could lighten up. A little.

Perturbed, she headed back to the lesson.

"Everything all right?" Amadi asked.

No one knew about the incident. Nichole had made her swear on their friendship. So, she ground her teeth to nubs, nodded, and climbed back into the ring. She bowed blindly and fought.

"Madelyn, focus!" Amadi ordered as Ekene's hand and feet flew at her from every direction.

The smug kid laughed, "Ha, she's all mine."

The presumptuous comment caught her attention by the throat. She zoned in on his movements and blocked his onslaught, save one kick that landed solidly in her core. Caving minimally from the impact she inhaled a jagged breath, pushing the pain deep inside. She rebounded with precision.

Two combination kicks herded Ekene to the ropes. "I don't hear you running your mouth now," she taunted. A three-combination hand-strike assault ended with a clean, but soft, thrust to his windpipe.

"That-a-girl, you neva give up!" Amadi called out from the rope's edge.

After a series of energized and well-aimed attacks, Madelyn took the match ten to eight. In her distracted and sub-par physical condition the win surprised her. The two fighters respectfully tapped gloves and bowed signifying the end of the lesson.

Not being the type to take anything seriously, Ekene grabbed her in a headlock. He administered a standard-issue noogie to the crown of her head. The hair on top of her head escaped its holder, forming a terrible nest of knots almost instantly. While fighting tremors of laughter, Madelyn tried to wiggle herself loose. Amadi began his palaverous speech about the importance of maintaining a clear focus.

They all ignored Deacon's low warning growl. It happened from time to time when a character he didn't care for crossed the gym's front. But the crack of impact and the explosion of shattering glass halted their friendly banter. Their heads snapped up to find the culprit standing tall in the gym entrance. Blood trickled from his balled fist while a knife gleamed in his other.

Deacon stood at attention, as did the hair along the path of his spine. His lips curled over long teeth and revealed healthy pink gums. With one word from Madelyn the fearless animal would own the situation. But she gave no such order. She was too horrified, angry, and confused to release him.

Forcing herself into action, she patted the nest of her hair down quickly and spoke, while the other three cautiously took in the drama. "Jim, what the hell are you doing?"

"Where is she, you stupid bitch?" He pointed the knife accusingly in her direction.

Angered and confused by the allegation, she fired back. "Have you even been home? I've known you to stay out and drink the night through. And I can smell the alcohol on you from here."

"I didn't put a finger on her. Where did you put her?" Jim barked.

Silence stretched taught to the point of snapping bones. He'd gone off the deep end. What had he done to her friend?

Jim took a step forward. "Tell me where she is or I swear I'll gut you."

"Enough!" Amadi roared.

Madelyn had enough of Jim Gallow's knife-wielding idiocy. And that threat crossed the line. Nichole was a grown woman. For better or worse, she could make her own decision. But it'd be a frosty day in the islands before she'd let that ogre intimidate her.

Before she moved, Amadi bounded off the ring's edge. He stopped three feet in front of Jim. An intense stare willed the belligerent man to take his shot. Jim, apparently not drunk enough to delude himself into thinking he could win the bout—though the two men stood eye to eye—turned and fled, trailing a litany of curses behind him.

Chapter Four

Nathan shoved through the door as though reliving his glory days as a defensive tackle for Ole Miss. The name placard that read Special Agent Nathan Brewer, complete with the noble FBI seal, rattled. If the thing fell off, he'd chunk it in the garbage. Maybe then people would leave him the hell alone.

He had to escape the incessant cheers, pats on the back, and "at a boy's" flying his way from every co-worker. Hell, even the damn mail boy had crossed over to the dark side, begging a high five like a two-year-old. Some jackass had even brought a cake. The red velvet confection looked like a man...a man with a bull's eye on the center of his forehead.

How quickly people forgot. He tugged at his collar. Only four days ago his friend and partner, for all intents and purposes, Keen Hunt, had been lying in the ICU in critical condition. The image of Keen's mother sobbing still floated in his frontal lobe. Her pain haunted him. The fear of losing her child had the regal woman broken and inconsolable on the hospital floor.

No one had been cheering then, and they shouldn't be cheering now. Yes, miraculously Hunt was in the clear. But he still had a long road to a full recovery.

Nathan dropped into the standard issue uncomfortable-as-hell office chair, ignored its protesting groan, and stretched his legs across the floor. He canted his head toward the piles of paperwork awaiting his attention. Each form wanted to know the same details over and over again about "the case" as everyone seemed to call it. He slumped deeper into his chair, not wanting to give the forms or the details his regard.

The partners were considered heroes where the FBI and U.S. government were concerned. They wouldn't approve the term. They'd simply done their jobs.

And nearly gotten Hunt killed.

The pair had tracked the notorious Cuban mob boss, Lorenzo Famosa, for the better part of two years. They had studied his behavior, his contacts, his hit men, and his investors. When this circus was finally wrapped up they would take down half the dirty underworld in a single move. Patiently and diligently, they had worked and waited until time for the take down.

Brewer and Hunt had planned it to perfection. Tactical units had been placed at the front and back of the abandoned warehouse where the transaction was set to take place. The units were waiting for the word to bar any escape. They had ambulances and federal vehicles stashed in an adjacent warehouse. And when the microphones and cameras had caught the dealing, they moved in.

Everyone was in cuffs and getting shoved into FBI vehicles in less than a minute. It had gone off without a hitch—until they were double-crossed by one of their own.

Nathan leaned over his desk and rubbed his fists on his forehead. The image of his friend lying in a pool of blood stained his mind. His fingers still felt the flesh and blood of his friend's near-fatal wound. He'd had to place two fingers in the hole to stop his friend from bleeding out. The bullet had demolished Hunt's right shoulder and clipped his artery. They were lucky the ambulance had been so close.

A squeaky hinge alerted Nathan to company. "Brewer, my office," the gruff voice of his superior demanded. He nodded in response.

Christ, what now?

Nathan went in with his guns locked and ready. "Sir, as I told you before. I had no alternative. Agent Helm and Famosa had to be eliminated as threats. Keen was—"

Williams' raised hand stopped his explanation cold. The hand told him to sit, too. Nathan complied.

Dr. James Williams, Ph D and MD, sat across from Nathan. His crinkled face told his story. He was born, he started working, and he never quit. Nathan had been working for the director for five years. He respected his opinion and his work ethic, to a point. But Nathan thought he could lighten up a little. A tight drink with a loose woman every now and then would do the trick, but he wasn't about to voice the suggestion.

He liked his job. Even when he hated it.

"I know you just got done with a doozy and I know you're down a partner. But we got a break in the Field-Dresser case."

Nathan's shoulders reared. His heart sat on his tongue.

"I need you to look into it," Williams continued.

Nathan swallowed. He sucked in a deep breath, and then another before he could speak. "You told me to back off. No, you ordered me to back off," he bit.

"We both take orders, Brewer. Sometimes, we don't like or agree with them. We do it anyway because order sets us apart from the apes. Just barely." Williams' hazy blue stare held firm.

"Who told you to back off and why?" Nathan asked with fewer teeth than before.

"They had their man. Just because you didn't believe it didn't mean they didn't have all the evidence they needed to go to trial."

"It's no coincidence that we're talking about this now, when yesterday was the anniversary. He's taken another one." Nathan nearly snarled.

"I flagged all missing persons reports for the island of Tortola in the British Virgin Islands back when you predicted it'd be his next location. It's up to you to discern whether it's the Field-Dresser's work or a shitty coincidence."

"The missing woman has dark hair, a pretty smile, and a long lean body."

Williams' upper lip twitched and it was all the answer Nathan needed.

"I'm sending Dick with you."

Nathan sawed his teeth.

"Y'all are wheels up at Homestead in an hour. I suggest you work out your differences in-air. I won't have the two of you screwing this up over a passed rivalry."

Nathan imagined opening the hatch mid-flight and shoving Special Agent Richard Kepler out without a parachute. "Yes sir." Talk about working things out in air.

Chapter Five

"Stay, bud," Madelyn ordered. Her whisper echoed in the marble entrance of the police substation, but Deacon's whine overpowered it. The silk of his ears nuzzled her bare calf. He'd stuck close all day, refusing to chase monkeys during her first two classes or play with her students at break. She supposed he only wanted to comfort her, but his somber mood seemed more foreboding than her rampant imagination.

She crouched as demurely as she could in a skirt and heels and cradled his head. "No dogs allowed. Do you want Mrs. Edna to yell at us again?"

His gaze lifted to the ceiling. If a dog could roll their eyes, Deacon had. Madelyn kissed his forehead, rubbed his fat jowls, and then stood. With a pouting huff he plopped himself down in a corner of the large corridor.

Madelyn left her only source of comfort on the chilly marble and clacked her way through the main hallway. The knot that had been growing in her stomach all day cinched tight.

Where the hell was Nichole?

Two men loitered in the building's foyer. A skinny man with a sideways stare and a terrible case of the shakes slouched in a corner chair. Track marks, both fresh and fading, marred his arm.

Desperation bloated his sunken eyes. An odd sadness washed over her. She couldn't imagine needing something so badly that it'd be worth your life.

The second occupant's leather vest boasted a screaming skull in flames. His steel-shackled arms paid tribute to Anita on one and Layla on the other. She wondered briefly if they were mother and daughter tributes or lovers dueling for the burly man's affections. She hoped her first notion was accurate because, given the evil scowl plaguing his face, she could not see how this brute's heart could seduce two women with its spell.

Madelyn hurried to the first set of double doors and peeked her head through the small, square window. Edna—the receptionist from hell—sat behind her desk tapping the skinny gold watch on her wrist. Squaring her shoulders she pushed through the door.

"Hi, Edna. How are you doing today?"

"I'm trying to keep Chief's schedule, if you people would oblige," the women snapped.

"I wasn't given a specific time to meet him. He told me to come after school," Madelyn explained.

"School let out an hour and forty-five minutes ago."

"Yes, but then I have tutoring."

"She told me all about it," Chief explained from his doorway.

"Well, why didn't you tell me?" Edna squawked.

"I've been a little busy, wouldn't you say?" Adrian Tau, better known as Chief, though he wasn't a police chief, stepped out of his office and motioned Madelyn forward with a wave. "Don't mind Mrs. Edna. She's just ornery because her husband wants to postpone their anniversary celebration for a week."

"No need to air my business," the older woman said.

When Madelyn approached, Chief opened his arms wide and she surprised herself by diving into his embrace. Her slender frame turned into a puff of smoke in his magic act, disappearing in his arms. The comfort was something she wouldn't have normally allowed, but she accepted the kindness she needed. She sank from the weight of worry. Emotions crashed against the dam inside her, but she wouldn't permit them to breach.

"I'm surprised he didn't postpone it indefinitely," he chuckled softly.

Madelyn collected her scattered thoughts and pushed back from the bear hug. "Hey, Chief."

The brackets of his mouth thinned as his lips pursed. "You look a little ragged."

"I feel it," she admitted.

"Well, come on in. We'll see if we can figure out what's going on." He stepped to the side and ushered her into his office with a hand on the middle of her back.

She tried to ease the tension in her muscles, but they didn't listen. She'd invited his touch by accepting his hug. The line had been breached and there was no going back. A full breath eased the worst of her discomfort...until she choked on the exhale.

A man leaned broad shoulders against the wall to the right of Chief's desk. One foot kicked over the other and his arms folded across his chest. His sharp khaki suit, striped shirt, and bold tie said, 'money,' and, 'turn up the AC.' His face, on the other hand, said nothing at all. His classically handsome features and dark eyes gave nothing away.

She paused in the doorway. Chief's soft belly bumped into her back, forcing her to continue into the office on her own two feet or on her face. "Sorry," she breathed. I didn't realize anyone else would be here."

Madelyn forced her feet forward into the small office, and then noticed a second suited man sitting in front of Chief's desk. He was beautiful in an overly obvious way. He looked like Barbie's husband, Ken. She squinted against the blinding shine from his blond hair, blue eyes, and perfect smile.

Chief skirted her and moved behind his desk, but didn't sit. "These gentlemen surprised me with a visit just a few short minutes before you arrived." He raised a palm to her, and then swung it toward the man at the wall. "Madelyn Garrett. This is Special Agent Nathan Brewer with the FBI."

"The FBI?" The shock translated into stilted syllables.

Nichole had hardly been missing for a day. Why was the FBI involved and why was the agent staring at her? He didn't smile like his counterpart. Did she have something on her face or did the mere sight of her piss him off?

Finally, his lips parted. "Mrs. Garrett," he said in the deepest, sexiest voice her ears had ever had the pleasure of absorbing. Her heart stopped beating. She wanted to clutch her chest to restart it. Upon further thought, she wanted to slap herself for being so senseless. He'd said two words. And he was a man. Just a man. And men lied. They cheated. They decimated futures.

"It's Ms. Garrett," she blurted. Trying to recover, she added, "You can call me Madelyn."

Before Chief could continue with his introductions, the second suit stood and snagged her hand. This guy gave everything away in a dashing smile, arched brow, and an overbearing lean. "Ms. Garrett, I am Special Agent Richard Kepler. Please don't be alarmed by our presence. We're here to help."

She shook his hand quickly, and then withdrew from his touch. He stepped closer and placed his hand on the small of her back, damn near her butt. In fact, his fingers brushed the band of her thong. "Please, have a seat," he nudged.

Madelyn glared at his hand. "Agent Kepler, I am perfectly capable of finding my own seat. You didn't have to show me where it was. It's attached to my body. Has been for years."

"Yes, ma'am." The agent's hand went up as though her ass had burned him. If only that were her super-power.

A single deep chuckle warmed the room. By the time she moved the chair nearest the door a few more inches from Agent Kepler and sat, all the men's faces were masks of concern or impassivity. She placed her purse on her lap and crossed her legs at the ankle.

"Why is the FBI involved? My friend has only been missing for a few hours. Is Jim involved in other crimes?" Madelyn asked.

"They're here to audit this interview." Chief glowered at each man in turn. "That means I ask the questions and you listen." Neither man spoke. "They'll question you later, if they choose."

The bear of a man swung his gaze back to her. "I entered Nichole's missing person's report into the system immediately. She's a woman of routine. She'd never abandon her students or husband. We know that. So, I didn't wait the mandatory seventy-two hours. The report apparently flagged due to similarities in an investigation. It's nothing for you to worry about, Maddy."

Chief sat and rested his forearms on his desk. On either side, stacks of files cluttered his workspace. A furrow creased his tanned forehead. "What crimes are Jim involved in that you know about?"

Madelyn fiddled with the tan leather strap on her bag. She'd promised Nichole she wouldn't say anything about her and Jim's relationship 'troubles,' as she liked to mildly refer to them. But she wasn't here, there, or anywhere, which suspended all pinkie promises.

"Domestic abuse," she said.

Chief's round shoulders straightened and he threaded his fingers. "Now, I've known Jim to hit the bottle pretty hard, but I've never seen bruises on Nichole. The times I've been called to the house their matches were verbal, not violent."

"It only happened once...that I know about. She made me promise not to tell anyone. But it was bad. She called me crying in the middle of the night. Before she said anything a loud crash disconnected the line. I got dressed and headed straight there. He'd beaten her so badly both her eyes were swollen shut."

"Why didn't you report it?" Chief demanded.

"I was selfish," she admitted. "I wanted to keep my friend instead of doing what I knew I should have. She refused to go to the hospital. Refused to get you involved. So, I took her home and nursed her for nearly three weeks."

"Six months ago she visited her sister in Spain." Chief balled one hand into a fist. The enormous fingers bulged like overstuffed sausages. A yellow tint discolored his skin as though the

constriction had cut all blood supply to his
extremities. But his face remained neutral. "She
never left the island?"

Madelyn shook her head. A sharp pang of
regret jabbed between her ribs.

"What was that look?" Agent Brewer asked in
a near whisper. Still, his voice stirred something
wicked inside her.

"I'm asking the questions," Chief barked.
"How'd you keep Jim from harassing you?"

"That night, I found Nichole stumbling down
the road almost a mile from her house. Jim didn't
know I had her, but it only took him two days to
come banging on my door. I told him if he pressed
her to come back...or ever hurt her again, I'd make
her vanish."

The room iced over at that little statement.
Agent Kepler stiffened beside her. Chief's chair
creaked. Agent Brewer didn't move, but the weight
of his stare doubled.

"What did you mean?" Chief Adrian Tau
asked.

"I meant he'd never see her again. Nichole and
I made a pact that first night. If he ever hurt her
again, she'd leave the island. She'd move someplace
he'd never find her and start over."

"Nichole doesn't have the means to do that.
She's a school teacher and Jim drinks through his
fishing money," Chief explained.

"I do," she said simply.

He waited for her to elaborate. When she
didn't, he sat up in his seat. "You're a school teacher
too."

She nodded.

"Fine," he huffed. "Is that what's happening
here? Did you make Nichole disappear?"

"No." Madelyn strangled her leather purse strap. "Like I told you on the phone, we left Paradise last night about an hour after Jim's tirade and that was the last time I saw her. She was supposed to meet me at the gym this morning, but she never showed. I held out hope until she didn't show for work."

"After we spoke I checked Nichole's house. No one was home, but everything looked normal. No signs of a struggle or that she packed in a hurry."

"Did you go inside?" Madelyn asked.

"No. I looked through the windows."

"Was her car there?"

"Who's running this investigation?" Chief snapped.

Madelyn sat back in her seat, surprised, but not deterred by the man's frustration. Actually, his resentment fueled her own. Her friend was missing and they all sat in a circle talking about it, instead of doing something to find her. Well, she and Chief talked. The other two—most qualified to handle the task—sat like spectators at a tennis match, watching the back and forth.

Chief cleared his throat. "Her car wasn't there. I checked local spots and her mother's house. I questioned Jim at work. Now, I need you to tell me what happened last night at the bar."

She recalled the scene just as it had unfolded. When the image of Jim dragging Nichole toward the door flashed in her mind, her conscience caught up with her. She should have insisted Nichole stay with her last night, but she hadn't. And now everything was a mess.

"What happened next?" Chief prodded.

"I goaded him so he'd let Nichole go. It worked like a charm," she said acidly.

"Now why would you go and do a thing like that? Jim is a very strong man. He could've really hurt you."

"It probably wasn't the smartest thing, but I had to do something to help her."

He shook his head. "Keep going."

"He let her go and came after me. Luckily, I hadn't had any more to drink than I had, and he'd had far more to drink than he should've. Bouncers intercepted his second attack and hauled him out the door."

Chief's voice turned into a reprimand. "You mean to tell me you grappled with Jim Gallow? Madelyn, he's nearly twice your size. Damn it girl, you're going to get yourself into a real spot one day walking around like you're Wonder Woman."

"Nichole and I left an hour later," she continued, ignoring his rant. "The bouncers escorted us out in light of the evening's events. Jim was nowhere to be seen. We both figured he'd found a quiet place to pass out. We got in our cars—I'd parked next to her—and pulled out of the lot. Nichole turned right toward her house and I went left toward mine."

They talked about the crowd, the music, the weather. When Madelyn was thoroughly exhausted with the sound of her own voice Chief got her a glass of water and they went over everything again.

She tried to keep focused on the task at hand, but restlessness had her eyes darting. Time and again they landed on the man leaning on the wall. The typical island man was more boy than man, long-haired and hippie like. That type was easy to ignore. But this specimen's brooding presence demanded her attention.

Her pulse quickened and she flushed with a forgotten heat. Hormones dormant for too long raged. Luckily, sanity body-checked her quick and dirty fantasy of exactly what she could do with that hard mouth.

When every detail of the night had been picked over like a carcass on the forest floor Chief leaned back in his chair. "Maddy, you've given me a lot to work with. I'll let you know the moment I have any information. Now get out of here. I know Deacon is waiting for you to go for your evening run."

Madelyn extended her hand to Chief a little too quickly, betraying her desperation to be free of the suffocating room and all the men inside it. "Thanks, Chief. Agents." She nodded at the strangers and then stood.

Agent Kepler hopped to attention. Madelyn turned away before he could say or do anything that would ultimately land her in jail. Through the glass she saw Edna's tapping foot and the hand on her hip. The woman's ample behind held open one of the double doors.

Please not now.

Before she fully opened Chief's office door the woman lit into her. "Ms. Garrett, we've talked about your beast before. It's a danger and shouldn't be allowed on the island. But it is most certainly not allowed in my building."

She'd tried letting her pup's good behavior and loving manner speak for themselves. She'd tried wooing the woman with her favorite goodies. She'd tried a community petition in which she'd logged over three thousand names. Madelyn breathed deeply, pulled the door closed behind her, and smiled. She was done trying.

"Service dogs are allowed in the building."

"He's a service dog?" Edna scoffed.

Madelyn conceded with a nod.

"Oh really?" Her haughty nose rose by the second. "What is his function? You're obviously not blind. Do you have seizures?"

"I suffer from multiple personality disorder."

The woman's eyes narrowed.

"Deacon's presence keeps Mary Lynn in check. Trust me," she said sweetly, "you want him around. Otherwise, she would break free and tell you in none too kind words exactly what kind of a bitch you are." She skirted past the dumb-struck woman. "Have a great day."

The tiny triumph she gained from besting mean ole Edna faded by the time she barreled through the station's main entrance with Deacon on her heels. Heat from the mid-day sun infused her irritation with strength.

Mr. FBI hadn't seemed the least bit interested in her or in Nichole's disappearance. He'd only asked a single question the entire two hours she was being interviewed. And he hadn't even taken notes. Agent Kepler was all too interested in her legs. He hadn't stopped inspecting them like bits of fiber under a microscope.

Bureaucrats just here for a paycheck.

Madelyn wrestled open the door to her Jeep. Deacon leaped inside and hopped the console to his seat. The pup's lolling tongue and intelligent eyes only amplified the pain of regret. If Nichole had been sitting there the night before, she wouldn't be missing. She slid into the seat.

Helplessness closed itself in the cab with her, despite Deacon's normally bracing presence. She snapped her seatbelt into place, determined to eradicate that feeling.

Chapter Six

"Wrap up for me." Nathan pushed away from the wall.

"But I have a date," Dick held up a hand.

"We just got here. How in the hell do you have a date?" Nathan snarled.

"I'm a friendly guy," Dick shrugged.

"You're on the clock," Nathan countered. He grabbed the knob, but the guy's hand on his arm pulled him up short.

"Where are you going? Oh, to get a date of your own. She's a man-eater. Watch your nuts. I think she'd crack 'em in a second." The bastard chuckled quietly.

"I'm following a lead." He stared at Dick's hand for a second before it slipped from his jacket.

"I want to talk to the man in charge of your circus, not the clown," Adrian Tau interjected from behind his desk.

Dick's face didn't look so pretty with an indignant bloom of red and a rumpled grimace. Nathan stopped the man's retaliation with the kick of a brow. Then he turned his full force on the cop. "I understand not wanting outsiders in your business, but you're too stubborn for your citizens' own good. If you don't accept our help, I guarantee this won't be your case in twenty-four hours. It'll probably be mine even if you do. So, enjoy shoving us around while you still can." Nathan turned away.

"What lead?" his non-partner asked.

He let the closed door do the talking as he hurried past Adrian Tau's grumbling witch of a secretary and down the hallway. By the time he made it outside a silver Jeep eased away from the curb with a mammoth-sized dog hanging its head out the window.

Nathan sprinted for the rental and yanked at his tie. Good Lord, he had a recliner bigger than the tin can. On the bright side, if he wrecked, they could use it as his coffin. And he damn well might wreck, driving on the left side of the road. He shrugged off his suit coat and tossed it the foot and a half to the other seat, crammed his body behind the wheel, and took off, playing a hunch.

The engine whined like a crazed child as he gunned it to the beachfront road. When Madelyn went right instead of left he pumped the brakes and earned a blaring horn at his back. He hadn't expected that. He'd predicted she'd head straight to Nichole's house to nose around.

His rental idled in the middle of the street while he thought it out. Then he smiled and veered left.

Women and their outfits. No way could she snoop in heels.

He followed the road past the docks and hooked another left at a fork, which led him away from the coast to where the other half lived. Only one wrong turn later he pulled past the driveway he sought. On the far side of the curve Nathan parked at the edge of the road, grabbed gloves from his bag in the sorry excuse for a trunk, and then strolled several yards back.

Natural vegetation overflowed the gravel in places, acting like a tunnel. The short drive allowed enough space for two cars to park one in front of the other with the bumper of the first nearly kissing the house. A realtor would label the place quaint, which translated into really small and old, but with potential.

Though no cars occupied the landing strips Nathan measured his footsteps. His gaze swept back and forth over the pale yellow house, paying close attention to the wavy glass windows and the woods surrounding the house. Two short planters brimmed with a flowering shrub bracketed the teal door. Above the threshold a painted placard read *Gallow*. It seemed Nichole worked to unlock the home's promise.

Nathan eased around the porch post, eyeing the scaly lizard that scampered across the banister. "Hello," he knocked. The entire house vibrated from the mild force of his knuckles. When no one responded he peered in through the window.

The one-room home didn't allow many places for a person to hide. Sheets lay only half on the empty bed, which could have been partitioned off by a white linen curtain pulled back on either side. A door gaped in the back corner of the house revealing a toilet and the edge of a shower stall.

He knocked once more, slipped on his gloves, and then tried the knob. Unlocked. People these days never ceased to amaze him. Just toss out the welcome mat. Hell, why not pack up your valuables and leave them at the curb for a thief? He stepped inside and closed the door behind him.

Booze and fish masked the faint scent of spice. A few feet from the door he walked between a table for two and small seating area with a sofa and two wooden rocking chairs. Paintings of island life tastefully filled the walls and were all signed with a frilly, 'NG.' One white shelf bulged floor to ceiling with books. Each stood upright in perfect alphabetical order by author, and then title, the wraps separated from some of the spines.

In the sink a fractured plate, a small cooked fish, and what looked to be cornbread mash with okra littered the basin. Nathan rubbed his stomach. What a waste. He'd skipped breakfast because of the crowded break room. The small jet hadn't offered so much as a peanut.

Nathan guessed that Nichole had made her husband dinner before going out last night. The jackass—in his drunken rage—had more than likely chucked the plate of food before heading to the bar to confront his wife.

He riffled through the wardrobe and then a small desk containing orderly receipts and account records. None of it showed what he wanted to see; blood, syringes, knives, or proof of purchase for spools of rope. But he hadn't expected it to.

The unmade bed and sullied sink in the otherwise tidy house told him something. Nichole hadn't come home last night. And judging from Madelyn Garrett's accounting of the previous night and the stench of whisky inside, Jim Gallow was too out of control to do the work of the Field-Dresser.

After returning the last stack of receipts to their folder, Nathan closed the drawer and headed for the porch. The latex gloves snapped at the ends of his fingers. He pulled the door closed with the wad, shoved them into his pocket, and sat on the single step. His wingtips settled onto the rocks. Slipping his phone from the opposite pocket, he checked the time.

It wouldn't be long now.

He clicked on the first waiting text. Dick wanted to know where the hell the car was. The corners of Nathan's mouth quirked. Scrolling down, he read the second message. "I just walked six blocks in dress shoes, you sorry asshole." A devious chuckle rumbled in his chest. Served him right for goosing Ms. Garrett on the ass. Not that she needed anyone to stick up for her. Hell, she'd practically bitten Dick's hand off and given it back to him with a smile.

A car rumbled in the distance. His ears pricked and his heartbeat kicked into gear. Nathan stowed the phone and rested his forearms on his knees. Sure enough a silver Jeep with a dog head sticking out the passenger window eased into the driveway. Legs nearly as long as his own—but far more silky smooth from the looks of her tan white skin—unfolded from the vehicle. Flip-flops dangled from pretty pink toes until she dropped to the ground. A tank top and athletic shorts displayed a tight body.

An almost imperceptible nod told the anxious dog he'd have to stay. If it were possible, the beast frowned, but obediently sat on his haunches. She'd pulled her thick brown hair back from her face. The long ponytail swished as she marched toward him. He dutifully ignored her pointed lips. The darn things had mesmerized him earlier to the point of falling off the wall. He focused on the dark eyes that showcased her fury.

"Madelyn, we don't have long before Jim Gallow gets off of work. So, I'll be direct," Nathan said before she could blast him. "What are you doing here?"

Her jaw fell open and her tongue toyed with a tooth at the back of her mouth. He'd seen the tactic many times, but always when someone struggled to rein the perfect words to put another in their place. "I'm here to look for my friend. Something you and your grab-ass partner—"

"He's not my partner."

"I'm glad to see you have some sense about you, but you don't seem to have much in the way of finding Nichole."

Talk about a kick in the goods. "How do you figure?"

"You sat—I'm sorry," she said, raising a hand to the sky, "—stood in that meeting and asked one question. You didn't even take notes. Who cares that a backwoods cop told you to sit and listen? Do you take orders from him?"

"Nichole wore a green sun dress with ruffles around the bodice, her favorite pearl earrings, and brown leather sandals last night." He paused, making certain he had her attention before continuing. "You first met at the farmer's market in front of the mango bin three days before you started work at the same school, and you became friends."

That sexy mouth of hers formed an O. Her breath caught in the back of her slender throat.

About the time he decided to get pissed at her unwarranted accusations he noticed a well of tears gathering in her eyes. She bit her pretty lips and sucked a deep breath. And suddenly he saw what she hid behind all that anger. He saw her sadness.

"It wasn't my interrogation. This isn't my investigation. Not yet anyway. And I'm not going to stomp all over someone else's jurisdiction. Not in front of their face, anyway."

She scoffed and magical smile lines creased her face. He wanted to see her smile. This conversation wouldn't manage that though.

"You're not in the US or even a province of it. You're already stomping on jurisdiction."

"We have the local and United Kingdom's permission to review this case as it relates to a three year investigation of crimes committed on US soil."

She blinked her tears away and propped a hand on her hip. "How do you know where Nichole and Jim live and when he gets off work?"

"It was a long flight. And contrary to your low opinion of my work ethic, I used the time to familiarize myself with the details."

Madelyn gnawed her cheek in contrition. With her hefty armor ever so lightly lowered, he seized the opportunity. "Have you ever been or are you currently in a relationship with Adrian Tau?"

"No." She gawked at him as though he'd suggested she sacrifice her first born to please the gods.

"How is it he knows so much about you and Nichole Gallow?"

"We're on the Community Development Committee together." She pinned him with a sideways glance.

"Which..." he prodded.

"Which meets one to ten times a month depending on the projects we have going. Last year we raised money to install safe playground equipment in the town's square. When we manage to raise enough money, we'll construct an actual football field next to the playground."

Her face lit and a smile tiptoed around the corners of her mouth. "It'll be real grass with two large net goals. Most of the kids have never played on a proper field. It will keep them from dodging cars and getting their balls run over." She paused, scrunched her mouth together, and turned the cutest shade of red. "Their soccer ball." She used air quotes and corrected, "Footballs."

"Is that or driving on the wrong side of the road harder to get used to?"

Her eyes nearly closed as she thought. "The sports references by far." She nodded and then looked around. As though she'd just remembered where she was and what she was supposed to be doing, her shoulders straightened. "So, are you at least going to look through the window or let me go in and see if he locked her in the bureau?"

He opened his mouth, but music erupted from her Jeep and Miranda Lambert's voice followed.

"Slapped my face and he shook me like a rag doll

Don't that sound like a real man

I'm gonna show him what a little girl's a made of

Gunpowder and lead"

Her wide eyes and hasty retreat were almost as telling as her ringtone selection. A picture of Madelyn Garrett's past formed in his mind and he didn't like it one damn bit. He'd wondered why she'd left her family behind and moved to a speck of land in the middle of an ocean. The answer glared in her every move. Someone had hurt her and done a hell of a job of it.

She climbed onto the dirty running board and leaned into the opened top vehicle. The song died before it hit the verse. Her hand clutched the top roll bar as though she'd never release the thing, but finally she sank to the ground.

Sensing her hesitance, Nathan stood and took one step in her direction. Her muscles tensed as though she might flee. He stilled. His hands rested by his sides.

"Sorry, I've had the thing for about four hours now and I don't know how to turn down the volume yet. It's been a while since I used one and it was about as big as your hand and only made phone calls and old-school texts." Madelyn Garrett's dark eyes swelled.

A smirk nearly betrayed him, but he bit it back. "Who set your ring tone?"

"The guy at the store showed me..." She placed the fingers of her right hand over her mouth. "The guy at the store."

"I need to..." they said in unison.

Nathan drew a deep breath. "I need to ask you some more questions, but I get the feeling you need to go."

Madelyn nodded that slight move of her head. And then she smiled. It wasn't a big one or maybe even genuine, but her lips curved on either side. As stupid and sappy as it was, he'd swear angels cried.

She flit her fingers in a wave, opened the door, and then met his gaze again. "I have questions for you too...later."

"I wouldn't expect anything less."

"I have some things to do tonight, but I'll be around tomorrow. Do you have a card or—"

"I'll find you."

"Will you find my friend?"

Just shank him in the gut and twist the knife. "One way or another, I'll find her."

Chapter Seven

The children's screaming laughter lifted Madelyn's spirits, even though they laughed at her. To be correct, they laughed at her and the poor kid groaning and rolling on the sand. She'd worked the football past mid-field and was clipping along at a good pace. She dribbled around a defender and on to the goal, but miss-stepped and slammed right into him. Not one of her best moves.

Granules scraped across her hand as she brushed away the sand caked to her sweaty legs. She rubbed away the soreness in her side where his elbow had connected with her ribs. Then she leaned forward, lopped her arms under Sauda's pits, and hoisted.

"Nice defense," she gasped.

The poor guy stayed crouched, bracing his hands on his knees.

Games usually lasted until lunchtime and often picked back up in the evenings as the sun began to fall off the sky. Guilt plagued her through the first match. Having fun while her friend was missing seemed wrong. But her mind had run marathons all night over Nichole's disappearance. She needed an escape. Football was just the thing to do that. It required energy and focus.

Sauda reset with the rest, ready to play. She hadn't had time to think. But the crowd thinned.

This was their last game and her reprieve would come crashing down around her.

The ball sailed just over her head, jarring her from the seeping worry. She jumped, bumped the canvas with her forehead, and then guided it down her body. Redemption. She launched herself down the field and straight for the goal. The kid she'd plowed braced for the impact that never materialized.

Madelyn rocketed the ball up over the goalie's head. It bounced off the tip of his finger and fell into the goal—the goal being an imaginary line in the sand the players knew by heart. The point sent her team into revelry with cheers, sweaty hugs, and chants. In the second line of their victory song she saw a most unusual sight.

Deacon was in his usual spot twenty yards away under the shade of a huddled group of palms, but his position was most peculiar. His feet, all four of them, jutted into the air and his head was half-buried in the sand. He emitted a laughable groan of pleasure. That noise, up until now, had belonged only to them. He made the sound on those rare occasions when he stopped moving long enough to relax and unwind with a belly rub. And now he was getting a belly rub from Mr. FBI.

She covered her mouth to keep from trenching sand with her jaw. Deacon, while sweeter than pie, was as messed up about people as she. Leaving the cheers behind, Madelyn went to reclaim her dog. "Deacon," she called from twelve feet out. He snapped to attention. Looking dutifully guilty, he hurried to her heel.

Nathan Brewer stood and dusted the sand from his worn jeans and University of Mississippi T-shirt. She stopped as though she'd run into a wall.

Boy had she. The abruptness of the impact stole her breath.

The agent tilted his head. His gaze studied her for a moment before turning that scrutiny on himself. He checked his fly and then patted his big hands over a taut chest. She wished his physique were the only shocker she had to deal with at the moment. Because it was enough.

"What?" he begged, coasting his fingers over the individual bumps of his abdomen.

Madelyn shook herself and continued toward him. "It's just. I haven't seen an Ole Miss shirt in a long time. It surprised me."

He crossed sturdy arms over his chest and twitched a brow.

"I went to college there, but I'm sure you've read that in my file."

"I haven't read your file."

"But you have it?"

"What happened to Deacon's belly?" His chin jutted toward the pup in question. "Those scars are pretty..."

"Grisly," she supplied, letting him change the subject.

"That's the word." Gaze zeroed in on her dog, he leaned forward. His arms unfolded and he stroked Deacon's head as if consoling him.

With him so close her words strained to leave her throat. But she swallowed and managed a response. "I don't know."

"Adopted?" Nathan asked, straightening.

"Rescued."

"How long did it take?"

"What?"

"For him to trust you?"

"Thirteen tanks of gas worth." She wrinkled her nose at Deacon.

"Did you lock him in the car and drive until he finally broke down and gave you a chance or what?"

"It just took a long time," she hedged, wishing she'd gone with that answer in the first place.

Nathan shoved his hands in his pockets. A mischievous smirk collected on his supple lips.

"It's a long story," she explained.

"I'm listening."

Madelyn shoved the loose strands of wet hair from her face, wiped the sweat on her damp shirt, and then realized she looked like hell. And for the first time in a long time, she actually cared. His gaze flitted about her face, but didn't seem to notice her ratty shorts or soaked tee.

"When I need to think, I drive. Finals were coming up at the end of my junior year. So, I hopped in my truck at the time—a gas guzzling 1980 Chevy Blazer—and started driving. I made it to the north side of Holly Springs National Forrest when I saw him hobble into the woods."

"That's damn near Tennessee."

"I crossed the state line looking for a place to turn around." She patted the top of her hair, realized she was primping, and then dropped her arms to her side. "I didn't have any food to coax him with. So, I pulled over and sat at the tree line. He laid about thirty yards away and watched me for three hours. It started to get dark. I called out to him, but he turned and limped away."

Madelyn threaded her fingers together. "He wouldn't come to me, but…" She watched the wind rustle the tips of the palms and considered her next words carefully.

"You saw your pain in his eyes."

The bottom dropped out of her stomach. He'd read her file. How else could he know? Which also meant he'd lied. For some stupid reason she'd believed every word that had come out of his mouth. At Nichole's house she'd experienced a bone deep draw to his no-nonsense manner.

Her gaze flew to Nathan's, but again he wasn't looking at her. His haunted eyes examined Deacon. How had she missed it before? Soul deep sadness made the eyes frown even when a person smiled. She swallowed past sudden rawness.

Special Agent Nathan Brewer stood a foot taller than her, mounds of muscles wider, and layers of hide tougher than she. But he hadn't always been a big strapping man. Madelyn bit the inside of her cheek to keep from tearing at the horrible images that flashed in her mind.

"And you see yours." she croaked.

His gaze met hers, and for a moment on the breezy beach, while the waves roared and children whooped, their pasts walled them in a transparent rectangle and sucked out all the air. His lids closed for a beat longer than normal. When his eyes opened the past wasn't gone, but he'd shoved it back. His lips curved and suddenly she could breathe again.

"You drove two hours a day to stare at this guy every day for two weeks?" he jutted his chin at her dog.

"Three weeks and two days in the middle of the summer and about two-hundred bucks worth of wet dog food, but he was worth it."

"He's awesome."

"He has his quirks, but then we all do." Madelyn dug her bare toes into the sand. Well, Agent Brewer, you didn't come here for my life story..."

"If I had, would you give it to me?"

"Nope."

He grinned. "Not yet."

"Not ever," she said.

"I'm starving. Is there a quiet restaurant nearby where we can talk about the case and eat?"

She could not believe she was about to say it, but it was the truth.

"We can eat at my house. It's just up the beach. In this town the quietest conversations travel the fastest. Besides, I have to talk to you too."

Madelyn scanned the area. "Your partner won't be joining us, will he?"

"He's not my partner."

Chapter Eight

Deacon wedged himself between him and Madelyn as they fell into step together. He got the message loud and clear. And if he didn't get it from the dog, he'd get it from Madelyn's constrained gait. Not much surprised him these days, but her invitation sank like a sniper's bullet in the center of his chest. And it seemed to have shocked her as much.

Just three football fields' distance from the game, about two miles from the small town center, a tiny house the color of honey-baked persimmon disrupted the tan sand and green of the jungle. Despite the color contrast it fit perfectly in the quiet nook of the bay, as though the earth had carved the stop out especially for her home.

She turned the knob, brushed her feet on a narrow rug, stepped inside and opened the door wider for him. Nathan stood, incredulous.

"You need to keep your door locked," he said in as even a voice as he could manage.

"I was just up the beach."

"Did you watch your door the whole time?"

She quirked her mouth.

"Where exactly am I going to put a key?" She gestured to her body with a hint of distain.

Given another surprise invitation, he seized it. His gaze stared at her pink toes and worked up the sculpted length of her legs. Sand clung to nearly every inch of available skin from mid-thigh down. Tattered shorts covered the junction of her thighs, but images he shouldn't have filled in the gaps. A baggy T-shirt covered her torso, but too many times when he'd watched her sprint up and down the sand it had billowed, revealing her tight abdomen and the hint of a grey sports bra.

He swallowed his lust and almost choked to death. Then he met her gaze. "Latch it to Deacon's collar or around your neck," he said with a rusty voice. "I don't care where you put it. You're a beautiful woman living alone." That got her back up. "And no matter how capable you are of defending yourself, there's no better place for someone to catch you off guard than your home."

"I lock it most of the time."

"Make it all the time."

"Come in before I change my mind."

Nathan shook out his flip-flops and stepped from the sand into the kitchen. Deacon nudged past him and sprawled in the middle of the walkway on the cool tiled floor. Nathan closed the door and twisted the deadbolt.

"You should lock it when you're home too."

"Anybody ever tell you you're bossy?"

"Once or twice."

He stood at the threshold and drank in the simplicity of her home. There were no shrines dedicated to family, no girlie décor. The colors of nature filled the space. Wood ceilings ran throughout with stone tiled floors. White linen curtains at every window rustled in the sea breeze. The house was so open it felt like an extension of the outdoors. Mother Nature herself breathed life in these walls. And that was a very bad thing. With all the windows opened who cared if she locked the doors. But he reserved that lecture for now.

Madelyn moved around the kitchen, washing this and grabbing that. Her shoulders relaxed. She poured them each a glass of water and motioned him forward.

"I really need to go wash up before I get sand all over the house. Do you like strawberry walnut salad?"

"Sure."

"Would you mind slicing these up?" She slid a cutting board with a mound of strawberries and a small knife in his direction.

"Not at all."

She hesitated, turned away, and then whipped back around. "You need to wash..." A long strand of hair dropped into her face as she stared at his hands, already sudsy over the sink. "Oh, right," she whispered before hurrying around the island, through a tiny living area, and past a heavy carved door.

Chapter Nine

Madelyn wanted to shower and change, but she didn't want to seem eager or too inviting. So, she only rinsed her legs, arms, and face. She resurrected her ponytail, which had managed to come almost completely undone during the fits of triumph on the beach.

Reentering the kitchen, she stopped. She'd expected Nathan to give up on strawberry chopping for more interesting sport like snooping about her home. Instead, he was putting the goat cheese on top of their otherwise-complete salads.

"You can cook?"

His eyebrow rose. "I wouldn't call preparing a salad cooking, but yes. I can cook, clean, and do laundry. Just like you can, I suppose. Cleaning and laundry aren't my favorites, but I'd get fired if I went to work naked."

She had a hard enough time concentrating around him without the mental picture he forced into her mind. With the image searing her brain, she worked overtime to keep it together.

He placed the bread he'd finished slicing on a plate and asked, "Where do you want to eat?"

"This way." Madelyn grabbed their drinks, thankful for something to do, and then led the way through her bedroom, which shrank like a funhouse with Nathan inside it. She quickened her pace and pushed through the back door and out onto the back patio.

They stopped in the shade of the house at a small bistro table. She set the glasses on the two-top and heaved a potted plant several feet, allowing her to reach the second chair.

"Entertain often?" He started at the dark water ring staining the deck.

"Nichole is the only person who's ever been in my house, until today."

His forehead wrinkled. She expected him to say something, but he nodded and divvied out the plates of food. He passed her a napkin, placed his in his lap, waited for her to pick up her fork, and then gulped down half his salad in only a couple of bites.

Madelyn stared at him in a fog of surreal disbelief. This big man with his rumbly voice, no-nonsense, yet soothing manner, made her home look like a doll house. He made her ordered life look like the ruse it was. She shifted in her seat.

"I'm afraid I'm about to make you more uncomfortable, but I'm not going to dress it up in flowers."

"Flowers die."

He tore off a hunk of bread and swallowed it down. "True enough. All right. I've been on the Field-Dresser case for nearly three years. A pair of murders occur every year, exactly one year from the last set. The pattern began in St. Thomas, and then moved to St. John a year ago yesterday. I believe he's begun the cycle in Tortola."

The metal fork clanged on the ceramic plate and then clattered to the table. Her heart beat so hard she'd swear it left impressions on her chest. Nausea rolled like a wave in her belly. "You think she's dead, not missing?"

"I honestly hope I'm wrong, but—"

"You are wrong." He opened his mouth to speak, but she forged ahead. "You're talking about the women killed by that maniac. He's in custody. Just last night they showed a snippet on the news about the beginning of the trail."

"It's not him," he whispered.

"What are you talking about? Granted, I don't have a TV, but I've heard people talk about it. And they said the prosecutor had all the evidence they needed to go for the death penalty."

Nathan set his fork on the edge of the plate. It didn't make a sound. He placed the napkin next to it, grabbed his thighs, and straightened. "They have every scrap of evidence they need. They have a verbal and written confession from Robert Inman. But one thing didn't match up between his story and the evidence. That thing is big enough to get the case thrown out. And it's big enough that when he told me, I wanted to cut him loose right then and there."

"Why didn't you?"

"Because I'm not self-employed."

"What was the thing?"

He simply shook his head.

"Fine, what does all that have to do with Nichole?"

"She matches the profile of the victims. Tall. Dark hair. Trim physique. The timing fits, along with some other things."

"Like?"

His chest expanded on a breath and he released it slowly. He wasn't going to answer her question.

Fine.

As the shock ebbed, reason seeped back into Madelyn's brain. "I think she ran away with someone...a man, maybe. That's why she didn't say anything to me."

"What makes you think that?"

"Well," she began. "You know her husband was abusive and jealous enough to make anyone want to leave."

"But she didn't leave him. You said it yourself. She wouldn't leave no matter how much you tried to convince her he would do it again and no matter how badly he treated her. She didn't leave."

She knew he was right. Nichole had been loyal to a fault. Still, she pushed ahead. "Yes, that's what I believed up until a few hours ago. Last night I did some investigating of my own."

His jaw clenched. His eyes clouded charcoal black.

Though the change was subtle, she noticed it immediately. She noticed it the way people notice the darkening of the sky before a storm. Gooseflesh prickled her entire body. "Before you lecture me about my place in all this, you should know I got a lead."

"A lead?" He ground the words between his teeth. "Who are you, Nancy Drew?"

"She was seen driving down the beach at two in the morning, Friday morning, with someone else in the car."

"Who told you this?"

"Mr. Malik. He's an old fisherman who lives west of here about five miles up the beach."

"Old?" His eyes narrowed.

"He's eighty, but he is sharp as a tack."

"Okay, what was this sharp eighty-year-old doing outside at two in the morning?"

Madelyn bit her cheek to hide her smirk. "I was curious myself. He said, 'Sugar, when you get to be my age you don't sleep much at night and you have to pee every few hours. I like to look at the moon and the stars when I pee.' He said it gives him a sense of being one with nature."

Nathan considered that. "If this pans out, you did better than I did last night. Nobody would talk to me and intimidation didn't go far either."

"I hate to be the one to break it to you, but you're not very intimidating." She hoped her bluff was working, because in truth he was intimidating the hell out of her. Every sentence he uttered in his dungeon-dark voice sent chills down her spine.

"I may not be," he agreed, "but my gun is."

She blew it off. "Don't take it to heart. You're not a local and you don't have boobs. So, nobody's going to talk to you."

"In that case," Nathan countered with a sly grin, "you only have half of the criteria." When she cocked an eyebrow he continued, "You're not a local. You only moved here three years ago."

"So, you read my file?"

"No. Di...Special Agent Kepler told me."

Her stomach knotted. "So, he read it."

"No, I have it locked up. But he did make nice with the courthouse receptionist. She pulled real estate and insurance records for him."

She nodded, unable to speak for the momentary relief. After a few moments she said, "The locals welcomed me quickly. For some it takes longer."

"It's the boobs."

"Excuse me?" Her cheeks flamed.

"Hey, you brought it up." He smirked.

"What?"

"That's why they welcomed you so quickly."

"No, it is not. I am a nice person and I have taken an interest in the island's culture, the community, and the children."

"Uh-huh."

How dare he talk about her boobs. They were body parts that had not gotten much attention in an uncomfortably long span of time. She'd all but forgotten about them. Even in her wardrobe they blended in like unfashionable accessories. And here this stranger was making her all too aware of their sudden wanting presence. She struggled to ignore the tingling, made worse by his knowing gaze and her constricting sports bra. Setting her jaw she tried to burn a hole in him with her gaze. Undisturbed, he gave her a killer smile and returned to his food.

"You need to eat," he said after a beat.

"I'm too irritated to eat. Nichole...my friend can't be dead."

They held each other's gaze for too long. She gulped the raw emotions clawing their way up her throat. "Are you finished?" Her hand shot out to take his plate.

His warm fingers encircled her wrist. Instead of going rigid and cold all over, the contact heated her someplace deep inside.

"I'll get these." Nathan's touch slid from her wrist, taking all the oxygen in her body with it.

He retrieved the plates and cups, stood, and looked over his shoulder at her. "Lock the back door on your way in."

Since when did she take orders from a man? Apparently, this was a banner day. She pulled herself up, sucked in a deep breath, followed his wide shoulders into her house, and locked the door behind her.

Nathan moved through her space with such easy assurance, like he'd been there a thousand times. But then that's probably how men moved through life, taking every bump and crossroad in his stride. He stepped over Deacon, placed the empty dishes in the sink, tucked her uneaten salad into the refrigerator, and then peered out the two wide slats of the window over her sink.

He turned and walked toward her, only stopping when he was within touching distance. "I need you to do something to help with this investigation."

"Anything. I want to help." Maybe contributing in some way would dull the helplessness plaguing her.

"Close and lock the bottom slats of your windows. Keep both the doors in your house and car locked whether you're in them or not. And stop your investigation."

Madelyn placed her hands on her hips. "Are you worried I'll take your job?"

"I'm worried you'll find something you don't want to find."

Her gaze dropped to his chest. She fought to block the gruesome images buffeting her mind.

"Hey." Her gaze found his. "I also need you to give me directions to Mr. Malik's house."

Chapter Ten

Excitement and dread coalesced, braiding Nathan's traps with tension. He waited for the snick of the lock before jogging up the beach toward the spot where he'd left the upgraded rental. When he got far enough away from her open windows that he wouldn't be overheard, he grabbed his phone and dialed.

"What do you want, asshole?" Dick grumbled.

"Still mad about the car, huh?"

"Hell, yes. I'm not your whipping boy, you know. I'm sorry Hunt got shot, but I can't change that fact. You're stuck with me for the duration of this circus, as that hillbilly called it. I can make this time as easy or as difficult as you want me to."

"You practice that speech all morning?"

"Dam—"

"Listen up, I need you to meet me at Paradise."

"We canvassed the place last night and didn't find out a damn thing."

"We're not meeting there to question people. We're going to grid off the west side of the island and start looking for Nichole."

"You mean her body, don't you?" For the first time since they'd arrived on the island, and maybe the first time ever, he heard sincerity and remorse in the man's voice.

"There's a chance it's not our guy and that she's still alive. But you know if the sick bastard is behind this, he's already done the deed and he's waiting for us to find her."

"I know."

"Look, I have to make a stop along the way to check out a source and hopefully get a physical description of our killer."

"No shit," he breathed.

"Hope not."

"Well, don't rush on my account. It'll take me a few hours to walk there."

Nathan opened his mouth, but a feminine voice cooed on the other side of the line. "I'll drop you wherever you need to go, babe."

"See? Saved by a good Samaritan," Dick said.

"If you'd slept in your hotel room last night, instead of with some stranger, you'd have seen the key I slipped under your door this morning."

"Drop me at my hotel?" he asked the woman.

"Mmm," she agreed.

"Have you done anything case-productive this morning?" The rustle of sheets or clothing grated on Nathan's nerves. "Dick for brain, pay attention."

"Huh?" the guy responded dazedly.

"Have you done anything productive this morning other than add to your collection of STD's?" Nathan hollered the question, drawing a snicker from the group of kids still loitering on the beach.

"He's screwing around," Dick explained. His voice sounded far from the mouthpiece. A bang acted as a gong in Nathan's ear. "I promise. He's a kidder. A joker." A slam sounded farther away. "You son of—"

"Say something bad about my momma," Nathan breathed. "I'll have another missing persons report on my hands." Dick panted his hostility. "Now answer my question."

"I've been going through files of Nichole Gallow's known associates and cross checking names with the previous victims. So far there's no commonality apart from the physical. But on this island there are several known associates that fit the killer's forensic height and weight profile."

"Who?"

"There's like ten names on the list."

"Well..."

"Well, I'll bring it with me, if I make it there. You jackass."

Nathan opened the door to the white SUV that was three times the size of the car he drove yesterday, slid behind the wheel, and headed toward Malik's house. Well, there was gold and there was shit. The two opposites existed in the world and in this situation.

The gold was the fact that he had a jump on this sick killer people referred to as the "Field-Dresser." To top that, Nathan even knew who the man's subsequent victim would be. He was in a prime position to catch him before he completed the second act of his twisted play. One Nathan was so intimately familiar with, he could almost see it unfold, as if on stage before him.

The shit was that if he didn't work fast and catch the sicko before his second act, the most alluring creature he had ever seen would soon be ravaged and eradicated from the earth.

Nathan had been on this icy case for nearly three years, but had managed to collect more bodies than clues. The psychopath left one pair of carved women each year hanging for the world to see, within two weeks of one another. No meaningful evidence was found at the scenes or on the bodies. No hair, fingerprints, DNA, or weapon.

The only fibers left were microscopic bits of cotton and the lengths of rope he used to hang them. Neither had been any help to the investigation because it webbed into a universe of possibilities. Camouflage heavy-duty utility rope stocked the shelves of every other outdoor and home improvement store around the world. The manufacturer didn't catalog dye lots. So, they couldn't narrow the point of purchase. Unable to refine the search or come up with any information to cross check against it, the heap had become useless. The cotton fibers found on the bodies all matched from scene to scene. The clues were two freight trains on the same track barreling head first toward one another.

A dead end.

Though the victims were dead, their bodies told an epic story of suffering at the hands of their killer. They also told a little about the killer himself. The man was large enough to subdue his victims with a single blow. Brains more scientific than his own had run tests and taken measurements on all the victims, then thrown around words like density, thrust, angle of the wound and so on. They determined the killer was between six-feet-four inches and six-feet-six inches tall, and in the neighborhood of two hundred sixty pounds. From the size they could rather accurately guess the killer's gender as male, unless there was an Amazonian woman walking around with a beef for her more petite kind.

Most importantly, Nathan knew the man's patterns. But would it be enough?

In order to succeed, he needed to get a grip and focus. He'd nearly fallen off the wall when

Adrian Tau removed his uniquely large frame from blocking Madelyn Garrett's striking features. And damn him to a lifetime partnership with Dick, but the more time he spent in her presence, the deeper her troubled eyes tugged on him.

She was a beautiful woman. He'd seen them before. Hell, he'd had them before. Which was why he couldn't understand his reaction to her. Perhaps it was because her life was in his hands, though she didn't know it.

****

"Maybe we need to take another look at the husband." Static crackled through the two-way radio and sputtered in the humidity. A bird screeched in the distance, as if echoing the Dick's belligerent opinion.

Thick greenery clouded his line of sight. Fallen branches and dead leaves grabbed at his boots. He was in shape, but the effort and heat caused his muscles to weep. Nathan shoved a thick vine out of his way and marshaled forward.

The scratch of the communicator blared again. "He's never hidden one before. They're always out in the open. Easy to find. Nobody likes being wrong, but maybe were making something out of nothing."

He'd swear the guy had given voice to the ramblings of his conscious. Nathan had never known the man to be so insightful, but the more boxes they X-ed on the map the more obnoxious those thoughts became. Yesterday afternoon they'd split and covered three square miles before the slipping daylight had forced them to stop.

Nathan plucked the walkie-talkie from his utility belt. He pressed the button, cutting of another of Dick's pleas. "I finished section seven and I'm wrapping nine. Where are you?"

"Finished eight and starting ten."

"You're slackin', Kepler," Nathan smiled and waited for the ugly words.

"You gave me the steep side of the mountain, jackass. If I plummet to my death out here, I'll haunt you forever."

Curving lines of topography polluted Nathan's map along with black Xs smeared from the raining beads of his sweat. "I agree this isn't his usual MO. Adrian Tau assured you he'd stay on Jim Gallow. If it turns out to be the husband, it's not our jurisdiction. So, we finished what we came here to do. Find out if it's our guy or not. We can't do that if we don't clear the woods, which is the last place Nichole Gallow was seen alive."

"If you'd told Tau, we could've had a human chain clear this sauna yesterday."

"And have any potential crime scene polluted with ten or more people's DNA. Thanks, but no."

"You don't trust him do you? Then again, you don't trust anybody."

"There's a short list of people I trust. Tau isn't on that list, but I'm betting he's on your list."

"My list?"

"Your list of people who fit the forensic profile."

"I forgot all about the damn list last night."

"We were both beat."

"Yeah to all of it. He's on the list, the husband, her karate instructor, that guy's nephew, a couple of bouncers at the bar, a few fellas at the gym, and a man who works with her husband."

"Only a tiny percentage of the population is over six feet tall and you're telling me all of them live on this island."

"I looked into it. The place used to be the number one exporter of sugarcane for the Brits. They couldn't work the fields themselves. So, like our lazy ancestors they shipped in slaves from Africa. And Darwin's theory pervaded for the next century."

"Meaning all the biggest and strongest survived, and then reproduced."

"That's about it."

Nathan slashed through the nine. They'd cleared another two miles this morning and only had two more to go. He put one foot in front of the other and pushed ahead.

Suppose he was wrong. Then Madelyn wouldn't be in danger. Through college, law school, his two years with Miami PD, and his six with the FBI, nailing the bad guy was all that mattered. For as long as he could remember it'd been his singular goal. And that suddenly paled to his desire to keep this woman safe.

All the saliva in his mouth evaporated and his skin fit as though it had shrunk in the excessive temperatures. Yep, dehydration caused his delusional thoughts. He needed to clear this jungle, get the hell off this island and back to work. His fingers coasted over the stamped piece of metal that hung beneath his shirt. The unforgiving edges reminded him of the vow he'd taken.

Renewed purpose quickened his steps. He shoved the paper back into his pack and scanned the dense undergrowth. Piercing yellow rays sliced through the forest canopy just ahead, adding to the suffocating sting in his lungs. Despite it, his steps propelled him in the direction of the thinned foliage. He shoved an armful of branches out of the way and stepped into a ten-foot circular clearing.

His steps faltered. He still, after all these years, had to wrestle a wave of sickness. He slapped both hands on his nape and huffed a breath. His skin chilled despite the temperature.

Like an arm shooting tall out of the ground with its fingers crinkled in every direction, the thick hardwood held the camouflage rope connected in a noose around Nichole Gallow's broken neck. At least that part had been quick. Her toes dangled about three feet from the ground. Blood tarnished the greenery, stealing the beauty of nature and that of the woman.

His gaze avoided her naked flesh, split chest, and splayed insides. He studied the rope and the small goat trail that led away from the body, down the mountain.

"Finished ten," Dick radioed.

Nathan reached blindly for the device and pressed the button. "Call Williams. Tell him we need that team and we need them right now."

Chapter Eleven

Walking into Chief's office, every hope Madelyn clung to had evaporated like ice on the surface of the sun. The solemn look on his face and the business-like persona radiating from Agent Brewer told her all she needed to know. Her friend was gone, never to return again.

She sank onto the chair. "How..." She paused searching for courage. "How did she die?"

"Well now, Maddy," Chief began, "don't trouble yourself with the details. That's what we're here for. You just need to take some time and grieve."

Nathan stepped from his wall post and leveled her gaze.

Madelyn tightened every muscle in her body, bracing for the impact of his words. Because she knew he would tell her what she needed to hear. He would tell her the truth.

In a surprisingly caring, yet firm, voice, he said, "Her death was quick, but before that she was raped repeatedly and beaten."

The news was a sucker-punch to the gut. Oxygen fled her lungs. Agony, instantaneous and fierce, radiated through her middle. Yet she hunched only slightly from its decimation.

Both men gave her silence. If they expected the news to settle, they ought to think again. Madelyn knew her friend was gone, but she couldn't make the reality fit into her brain. She'd seen Nichole alive, happy, and vibrant days ago. Damnit, she still had things to talk to her about.

There were confessions of her heart and secrets to share that now had no recipient. There were drinks to be had and a lifetime of friendship's memories to be made...that never would be.

Someone ended Nichole's life incomplete in its possibilities. She would never laugh or cry again. She would never feel her abdomen swell full with a child, something she'd always longed for. She would never come to terms with wrinkles, sagging boobs, or varicose veins, things she'd always dreaded.

Dead at twenty-five. The notion paralyzed, but Madelyn wouldn't remain immobile. She couldn't. Not now. She straightened to her full height. Her head rose and her gaze found Agent Brewer's. "I want to see her. I need to...say goodbye."

"You wouldn't recognize her," he said.

Understanding seeped into her bones like a cancer, eroding every good memory, tainting her present, and destroying her future. But still. She needed closure. No matter how painful.

Madelyn set her jaw and stared into the storm of Agent Brewer's eyes.

"She's with forensics now. I'll take you as soon as she's ready."

Chief began again, "Maddie, I will be looking in to other possibilities, while Agent Brewer here chases his ghost." Chief stubbornly continued even when his gaze met the agent's stalling glare. "I believe Jim Gallow is a person of interest and should not be overlooked in this case. They have a history, as you pointed out."

"My team will look into every possibility, Inspector. You're officially off the case. This is now a federal investigation." With the calm of a lapping surf and the tumult of its unseen riptide, Nathan stole the man's footing. Chief folded his arms and glowered, but gave no indication of his willingness to cooperate. Yet, she got the impression he would abide and not like it one darn bit.

Madelyn's gaze jumped back and forth between the two men. Then a light bulb exploded in her head. "What if Jim heard about the other murders and made Nichole's murder out to look like the others. You know, to cover the murder?"

As Agent Brewer inhaled to state his case a chirp stopped him. After a glance at the display he headed for the office door. "Let's go, Ms. Garrett."

With her heart wedged between her ribs, Madelyn stood.

"Madelyn, I don't agree with this," Chief gruffed. "You don't know what you're getting yourself into."

She inhaled a shallow breath. It hurt less. "I know what I'm doing."

He aimed a hammy finger toward her chest. "You may have seen a dead body at a funeral, but you haven't seen one carved up. It's a whole other deal."

"Actually, Chief," she said, "I have."

Chapter Twelve

She turned on her heels and sauntered through the door Nathan held open as though she hadn't just pulled the pin on a grenade. From the slack jaw and near cross-eyed expression on Chief's face, he hadn't seen that one coming either. Nathan shook himself and hurried to catch Madelyn.

The bitch of a receptionist braced her large bosom and even larger mouth with her hands. Guess she'd caught the news too. His wingtips clacked on the tile floor. He increased the tempo to gain on her slapping sandals. The one who'd had the closest connection with the victim seemed the least affected by the recent exchange. And that troubled Nathan in more ways than one.

"What did you mean by, 'I have?'" His baritone echoed in the deserted hallway.

"I meant I'd be fine in the presence of a dead body." Her steps continued on toward the foyer where a big lump of fur waited in the dim light.

"I gathered that."

"Then why'd you ask again?" She shoved through the glass doors. Deacon sprang to his feet with his ears pricked and his tail wagging.

"You know why I asked," Nathan growled.

The dog's ears slicked. His chest puffed.

Madelyn ignored him and planted a hand on the heavy entrance door.

Nathan's arm shot out. His hand cemented hers to the cold metal, boxing her in the frame of his body. Her rigid heat brushed his side. The contact offset the chill and made the day in the jungles seem downright tepid in comparison.

"Answer me," he demanded.

Her dark hair swayed under his breath, tickling his chin. And if touching her wasn't enough to make him dumb, he'd blow a one-point-oh on a Breathalyzer from the intoxication of her scent.

A quiet snarl reverberated in the tiny room.

Though really Nathan wasn't one hundred percent certain which of the two had given the warning, he shifted his gaze to meet Deacon's. "Pipe down. This is for her own good."

The noise quieted and the dog sat.

"How in the hell is this for my own good?" She whipped her head around and tried to bore a hole into him with her dark eyes.

"If I don't know your story, how can I protect you?"

"I don't need protection. I need to see my friend."

His gaze dropped to her mouth, which was way too close for either of their own good. Luckily her supple lips formed a hard line. He let his fingers slide over the smooth back of her hand. "Let's go. Deacon, you're in the back."

He started forward, but bumped into her stalled backside. "Sorry."

"I'm taking my own car." She shoved through the door and angled for her Jeep.

"I don't think that's a good idea."

"Because?"

"High emotions and operating a nearly three-hundred-horsepower machine don't mesh well."

"I'll be fine."

"You keep saying that."

She opened the door, let Deacon load, and met his gaze. Absently, she rubbed her palm over the back of the hand he'd touched. "I keep saying it because one day it'll be true."

Chapter Thirteen

Grey clouds blotted the sun's dying rays. Madelyn downshifted, an especially difficult task with a big blockhead in her lap. The moment she'd fastened her seatbelt he crawled over, straddling the console with his extra large body. He knew. Without her having to say a word, he knew something bad had happened. She stared at the road and followed the SUV around a curve to keep from thinking.

All too soon they pulled in front of a massive green military-style tent in the center of an empty lot. Agent Brewer slid out of his rental. Its door groaned like an ancient relic as he heaved the door with a bit more force than necessary.

Madelyn lifted Deacon's head to her mouth and smacked a kiss between his brows. "I have to go for a few minutes. You can't come with me. I'm sorry." She scooted out the vehicle. He pulled the rest of his body over the hump and curled into the driver's seat.

"Are you sure you still want to do this?"

He'd lost the coat, but his sleeves were still buttoned and his tie pulled tight. She'd wanted to yank him by it earlier and scream for him to mind his own damn business. But he'd found Nichole. One way or the other. Just like he'd said. So, she'd kept her hands to herself.

"I'm not going to fall apart," she said.

"It's okay if you do."

Experience wouldn't allow her to lose her cool in front of anyone, except her dog.   When she didn't respond he frowned and walked ahead. "This way." At the makeshift doorway he pulled the flap back and ushered her inside with a wave of his hand.

Stale air infused with chemicals stung her nostrils. Mobile air conditioners at war with the heat and humidity hummed. A person covered hair-to-toe in a white hazmat-style suit shifted back and forth at a row of machines at the far end of the tent. Two agents—she guessed by the black T-shirts with the letters FBI stamped over the breast—talked quietly over a map.

She followed Agent Brewer as he made his way toward the rear of the tent. Reaching a partition, he called out, "Artie." Ten seconds later a short bald man appeared from behind the green canvas. Crow's feet laced his kind blue eyes.

The man reached out his hand. "You must be Madelyn Garrett. I am Artie Stergin, the team's lead forensic analyst and coroner. I am very sorry for your loss. But you know you don't have to do this. She has already been identified by Mr. Gallow."

Madelyn's stomach rolled like a sailboat caught in a squall. She pictured Jim smiling over Nichole's lifeless body. Identified by her killer. The sentiment was wrong in every way something could be wrong. Somehow, she didn't give in to the urge to flee or vomit.

"I am here...to say goodbye," she whispered.

"All right." The old man nodded. "I've cleaned Mrs. Gallow up as much as possible. You can take all the time you need. Whenever you're ready..."

Scared that with more time she'd lose her nerve, she jumped in. "I'm ready."

Nichole's body lay covered on a table in the center of the room. Tables filled with beakers, microscopes, evidence bags, and other analysis equipment lined the canvas walls of the room. Artie walked around the table and faced Madelyn, while Nathan stood a few feet back to her right.

Artie canted his head. She nodded for him to proceed. The white sheet rolled gently back and her friend's swollen and sallow face came into view.

Madelyn wanted to scream and cover her own face. She wanted to turn and run. Forever. Instead, she looked more carefully. She blocked out the horrors in front of her and searched for her friend's familiar features, the things she'd loved.

She found the beauty mark just below Nichole's left eye. She found the smile lines framing her friend's lips. Nichole had called them 'preemptive wrinkles.' Those were the things she would remember. Those were the things she would miss.

A weight heavier than the sea crushed Madelyn's spirit. She didn't want to say goodbye. She swallowed the tears threatening to escape.

I'm sorry, Nichole. I wish I could have, no, I wish I would have done more to help you. I can't change this, but I can make sure he doesn't get away with it. I miss you already. I will miss you forever. Thank you for being my friend. I love you.

A fissure formed in Madelyn's stoic resolve. Sadness welled. She turned hoping to escape the tent and the torrent of emotions dogging her heels. Agent Brewer's wide chest brought her and her seeping waterworks up short. Sometime in her goodbye he'd closed the gap between them. Only his firm grip on her shoulders kept her from crashing into him...or the ground, in an effort to add distance between them. Quite literally the man threw her off balance.

His eyes were hooded with concern. Refusing to hold his gaze for fear her mental state would disintegrate, she dropped hers to his stubbled chin. The proximity and shadow of hair revealed a dip in the cleft of his firm jaw that she hadn't noticed yesterday.

Silently his hands dropped and he stepped back. Without a glance Madelyn bolted, retreating through the doors. When at last fresh air filled her lungs, the sky loomed as black as her heavy heart. Desperate to alleviate the stench of death she heaved several breaths.

"Madelyn." He hadn't called her by name before. It resonated in his deep tones and raised a flush across her skin.

She stopped walking only when she reached her Jeep, and then turned to face him. Her weak grip latched onto the door. The hunk of metal and Deacon's mossy scent steadied her weak knees. "Thank you for letting me say goodbye."

Again he'd come closer than she expected. His shoulder nearly grazed the side mirror of her vehicle. And again his deep gaze yanked her under. Yes, sadness haunted his dark eyes, but the textured layers of intensity, lust, and sincerity made interesting textures. She needed the reprieve from reality. His gaze eased its crippling weight.

"Madelyn, you need to go into protective custody."

Just like that, reality crushed her. That she remained upright after the blow only attested to her resolve not to reveal the storm raging inside. But she couldn't hide her puzzlement. "What! Why?"

"I think you could be his next victim."

"Jim won't touch me."

"I don't think its Jim."

"But you don't have any proof that it's not."

"Please, listen." The striated muscles of his jaw flexed.

Biting her lip to stave off the rain of tears, she did as he asked.

"You'd be taken to a safe house until we get this guy. A couple of weeks max. We're so close to getting this bastard. We would set up a decoy in your house and catch him when he makes his move."

"I'm not going to let anyone run me off again. So, Agent Brewer, you do what you need to do to catch *whoever* did this to my friend."

With that she retreated to the safety of her car. Agent Brewer stood like a statue of a Greek god, or perhaps a gargoyle, from the sneering expression on his face, and watched her leave. She wheeled onto the main road out of the agent's sight and Deacon turned to face the back of the Jeep. He hung his head low and whined a pitiful song.

Chapter Fourteen

The clack of her bolt sliding into place shattered the last of her resolve. Waves of guilt and loss knocked Madelyn to her knees. The unforgiving impact of the tiles stung inconsequentially compared to the ache in her chest. Her purse slipped from her shoulder and crashed to the floor. Its contents scattered. A tube of lipstick she never wore pirouetted. Tears distorted the mess into marbled gobs.

Her fists beat the cool floor until her breaths became so labored she splayed them on the burnt orange clay to keep from flattening her nose on them. A screech so animalistic it belonged in the wild pinged off the terra cotta. Wetness pooled beneath her fingers. When her tears ran out and fatigue dulled the rage she curled into a ball.

A chill settled in her marrow. How had her neatly ordered life come crashing down around her? Why did hell's hounds gnash at her heels? She knew the answer. Madelyn slammed her eyes shut in the dark house to block out the undeniable truth. Still it seeped in like the cold.

Because you're a murderer.

The old wounds gaped as though never healed. And they weren't. And they never would be.

Silent and tearless sobs wracked her prone form. Just when the cold and solitude became too much to bear the quiet tap of paws shuffled her way. Humid breath coursed through her hair and onto her neck. Then, in a heap, Deacon piled himself against her knotted arms and legs.

Relief from the cold came little by little, thawing her bones and stemming the hopelessness that was tomorrow. Her lids grew heavy. Her will to move faded. And so a dreamless sleep claimed her.

Stiff lids opened to the break of day spilling in through the windows. Deacon's big striped head lay a few inches from her nose. She tightened the arm she'd draped over the pup at some point in the night.

"I don't deserve you."

The words came out as a grumbled croak. Her throat burned as though she'd swallowed a cactus bulb and washed it down with acid. She nuzzled her face in the dog's neck and held him close for as long as her screaming hip could stand. Rolling onto her back, she took in the wood ceiling, the underside of the bar, the scarred legs of the two-seater table across from it, and the tiny granules of sand that had migrated in from the beach only a couple of feet away.

Her gaze jumped to the clock on the oven. On any other Monday she'd be zooming around the place trying to get out the door to meet Nichole at the gym. Today there was no point. She wouldn't be there. Ever again.

Numbness traveled from her hip and shoulder, blanketing her in a shroud of apathy. At the very least she needed to get up and get ready for work, but she couldn't find the will to move.

Finally she flayed herself from the floor and shuffled into the bathroom. Madelyn stared at her toothbrush for several minutes before turning away. The bathtub knobs squeaked under her hand and the water rushed from the faucet. She popped the diverter and the shower rained like her tears had last night.

Maybe she'd cried them all out. Because she couldn't summon even a mist of emotion. She closed the toilet lid, sat, and peeled off one item at a time. Exhaustion taxed her muscles, making the simple task seem as though she were doing it in a vat of syrup.

When she stepped into the shower cool water jolted her indifference. This wasn't about her. There were children depending on her to explain the inexplicable. There were children who would undoubtedly need a shoulder to cry on or a coherent party to listen. She had to be that for them. And that necessity was the only thing that got her dressed.

If Madelyn thought the night was bad, the day was one hundred times worse. The entire school reeled from the news. Children wept, some to themselves, others in groups, while tiny tears drenched her shirt. It was a bit of hell on Earth.

The sun shined, but the day clouded with grief.

The night brought fitful sleep until exhaustion took over. But she didn't wake refreshed. She woke in a vengeful fury. Hate replaced sorrow. Her jaw clenched tight and her nails dug into her palms.

The spark of Nichole's murder ignited a long-dormant rage. She dressed in record time and sprinted, churning sand all the way to the gym. Deacon didn't circle her once. In fact, he kept his distance.

A rectangle of plywood used to fortify the storefront in case of a hurricane covered the broken glass door. Madelyn yanked the handle and hoisted it open. Jim had wrecked her world. The blatant evidence in the four walls of a place that had represented her new beginning ratcheted her misfit temper.

Amadi was nowhere to be seen and for that she was grateful. He would have wanted her to calm down and find her center, but she didn't want peace. Her fists, still squeezed tight, coaxed small hues of red to the surface of her skin where the fingernails cut into her hands. The whites of her knuckles turned red. Her jaw clenched tight as the anger stirred. She wanted blood and fury.

Today the bag would not do. She needed a person to unleash her hell upon. She jumped on the edge of the ring where two men rehashed the details of their previous triumphs. These were the kind of men she typically shied away from. They fought dirty and took wins however they could get them, but today she didn't care. She leaped over the rope. The larger man backed away from his friend with a condescending smile. "I'll let you take this one."

Her opponent outweighed her by eighty pounds. The gusts of his meaty arms nearly threw her off balance. One blow would stop her misery cold in its tracks. He planted his feet in the center of the ring. His crooked nose and narrowed eyes taunted her to step into the reach of his fists.

He was strong, but she was fast, focused, and pissed at the universe. She swept his feet from under him and planted her foot a few inches from his temple, winning the match only a few minutes into the bout. Thirsty for more, she didn't relish the win.   Luckily, his friend wanted to prove his worth. He traveled the ring, dogging her into corners, and forcing her to fight her way out. The sting of her overworked muscles distracted her from the ache in her chest. The burn of her lungs overtook the sizzle of her rage. She lost the bout four to five, but exhaustion numbed the loss that had nothing to do with punches and kicks.

Arms draped over the top rope, Madelyn sucked in steady breaths. Heavy-hitter and his hard-nosed friend ambled from her right. When she turned to meet their gazes she noticed the audience they'd gathered on the other side of the ring. Red fury had eroded her peripheral vision. Ekene and Nathan Brewer sat on a wooden bench at the ring's edge.

Hard-nose offered his hand. "Nice work. You pack a whole lot of anger into that little frame."

She shook his hand, but didn't say anything. What would she say to that?

Wish I didn't.

He and his friend headed toward the lockers and she put her newly found powers of observation to work on Agent Brewer. He sported the same scowl he'd had the night before, but he'd changed from the suit. A nicely worn pair of jeans hugged his thighs. His T-shirt tattooed the FBI crest to his left pec. Sun-kissed arms jutted from the sleeves and stretched them taut.

Luckily, Ekene's boisterous claps cut her study short. He whistled through big lips. "Nice... you nearly mopped the floor with their guts, girl. You know, Amadi would give you hell for that little fit." He shot her a sly smile and turned up his palms. "But he's not here, is he?"

Nathan stood and braced both hands on the canvas. "We need to talk." He bit the words between shiny teeth.

"Hop in." She nodded toward the middle of the ring and gave a sweet smile.

Chapter Fifteen

In the face of loss and imminent danger most people would give over any freedoms they possessed to be safe, but not Madelyn Garrett. Nathan had opened and closed her file about five times the previous night. He needed to know what made her tick. Then maybe he'd find a way to get her to concede and let them put her into protective custody. Because this was no copy-cat.

The Bureau omitted a great deal from the media over the years about the severity and brutality of the crimes. But this guy hadn't missed one sick trick. As though the bastard studied his previous killings every night in his dreams, he'd carried this one out with enraging perfection.

And his next victim stubbornly refused protection.

As things sat he might have to knock her out, toss her over his shoulder, and march her to the safe house to get her to comply. Nathan leaped onto the mat and rolled beneath the ropes. When he stood the mirth fell from her lips.

"When I win, you leave me alone." Her hands banded her hips.

The breaths she sucked in long, even pulls forced her full B-cup against the sweat-soaked material of her tank top. Tiny nipples stretched the blue fabric at the center of those pretty swells.

"You won't win," he groused.

"You're awfully cocky." She bounded on her toes and shook out her arms.

"I'm motivated."

The tension in her muscular legs telegraphed her movement a split second before her body lurched in his direction. She came in like a bolt of lightning. Her balled fist acted as the electrified leader ready to decimate everything in its path.

Nathan shifted to the outside. The wind from her punch tickled his cheek. The nearness of her arm brought a line of small freckles into perfect view. He grabbed her wrist in his right hand. One step back and a shove to her shoulder sent her reeling. A twist and lift ended the fight she'd gathered in her left hand and foot. She met the mat with a thud.

He stood over her prone form and held his grip. "You need to let us protect you."

His leg buckled. He teetered toward the canvas before his nerve endings registered the burn of pain. He landed on all fours. The muscles in his calf knotted in retaliation to the blow.

How in the hell she'd worked past the agony of having her wrist locked to be able to knee him in the calf was beyond him.

"I don't need protection." Madelyn rolled onto her back. The end of her ponytail fanned out to one side of her head, while other sprigs stuck to her face. Her brows crinkled and her dark eyes sparked.

"Will you at least listen to what I have to say?" Nathan used his good leg to stand and offered his hand.

She stared at his hand for a long minute.

"Are you going to bite it or take it?" he asked.

"Neither. We can talk on the steps." She twisted away and stood under her own steam.

Anger rolled off her body in waves. As did a subtle, but potent, sex appeal he had no right to notice. It wrapped itself around his brain and siphoned his ability for higher thought. He apparently needed few brain functioning cells to follow her out the door and into the sweltering morning heat.

Madelyn sat on the top step. Nathan did the same, but put as much distance between them as the width of wood allowed. Deacon plopped down between them with a fifth of the spunk he'd shown only a couple of days before. His person picked at the seam on her shorts and stared into the distance.

Almost as repressed as her allure was the grief she hid behind the impenetrable wall of rage. So he wouldn't come off as the creep he apparently was—itching over a women who'd just lost her best friend—Nathan honed in on that defense mechanism and attempted to exploit it.

"Madelyn, each set of murders occur a year apart. On the night Nichole went missing it had been twelve months since the murder on St. John. There are always two victims per island and the victims have close ties, connections to one another. The two on St. Thomas, Trisha and Summer Sutherland, were sisters."

She didn't move. Didn't attempt to speak. So, he continued. "Trisha was killed first. Her body was hung on the flagpole in the square of her small town. Two weeks later Summer was found hung in a tree behind the local school. The two on St. John, Nancy Starks and Robin Young, were friends on the same volleyball team. Nancy was hung on a light pole on the main thoroughfare of her town. Robin was found two weeks later on a light pole next to the beach where they used to play. You fit his profile and you were close to Nichole."

He turned to see if anything he'd said made an impact. She still picked her shorts' seam and stared into the lighting sky. "You didn't see what Jim did to her." Her tone matched that of a funeral dirge. She hiccupped a breath, and then fortified herself before continuing.

"Her eyes were swollen shut. As she felt her way down the side of the road, she left a trail of blood. It was a week before she could chew semi-solid foods. He left scars all over her body. I had to feed her, dress her, and even take her to the bathroom for weeks. She was as helpless as a child."

She blinked several times and then turned her haunted gaze on him. "I think this time he just finished what he started." Her hair swished back and forth with the shake of her head. "I don't think she's connected to your murders. I don't think I have anything to worry about, except a dead friend. Thank you for your concern, Agent Brewer, but I can take care of myself."

She pushed off the step. "Come, Deacon." When the dog followed she broke into a run.

Nathan yelled, "Call me Nathan, you stubborn over-confident pain in my ass."

He couldn't deny it any longer. There was something about this woman.

Women in general gave Nathan his way. In fact, his mother was the only woman who'd ever stood up to him. She always told him he might as well turn himself around because his handsome face and sly smile wouldn't work on her. Whereas his high school principal, Mrs. Monroe, told him he could make it to the presidency with his charm.

Madelyn stood up to him. She was bull headed, reckless, and annoying as hell. She was gorgeous and raw. She was real. Smart. Tough.

Loyal. Caring. Interesting. Nathan wanted to be
close to her, know more about her, and above all he
wanted to protect her.

Chapter Sixteen

Work blurred past. And not because it went by particularly quickly. Madelyn remembered people offering condolences, but she didn't remember what they said. She remembered people, especially the students, asking questions about the horrible details of the crime, but she couldn't make herself remember them.

The fog stayed thick until she grabbed a beer out of the refrigerator. She popped the top and relaxed back in a chair of her thick wooden dining table that rarely sat the two it could. She sipped her Carib Lager and rubbed the head resting in her lap. The familiar bristles of Deacon's coat soothed her as she sifted through the muck in her head. But the more she sifted the higher her anger built.

Regret at not inviting Nichole to stay over Thursday night gnawed at her resolve. Helplessness taunted. Rage at knowing Jim Gallow walked free while Nichole lay in a morgue assaulted her senses.

The anger took over again. She hated the rage inside her. It ate at her soul. She poured the beer down the drain and decided a run would expel the jagged rage.

The falling sun turned the sky into the best version of a Monet she'd ever seen. The sun's orange met with red. It faded into purple and blue, and then reflected off the sea and clouds. She breathed it all in—the wet air, the fresh scent of the banana and palm trees. Her anger melted away as she lengthened her stride.

Two miles was her usual share of beach. Wanting more of the simplicity, she pushed on. Deacon must've called it quits. His paws no longer churned the sand behind her. He probably passed the time digging for fiddler crabs near ocean's edge.

Slowly the colorful sky darkened.

Striding down the shore, she didn't anticipate the collision. It came from behind. Her face met the sand. The air deserted her lungs. She struggled to orient to the new position. Madelyn lifted her ringing head and gasped for air, but a large hand pinned the back of her neck. It restricted her movement, her vision, her life.

She inhaled bits of sand. Choking on them she grappled for calm. If she panicked, she'd die. Through shards of pain, she collected a clear breath. Then another. Madelyn barred her hips off the earth, but the weight of a large body trapped hers.

Click, click, click, click.

The tiny sound reverberated in her skull. Cool metal manacled her wrists. Panic devoured her whole. She thrashed against the bonds. The ligaments of her arms stretched unnaturally behind her back. Her body sank deeper into the quicksand.

Not her hands. How could she fight if she didn't have her hands? It would've been wise to take Agent Brewer up on that protective custody offer. But now wasn't the time to lament past mistakes.

Madelyn prayed for the first time in a very long time—to the God she wasn't too sure gave a shit about her—that someone inhabited the marvelous mansion behind her. Maybe they would call Chief and he'd arrive in time to save her. And if she were really lucky, the owner would come out with guns blazing to protect their opulent home.

She shifted her head in the grit. Like so many times before, her prayers were dashed in darkness. Her slanted glimpse of the house showed blackness. Void of life. And soon, she might very well match.

Madelyn ground her teeth into her waning courage. No, she didn't have her hands. But she would use whatever she could to fight. However she could manage, she wouldn't give up.

With a face full of sand, she decided to fight.

He grabbed her screaming shoulders and flipped her over. His weight only lifted for a tiny fragment of a second.

Her attacker's face loomed. A black mask hid his identity. Only his dark eyes peeked from the shroud. Her fingers itched to gouge them out. With his hands on the tops of her shoulders he lowered his head to hers. Fear churned in her gut as he moved in closer.

Madelyn choked it down and waited. His obscured face hung inches from hers. With all the force she could generate while backed against the sand, she lurched forward and slammed her head into his.

Pain crackled through her brain. Her attacker grunted. His grip released her shoulders. Without thought she planted her feet and thrust her hips up and over, flipping him onto his back.

Instantly, she curled her butt off the sand and slipped her feet under the loop of cuffs. She could run, but maybe he could too. Maybe she wouldn't get away. Or maybe he would.

In one smooth motion she flipped onto him. Straddling his waist she reared her arms to the sky and battered down toward his face. The cuffs jerked to a halt mid-strike. Her wrists wracked against the metal. A cry escaped her lips.

"Damn it, Madelyn, you busted my lip!"

Confused, she struggled to gain control of her hands, promising to do much more than just bust his lip. He held the cuffs tight with one hand and with the other pulled off his mask.

"What are you doing?" she shrieked.

"Proving a point." Special Agent Nathan Brewer hurled the words.

"What, that you're insane?"

"No, that you need protection."

"Me? Who has the busted lip?"

"Who's in hand cuffs?"

Nathan released his hold on the manacles. Her hands fell slack on his hard abdomen. He shifted his hips and took advantage of her stupor. She rolled listlessly onto her back. Holding himself directly above her, he stared into her eyes.

"You didn't leave me much choice."

Madelyn willed her brain to catch up with the action. She couldn't figure out if she was pissed or completely aroused. He mounted her spread legs like a lover. His weight rested in the cradle of her thighs. In a place where weight hadn't rested in a long, long time.

Heat flushed her body from the fight. From the fall of adrenaline. From the contact of their bodies.

Madelyn tried not to get lost in his penetrating stare. And it was the hardest thing she'd ever done in her life. Finally, she decided pissed was the best option for the moment. Putting on the meanest look she could muster, she tried to let him have it.

"You know, you're a real ass." She planted her cuffed hands on his firm chest and pushed. "Get off me."

He didn't budge. His gaze just bore deeper. "And you're real stubborn." The slightest grin tickled his hard expression. "Do I have your attention now?"

"Yes, you have my attention. Now please..."

He removed himself and sat facing the ocean next to her sprawled body. "You need some help with those cuffs?"

No. She needed help with something else—the need raging inside her body— but she wasn't about to ask him for that kind of help.

"Uh-uh," was all she could muster.

Madelyn sat and sand rained from her body. She blew it from her face and brushed it with her bound hands before turning toward the water. Offering him her hands seemed more intimate than letting him rest in the junction of her thighs. So, she interlocked her fingers and watched the white caps glimmer in the moonlight.

They sat side-by-side staring at the starry sky, the crashing waves doing her talking for her. They screamed her disbelief. They roared her outrage. They sang her desperation.

"The cuffs were the point," Nathan said. "If I could get close enough to cuff you, then he could take you. He sedates his victims with a shot of Versed. Traces of the drug have been found in every autopsy. We believe he hauls them to another location because there is so little evidence where the bodies are found. In that second location he takes his time."

"He rapes and tortures them, for hours. When he's had his fill he takes them to a third and final location, where he kills them by hanging. He'll use a tree, light pole, or flag pole. He's not picky. But he doesn't stop there. He cuts them open from end to end, removes their insides, and leaves them for all to see."

He turned to her. Stubbornly, she stared straight ahead, afraid the tears collecting in her eyes would spill over. Nathan's warm hands settled around the cuffs. One at a time he released the lock, and then slid them from her wrists. They slid onto the sand.

His thumb caught her chin and tilted it up to meet his gaze. "I'll protect you. You don't have to go to the safe house, but my team will set up a perimeter at your house and I'll be your bodyguard. I've seen too many dead bodies at this sicko's hand and I won't stand idly by while he rapes, tortures, and murders you."

She couldn't speak or she'd sob.

"Madelyn," he begged.

She finally choked. "I...I have to think. I need some time to think."

"You don't have time," he growled.

When her tears began their muted fall Nathan released her chin. She buried her head on her knees and wrapped her arms around her folded legs. The tears weren't for her. They were for Nichole. They were for the other women who had suffered the injustices of the killer's twisted mind.

If she had taken all night to grieve, Nathan probably would have watched over her. His presence was unshakable. She only gave herself a couple of minutes, before lifting her head and clearing away the tears. She turned toward him. "Walk me home?"

He didn't speak, just stood and reached for her hand.

They walked in silence until they reached the two-mile marker. Deacon wasn't there digging for crabs. Her eyes searched the shoreline. No sign of him.

Madelyn's head snapped around. "Where's my dog?"

"There." Nathan pointed to the palms.

Under the palms was an unconscious mass of fur and muscle. Madelyn sprinted to Deacon. She placed a hand under his leg and searched for his heart beat. "What did you do?"

"Only a fraction of what this killer would do to you," he replied with a no-nonsense stare.

She didn't pay the comment its due attention. She focused on Deacon. His chest rose and fell and his heart drummed easily against her palm. She lifted his leg and released it. His big paw slapped down with no resistance. He was out cold.

She stood and glared at Nathan. Then she added an evil smirk. "You're carrying him back."

Chapter Seventeen

Nathan was in shape, but hauling an extra ninety-five pounds over the sand for two miles took its toll. By the time he laid Deacon onto the plush dog bed in the corner of the living area, his mouth was dry and his stomach wept for sustenance. She hadn't said much on the walk back. No doubt she was pissed, but hopefully she gave some serious thought to what he'd told her.

Madelyn dumped the sand from her shoes and set them next to the front door. When she finally turned into the small house her gaze skated over his head. Yep, still mad. She headed for the fridge. The clank of glass bottles lit the air. Nathan almost groaned. He wasn't above begging.

As she rounded the corner, her sultry, sad eyes narrowed on him. She held out one of the two beers she held.

He hesitated. "You slip something into it?"

"No."

He reached for it, but she jerked it back. "I should knock you over the head with it though." She shoved the thing at him and worked her jaw side-to-side.

Nathan snagged it, twisted the top, and then handed it back to her. "Perils of the job."

Surprisingly, she traded bottles with him. He'd half expected her to remove the cap with her teeth, just to prove she didn't need help.

"You're not leaving until he wakes up, which means you're staying for dinner. So, go light the grill while I figure out what you're going to cook."

"I'm on it." He nodded—liking the idea of this domestic scene a little too much—and headed for the patio before she changed her mind. When he stepped into her bedroom his gait eased, allowing him to catalogue the nuances of her intimate space.

A hint of lavender hung in the air. Strings of tiny lights hung above the patio and reflected an ethereal glow in the space. It lit heavily on a queen-size bed shoved into the corner of the small room. She'd look so damn good spread out on the fluffy white comforter, all pliant, and needy. But it'd take more to get her there than he could give.

So, he adjusted his pants to accommodate his swollen cock, grabbed the knob to the back door, and twisted. Nothing happened. A satisfied smirk curved his lips. She did listen to him. At least a little. He flipped the bolt and made his way to the grill.

About the time he got the coals lit and the edges charred white, Madelyn breezed through the door. She placed a platter of shrimp and vegetable kabobs onto the bistro table, and then disappeared into the house without a glance in his direction. He stared after her sweaty, sand coated form.

The more he puzzled over Madelyn Garrett the more he wondered what he'd give—if he could—to be with her.

Nathan watched the black squares turn white, the vegetable and shrimp sear, and brooded. If he lost focus of his goals, the bad guys would win. And no amount of lust could override his need to see sick sons-of-bitches like Famosa and the Field-Dresser rot for their crimes.

The back door opened and closed again, but he didn't turn around. He pulled the last of his beer and turned the skinny wooden spindles.

"Why do you care so much?" Madelyn's sultry voice taunted him, while her words hit a little close to the mark.

"It's my job."

Her arm brushed his, inciting the throb between his legs that had only grown more insistent. A beer bottle hung between her fingers. He grabbed the offering and prayed she'd retreat. The scent of her sweat overrode his hunger for food. He licked his lips to keep from licking her mouth. The mouth that had pulled him like a bull to a matador's cape when he'd had her flat on her back, nestling his dick on the beach.

"Not many people show so much dedication to their work." The breath of her words danced over his bicep.

"Not many jobs protect the innocent and see that the guilty are punished."

"Why is that so important to you?"

His grip on the beer doubled and he couldn't decide whether her proximity or the sensitive subject matter had him on edge. "Dinner's ready."

"Hum." She stepped back. "I have plates on the table. Let me grab them."

"Hum?" He turned toward her retreating back.

Her pony-tail gyrated with the bob of her head. "You have this unearthly calm about you, but you can be pushed just like everyone else."

"I don't know that I like being lumped into the general population. Especially since you seem to have an aversion to them."

Madelyn shoved a plate at his middle and ducked around him. Her gaze darted high and low in front of the grill.

"Looking for these?" He clamped the tongs together.

"Yes," she bit.

Nathan reached over her shoulder, pinning her between him and the grate. Her breath hitched. He plucked two skewers from the low flame and set them on her plate. She stayed perfectly still as though he loaded her with dynamite instead of grilled deliciousness. He pulled the last three from the heat, heaped them on the plate, and then stepped back.

"Shall we?"

She walked to the table with a rigidity normally reserved for the dead. It loosened after gulps of beer and a few bites. "It's very good. Thank you."

"That's all you. I just heated it. But I have to warn you..." Her eyes shot wide. "If this is what I get for tranquilizing your dog, tackling you, and smashing your face in the sand, you had better keep a good eye out."

A genuine smile bowed her pretty mouth. Too soon it fell away.

"You honestly don't think Jim killed her. I get that. But when will you know for sure?"

He tossed a pita triangle heaped with some sort of black spicy dip she'd added to the table into his mouth and chewed. His head shook before he could speak. "You really don't trust anyone, do you?"

"I trust him." She hiked a thumb toward the unconscious dog in the house. "And he trusts me."

"Your trust is hard earned, and I can respect that. What I can't understand, is why you'd risk your life when all the signs point to the Field-Dresser."

Madelyn pushed her half-eaten meal away. "Because I went with the superficial once and lost everything for it. I don't have much to lose now, but what I do have I intend to keep."

Nathan shoved her plate back in front of her. "Eat. It's not the husband. Not unless he's the serial killer. And I don't think he is. This guy is patient. Jim Gallow has a world of impulse control issues. But if you need actual physical proof, I'll have it in a couple of days."

When he'd finished every bit of food on his plate and the tray of dip, she reached for the dishes. He caught her hand in his. "I don't suggest waiting that long to go into protective custody."

It could have been a trick of the light, but he'd swear her pupils dilated. "Noted," she breathed. He released her hand. She snatched the plate and stood. "I'll go clean these up."

"I'll take care of the grill."

"Thanks." She ran like the mountain behind her house had just erupted. With a stack of breakables, the display made him chuckle.

He dealt with the coals, cleaned the grate, and locked the door behind him, along with every window in her bedroom. In the kitchen dishes clanked and clattered and water drizzled from the spout. Deacon stretched his legs over the edge of his dog bed. Nathan sat next to the groggy pup. He braced his back on the tiniest sofa he'd ever seen and stroked the big guy's scarred belly.

Little by little the dog wiggled his way off the dog bed and to Nathan's side. "Sorry for the fake out, buddy. Sometimes we all have to take one for the team." He found the particularly sensitive spot at the top of Deacon's sturdy chest and scratched.

The big guy's tongue lulled out the side of his head and groaned as though he'd found an unattended Christmas ham. "I suppose this'll get us square?"

Deacon lifted his head and plopped it on Nathan's thighs. After a few wiggles the top half of the pup's body fixed him to the floor.

"Real talk. I like it." Nathan scrubbed the dog's head. "So, wanna tell me how to get Madelyn to trust me?"

The mighty beast heaved a sigh.

"Pray for a miracle? Yep, that's what I thought."

The water in the kitchen shut off. Silence descended in the tiny dwelling. Nathan kept his mouth shut to head off any beating Madelyn would dole out if she heard him pestering the dog for information. A few cabinets opened and closed. The soft pads of her footsteps announced her arrival a few seconds before she appeared.

She'd washed her face and let her hair down. Some clung to the tops of her breasts while the rest cascaded down her back. A huge smile parted her lips and warmed her somber eyes.

Lord, he was in trouble.

"Why didn't you tell me he was awake?" She skittered across the room and dropped to her knees beside him. "Hey, bud."

Madelyn leaned forward, cupped Deacon's head in her hands, and lowered hers to meet it. Her hair draped her face. It forced a rush of air thick with her scent straight up Nathan's nose. He ground his teeth to keep from groaning like a dog.

She sat back, still holding Deacon's head and smiled. "You have my permission to bite him," she whispered.

"Not a chance."

"You're right, he wouldn't." Her gaze met his. "He likes you a lot and that's out of character for him. He only appreciates a few people, but not this openly." She gestured toward his current position.

They shared a smile that—despite its innocence—charged the air between them. This close, the pull grew bold. His fingers itched to tame her hair in his grip. Her gaze darted to his mouth, and then back up. His breaths came shallow, flaring his nostrils.

Madelyn's lips parted. She cast her gaze at the dog and gnawed on her cheek.

"I won't bite you, you know?"

Her hand brushed Deacon's fur in a light, distracted stroke. The caress transferred through the dog's body. Nathan's thigh tingled.

"Would it sound crazy," she whispered, "if I said I'm worried you won't bite."

"Not if you explain what you mean."

She continued to rub the dog and drive him mad without a word.

"I can bite...and make you like it."

Her cheeks flamed red. She zeroed in on him with wide eyes. "I didn't mean it like that." A sigh drew her shoulders. "I mean if you acted like most men it would be easier."

It was worth a shot.

"Easier?" he asked, quirking a brow.

"I wouldn't feel bad about slamming the door in your face or telling you to fuck off."

"So, you haven't told me to fuck off?" He grinned to lighten the mood. "I'd hate to be the bastard that got the blunt rejection."

The pulse in her neck made the skin just below her ear throb. One little kiss couldn't hurt. Could it?

Nathan sat forward, bringing their faces a breath apart. His hand released the prickly fur for more tender locks.

"Deacon is awake, so you're free to go."

"Do you want me to go?" He stilled, stared into her soulful eyes, and waited.

"You should go," she murmured.

"Do you want me to go?" he repeated.

A war raged in her flitting eyes.

"Yes." Her gaze met his. "I need time to wrap my head around all this. This kind of stuff doesn't happen to me. I am a simple person. I lead a simple life. And all this..." She stood and raked her hands through her hair. "It's just crazy. I mean you—the FBI here—Nichole gone, Jim, and your killer. It's too much."

"It's not more than you can handle. You are a strong woman. You just have to trust us to take care of the situation. You have to trust me."

"Trust doesn't come easily. Not for me anyway." She shrugged.

"Me neither."

"I want to trust you." Her arms crossed over her chest, plumping her breasts.

But I'm a rat bastard with a fixation on your body that can't be trusted.

"But?" he asked.

"But it's hard to give up control. I finally have control over my life and here's another man..." She ground her lips together. "You're asking me to relinquish it. I...I need time. Lock me in here tonight and take a look around outside. You said yourself he strikes two weeks apart, so I have a little time. Just give me tomorrow."

He hoisted himself and Deacon off the floor. "Where do you want this lug?"

"Will you put him on my bed, please?"

Nathan nodded and hauled the dog into her room. Madelyn stayed put. He laid Deacon on her plush comforter and rubbed his head. "You lucky bastard."

He returned to find her holding the same locked down—a.k.a. breasts out—position. "Hold out your hands."

She scrunched her face and cocked her head to the side.

"Do it."

She huffed, but did as he commanded. And wasn't that hot.

He placed a walkie-talkie in her hand. "I'll be close. You need me, for anything, use it." Her cheeks turned pink. "Seriously, you think you hear something outside, you think you see something, don't wait."

In the other hand he placed a Glock 27. "In case I'm not close enough."

"Oh."

"Do you know how to use one of these?"

"Yes."

"Show me."

"You want me to shoot you?" Her pretty mouth bowed, and not in a smile. "I took a gun safety course and shot nearly every day in Mississippi."

"That was a while ago."

Madelyn clipped the radio onto the waist of her shorts. She cradled the gun like a professional. Her small hands wrapped firm around the slide. One finger hit the slide lock. She stripped and reassembled the Glock in military fashion in under thirty seconds.

"Hot damn, I think I'm in love."

She held the pistol by her leg, covered her mouth with her other hand, and giggled. "I think you're crazy. Truly." Her head shook back and forth. "And now that I'm armed, don't tackle me in the dark."

"Only if you ask." He grinned and stepped around her slacked jaw. Before he let himself out he called over his shoulder, "Lock the door behind me."

Chapter Eighteen

His large frame sat hunched over the sullied kitchen table. The last rays of sunlight dissipated from the shallow room. Cigarette smoke hung heavy, clouding the stagnant air, while fresh fumes constantly rose from the bidi laid on his linoleum-topped office space. A static-laced tune filled in the smokeless holes. The delicious and haunting voice of Billie Holiday diffused from the turntable speaker plopped in the center of the adjacent living room. Over and over she sang of the strange fruit and the blood on the leaves.

His hands worked over the spool of rope in front of him. A row of twelve spools sat lined against the wall, awaiting their useful day. Around his wrist he twisted the tight knit fabric until his skin was masked with the wrapping. Taking the loose end firm in his opposing hand he wiggled the slack for a brief moment. Then, with mighty force, he yanked it taut. The boa constricted around his wrist burning his flesh as it moved rapidly across it. His fist clinched down on the rope and his eerie bellow rattled the walls.

When his demented joy subsided he moved the rope to his exposed thigh. He repeated the ritual again and again over his body. With each pull of the slack his mind erupted in joy at the thought that his pain was nothing compared to theirs.

His thoughts during his ritualistic ecstasy always flew to his first witnessed kill. His father had taught him well. As a boy every one of his father's kills he'd been privy to had been a show of artistry.

He could still see his father's skilled hands toil over the white-fronted capuchin. His innocent eyes had been wide with disbelief as his father slowly and methodically tortured the small monkey. Cuts and burns, abrasions and punctures stained his young eyes. The screams his father had persuaded from the animal still rang in his ears. It had taken seven days for the animal's death.

His father was his hero. And now as an artist himself, he could appreciate his father's patience and zeal for perfection. It took a surplus of control to extend the pleasure as long as that man could. He'd tried to hone that particular skill and failed at each attempt. Through childhood he'd tested his restraint on small animals. When they lost their luster he moved on to larger ones. He used goats and cattle, cats and dogs to get his adolescent rushes. But each time he couldn't restrain the urge to end them much more quickly than his father would have.

In his adult years, his environment expanded and he learned more about the world. He was finally introduced to the concept of right instead of wrong, good as opposed to bad, happy versus sad. And the ideas stuck for a time.

He lived the straight and narrow for years, blending in with the people around him. He molded himself into a conventional man. College had been a liberating experience. It had allowed him to see good in the world and even to create happiness in his own.

But the demon would not be long denied. His hunger returned more ambitious and greedy than before. The tricks of his youth no longer held his attention. He needed something more.

When he crossed over into the human realm he met the devil inside himself. And he liked it. These pawns were so much more fulfilling than the ones of his youth. He could frighten them with one touch, one word. Even a look could conjure a beautiful plea.

Each beauty he enjoyed reminded him of his mother. Long, dark hair flowed down their backs. Their kind hearts and sweet smiles coupled with their feminine curves and lines. But the thing that reminded him most of his mother was the feel of their blood.

His loving mother ended her own life when he was just a boy. It happened shortly after his father had shown him his intricate hobby. He'd returned from the bus stop, a mile trek to where he was shuttled back and forth to elementary school, because he'd forgotten his lunch bag. He opened the front door and saw his mother hanging from the living room rafters.

Blood dripped from her wrists. Her favorite Billie Holiday song livened the background.

When he couldn't get a response from her he laid in the pool of her blood, scrolling his fingers through the congealing liquid until his father came home from work. He liked lying there because he could see the slight smile on her paling face. Sure, his father had been angry with him for not going to school, but he hadn't beaten him. He'd simply cleaned the blood off of them both and put Momma to sleep in the ground behind their house.

Today's beauties reminded him so much of his momma. They were certainly more difficult to come by than cats or dogs. But the reward far outweighed the labor involved. On occasion their fight was more too. He had gotten a bloody lip and even a broken finger carrying out his devil's will.

He was constantly challenged. From planning to execution, he methodically laid out each step of his pleasure's feat. Crowds were a constant nuisance and the authorities were a hindrance. Several times he had to change tactics on the fly, which he hated to do. But it was all worth the trouble.

The joy of their cries tickled his ears. The sight of their struggle gave life to the mundane. Their begging stroked his ego. But nothing compared to that gleam in their eyes. Standing under their hanging spot, when the last thread of hope vanished, their eyes gleamed. He lived for the realization that came just before the noose tightened around their life and all was lost. No shining knight would come to their rescue. No one would save them.

He saw in their eyes the acknowledgement of pure evil in the world and the recognition that he was the conductor of it all. When that gleam flashed in their eyes and they accepted their fate, he was victorious.

His body rocked as the memories and power washed over him. Putting his spool aside for the moment he placed latex gloves on his large hands. Their pop stung the air. The bottle of all-purpose kitchen cleaner squeaked as his hand depressed the nozzle and removed any evidence from the table. When the site was clear he picked one of the waiting spools from the wall and placed it on the linoleum.

He sat in front of the heap of rope. He sang Strange Fruit with Billie while he made his next noose. He would get to use it sooner than he'd thought. The corners of his mouth turned and a deep laugh escaped his throat. Once again he was working on the fly, but he would enjoy it no less.

Madelyn angered him and she would pay. He hadn't seen a glint of terror in her eyes. Not enough sadness for his pleasure. She was stronger than the others. She needed a more penetrating threat.

Chapter Nineteen

"Do we really have to take both tests tomorrow?" Yaniel whined.

Madelyn continued writing the review pages for their test on the abolition of the Caribbean slave trade. "Yes."

"But...with everything that's happened... I don't know. I figured we'd take time to mourn Mrs. Gallow," the boy continued.

Talk about a low blow. Madelyn snapped the cap on the dry-erase marker and then wiped the stray ink from her fingers. She faced the class and centered her no-nonsense glare on the boy in the back of the single-room hut. "We won't just mourn her, Yaniel. We'll honor her with high marks on our tests."

No one had a good comeback to that. She smiled. "Make sure you have these page numbers in your notebooks and that you study them tonight. Now, on to my man Hamlet."

"I need to use the ladies'," Martha interrupted.

"We break in ten minutes. I'm sure you can hold it that long. Now, who can tell me which characters survive at the end of the play?"

A few hands raised, but Martha's hand whipped through the air.

"Lin." Madelyn called on the girl in front of the student whose eyeballs apparently floated in urine.

"Horatio and Fortinbras." Lin beams.

Almost.

At least the pandemonium allowed little free time to think about the sorrow, the decisions to be made, the fear, and the unexpected spark that Nathan Brewer's presence ignited. A spark that seemed to burn her from the inside out.

Martha flailed two hands and added her head in the mix, shaking side to side.

"Okay, Martha." Madelyn held up a hand. "Answer the question correctly and you may be excused."

"Thank you, Ms. Garrett." The girl's hands gripped the edge of her desk. "Horatio, Fortinbras, the English Ambassador, and likely Osric."

"Nice work." Madelyn nodded. "You may go, but if you make less than ninety percent on the test tomorrow you won't get to go again."

"Yes, um'." The girl slid her seat back.

"Ms. Garrett?" Zuberi's voice turned her attention to the back of the room. "If I answer a question right can I go to the bathroom?"

Two other hands shot up. Kids. They saw a perceived crack in her armor and took aim. But watch out for the chasm beneath. She smiled. "Sure. You just have to earn a one hundred on the test tomorrow or you lose your bathroom privileges for the rest of the year."

The two hands sank. Zuberi puffed his chest and jutted his chin.

"All right," Madelyn conceded. "Compare and contrast Hamlet with Horatio, Fortinbras, Claudius, and Laertes."

He balked, but she knew he could answer the question. Despite his macho swagger, he paid as close attention to their reading of the play as he did Martha's short skirts. Well, almost.

"So," Zuberi started, "Horatio is—"

A shrill scream sliced through the orderly classroom assembly and severed the boy's answer. The sharp pitch radiated from the young girl lurching from the gaping classroom door. She backpedaled, slammed into an empty desk, and fell to the ground.

What on earth... Then Madelyn remembered that this was no ordinary day. Nathan's warning flashed in her mind. She sprinted hard and fast, clearing the long room in a few strides.

"Are you okay?" Madelyn kneeled next to the girl. Her gaze searched for signs of injury, but found none. Martha's bloated eyes focused on a point over Madelyn's shoulder outside the classroom.

She turned and the reel of her life hitched. Everything slowed. A frame per second ticked by. The bright Caribbean sky framed the doorway. A ghastly silhouette absorbed the sunlight. Camouflage rope knotted around the wooden rafters of the porch. The noose, tight around his neck, severed life. His. Hers.

No!

The word ricocheted in her skull. It rang her ears louder than the roar of the sea. And yet, she didn't make a sound as she stared at Deacon's suspended bulk. Her only friend left in the world hung limp. Lifeless.

No!

This time the silent word boomeranged as a command. Like her will had the power to change reality.

The wicked laugh from her past echoed. A chill settled along her spine. Her gut flipped. And she'd swear his ghost stood over her, mocking the seed of hope as he'd done so often all those years ago. He'd beaten down every sprout of hope in the desert that had been her life. That was quickly becoming her life again.

No.

"Deacon." Madelyn scrambled across the distance. Her bare knees stung from the traction of the rough floor. One of her sandals slipped from her foot, but she made it to the door.

She lunged for Deacon and wrapped her arms around his narrow waist. A shiver rocked them. Madelyn gasped. Her tongue threatened to lodge in her throat. Was that his shiver or hers?

His belly still radiated heat.

"Deacon?" she cried.

When he shuddered under her hand a sob choked itself off in her windpipe. She gathered as much of his haunches and middle as she could with him hanging so high and lifted. His uneven weight tattered, but she held strong. She waited, hoped, begged that she hadn't hallucinated the fight left inside him.

"Deacon!"

He reared against the rope. She shuffled under him, struggling to keep the rope from cinching around his throat. The rope some psychopath had placed there. In the daylight. Silently. With her and her children only ten feet away.

Her gaze scanned the dirt yard, the other huts, the woods surrounding the school. Was he there, watching and waiting?

"Martha," Madelyn hollered.

"Yes," the girl squeaked.

"Tell Sauda and Zuberi to come here and everyone else to close the windows and get into the supply closet now," she commanded.

'Yes ma'am's' murmured behind her. Then the shuffle of adolescent feet scattered. Apparently, she'd gathered a crowd. The boys she'd requested stood before her. Sweat dripped from Sauda's dark chin.

"Is he..." Zuberi rang his hands.

"No, but I need your help." Her heart beat so forcefully against her chest it stole all the oxygen from her lungs. Stars danced in her periphery.

"Name it," Sauda pled.

"A chair," she panted.

They scrambled.

Her shoulders sang. The feeling in her fingers faded down her arm. Madelyn straightened her back and reinforced her grip. "You'll be okay, bud. I've got you." A tear slipped down her cheek, but she rubbed onto his fur. She couldn't lose it now. Her kids needed her.

The clattering of a chair hitting the porch sent a fresh shot of adrenaline through her body.

"Sauda had to help with the windows. Most of the scaredy-cats made for the closet." Zuberi laughed as he rubbed at the tremor in his hand.

"I'm scared too," she whispered.

"Ha. You don't sound scared or look it." He scooted the chair closer and hurried atop it.

She grew up scared, every second of every day. Crisis mode became her twisted little comfort zone. She learned to operate under pain, and terror, and his ever-watchful eyes.

"You ready?" he asked.

"Yes." Madelyn loosened her stance to catch his falling weight. "I'm ready." Her breath seized and she waited.

And waited.

Her torso quivered under the weight of Deacon's body and his sluggish struggles. "Calm down. It's okay. Everything is going to be okay," she said in a light, even tone for all their benefit. If only the cramp in her side would agree.

"I'm sorry, Ms. Garrett. But the rope... I can't get it loose. There's not enough rope between the noose and the rafters."

Sweat tickled her brow. Her entire body quaked. She couldn't hold on much longer. But she couldn't let go. Not for a second. Not for anything.

"Scissors," she ground through clenched teeth.

The boy leaped from the chair. His too large feet for his body clopped inside. "Scissors," he yelled. Seconds later the rumble of feet approached. "I have them. And Sauda can help now."

"Great. Please, hurry." She swore she wouldn't rush them, but the last bit of feeling fled her hands.

Sauda, the taller of the two, bracketed his hands on the lower part of Deacon's chest. The white of his eyes grew, contrasting against the charcoal of his skin. "Cut it already."

"I'm trying," Zuberi huffed. "It's not like cutting paper."

"It's okay," Madelyn said. But her voice came as little more than a whisper. A wish. Her eyes closed on the hope. One of the boys growled in frustration.

Deacon's bulk gave way. It crashed down hard on her face, but her arms stayed locked around his back end. She shuffled to balance the awkwardness of the grip. Sauda shifted. He sidled closer to her and encircled Deacon's chest.

"Inside," she huffed.

They stumbled into the building and Zuberi slammed the door behind them.

"Put the chair in front of the door." Madelyn turned to make certain the child did as she asked.

Her foot landed on the side of Sauda's. In an effort not to hurt him, her ankle rolled. The mass in her arms flailed. The classroom tilted.

Madelyn landed hard on her elbow and Deacon landed on her chest. The impact drove her flat as a paper doll onto the floor. Two feet of the sturdy wooden chair and the stiff back of the top wedged between the knob and the floor. A shard of relief slipped into place. "Thank you. Now, in the closet boys."

"But who's doing this to us?" One of them begged.

"Closet now. Questions later."

She rolled Deacon onto his side and scrambled to her knees beside him. His breaths came shallow and slow. But they came. Distance glazed his eyes. His pulse bumped lazily against his chest. A drop of water splashed against his cheek. He blinked mechanically.

A sob shook her shoulders and she realized the water was her tear. She sucked back the emotion. Her gaze darted around the room looking for her students. The desks stood empty. A few pencils littered the floor along with a piece of paper and a half eaten banana.

Why hadn't she trusted Nathan? Now her dog and her children were in jeopardy.

Nathan.

Madelyn wasn't the damsel in distress type, but a vicious, sadistic killer was out of her league. She dove for the closet, frantic for the radio he'd given her last night. Too bad she'd left the gun nestled under her pillow.

She flung the closet door open. Several kids gasped, while others lifted makeshift weapons in their trembling hands. Broom handles, yardsticks, and scissors were better than nothing.

"Someone hand me my bag," she begged in the calmest voice she could manage.

Arms reached in every direction. Someone yelled, "Here. I got it!" A collective sigh lightened the thick air. They crowd-surfed the woven bamboo tote. Her hand dove into its contents, roving for the feel of hard plastic while she surveyed the perimeter of the room.

Sweet success tickled her fingertips. She yanked the contraption from the bag and closed the closet door. She leaned against it for fortification, pressed the button, and hoped. "Nathan?"

Chapter Twenty

Broad daylight. The boldness of it had excited him. The reality of it boiled the blood in his veins. He'd been so close to getting caught that the *clink* of the cell door being slammed on his ass echoed behind him. On top of that he'd been interrupted before he'd split the dog in two.

Reliving her reaction in his mind aroused and irritated him further.

Her body jerked at the sight of his glorious work, as though caught dead center by a bullet. Those lips, so often smiling or smirking, formed the terrified O of Edvard Munch's pastel-painted scream. Damn her to hell. Just like the painting, no shrill screech or throaty cry poured from her stretched mouth.

Had Deacon's blood been splattered across the porch, had his insides been on display, maybe then that sweet song would have caressed him like a greedy hand wrapped around his dick.

He stomped through the woods and came out on the other side of the thicket near the beach. A woman toting a large bowl of fruit on her head gave him a friendly smile. He returned the gesture while inside he seethed, his body suddenly too small to contain the rage. It took every bit of restraint he possessed to let her walk past him without grabbing her in a choke hold, dragging her into the woods, and finishing the work he'd spoiled for today.

The patience he'd strived for revealed itself in that moment. He looked through the fury to the future. To the ultimate prize.

He would break Madelyn Garrett. She would scream for him. She would beg like all the others.

Turning his back on the sorry substitute, he slid into his father's old truck and started the engine. He pulled from the undergrowth to the edge of the road. An SUV barreled at him.

Fuck it all, but his palms slicked on the worn steering wheel.

Special Agent Nathan Brewer had been on his trail for a while now. He liked toying with the man, leaving just enough evidence to send him in fitful circles. Only he'd never been this close.

Framing Roger Inman should've gotten the man off his tail for good, if not for enough time to finish the women so close to home. So close to his heart. His jackknifing heart.

"Fuck." The vehicle drew closer. Its headlights flashed. He slipped his left foot onto the brake and hovered the right over the gas.

He inhaled, ready to flee, but the rush of oxygen dissipated the fog of adrenaline and the cloak of disappointment.

"Don't be a rookie. You can explain why you're here in this inconspicuous car. Even if it got his suspicions up, he wouldn't have enough to hold you. And you'd have plenty of time to clean away any evidence."

He dragged his palms over his pants and sat straight. The man zipped past with an expression that could have fit perfectly onto that of any of the four horsemen.

Interesting.

Either the man got wood from the possibility of catching him or from looking at his woman. Didn't that make things more interesting? A challenge. He was up to the task. In fact, he was up for two.

Chapter Twenty-one

God-fucking-damnit.

The ugly words bubbled on Nathan's tongue every time he looked at Madelyn. She sat behind a hefty desk, whispering to the young girl wrapped in her arms. Martha, the student who'd most likely stopped the killer from quartering Deacon, buried her face in Madelyn's curls. After a full six hours of lockdown in which his team questioned students and collected evidence, the woman's stiff spine and rigid jaw showed strength. But the clutch of her fists told Nathan she rode the fine edge of rage and sorrow...again.

Though he knew in his bones if he'd tried forcing her into protective custody he'd have lost the battle, it didn't stop culpability from gutting him. She'd been ten feet from unbridled evil. She'd been vulnerable because he'd given her the time she'd requested.

He'd thought they had a little bit of time. But no. The Field-Dresser changed his methods. Why? Did he know the FBI was on his tail? And if so, how did he know? Until yesterday there hadn't been an obvious Bureau presence on the island and the bastard hadn't spun this idea overnight. Most importantly, would he change his timetable?

"Richard Kepler is the Field-Dresser," the crime scene tech leaning on the doorframe whispered.

"What?" Nathan's head snapped around so quickly his neck *popped*.

"Well, that got your attention." The blonde smirked. "Since my rockin' ensemble didn't work, I had to say something to snap you out of it." She wiggled spirit fingers encased in surgical gloves and aimed them at the booties covering her feet. "And my report wasn't registering at all."

"What?" he barked again.

"Here." She shoved a clipboard into his hands. "I need you to sign these before I can run the tests."

"Look," he began to protest and then stopped. Damnit. He hadn't been listening to a thing she'd been saying. "I'm sorry. We've never been this close before. And I really want to get this piece of..."

"...shit, rat-bastard," she supplied.

"Spot on." He nodded.

"Then you might want to bring it down a notch." She snapped off the latex gloves. "You were grinding your teeth and huffing like the Big Bad Wolf ready to blow the island down to find this guy."

"That's not an altogether bad idea," he said, taking pains to even his breathing.

"Yeah, and my ex-husband thought a tattoo wasn't an altogether bad idea, until he ended up with a Florida State Seminole that looked far more constipated than fierce."

Nathan almost smiled. Almost. "When will you have the results? And, I'm sorry, I didn't catch your name."

"It's Pippa." Nathan's surprise must have shown. "Don't start. You have more important shit to think about." She studied the horizon. "From the looks of things, I'll get back to the pitiful excuse for a proper lab by sunset. If I pull an all-nighter to get them started, some of them will finish tomorrow. But the ones you want, fiber analysis and DNA, will take longer." She swatted at the pixie cut that matched her face. "But I'll let you know as soon as I have the results."

"I'm really sorry to interrupt. Martha's mother is here." Madelyn said. The girl who'd been crying for hours stood tall and dry eyed next to her teacher. Only her grip on Madelyn's hand betrayed the calm veneer.

"I'll take you to your mom." The tech's bright blue eyes smiled at the girl, and then she winked at Madelyn. "I don't think your teacher is finished up just yet."

"Oh," Madelyn said in surprise. "I'll see you tomorrow, Martha."

The girl nodded and took the petite hand offered her. When they walked into the fading sunlight, Madelyn wrapped her arms around her middle and stared after them.

"What did you say to her?" Nathan asked.

"Who?"

"Martha, to get her to stop crying?"

"People can only hurt us as much as we let them. If we let them, they win."

"Who hurt you?"

Her hands dropped to her sides and her gaze met his. "No one." She swallowed, opened her mouth to add something, but turned away and retreated toward her desk.

"Do you really believe that?" He needed to know if denial was her way of dealing or a deeper seeded issue that could get them killed. The question stopped her progress.

"Some days," she whispered.

"And today?"

"Not for a minute."

"Good."

A mirthless laugh shook her shoulders.

"The hurt will power your fight, give you the tenacity to get through this. And hopefully it will sharpen your focus, so you can tell the good guys from the bad."

"I know what you're thinking," she huffed.

Let me lay you down, spread your legs, and fuck you until we forget our own names.

"I highly doubt that." Nathan stared at the leanly muscled legs jutting out from her sundress. She turned slowly enough he could have raised his gaze, if he'd wanted to. But her legs shifting and flexing elegantly in her strappy sandals was too enticing.

"I suppose I was wrong, but whatever you're thinking now, it's not going to happen."

"Yes." He raised his gaze and centered hers. "It is." He stepped toward her. She negated his progress with a backward step. When he took another and another she soon found her upper thighs against the heavy desk. Nathan stopped inches away from her flushed cheeks and open mouth. He spread his hands around her narrow waist and then lifted.

"This isn't a good idea," she gasped.

He quirked a brow. "Why not?" While her tongue toyed with a tooth at the back of her mouth —a trait he'd noticed already, and found too damn endearing—he set her on the edge of the tidy desk. Though he shouldn't, he let his hand skim so close to her lush bottom that the heat nearly melted his fingerprints. His hands hooked the back of her knees and lifted slightly. "I can clean these cuts or take you to the hospital. Your choice."

"My cuts?" Her heavy lids lifted along with a brow.

"How'd you get these?" He gestured to the jagged cut on one knee and the scrape on the other.

"I don't...I was on the floor with Martha and then I saw Deacon. I just got to him as fast as I could."

"Do you have a first aid kit?"

"In the closet. Bottom shelf on the right." She fidgeted with the hem of her skirt.

"I'll be right back."

Nathan hurried to the closet and found the small red and white bag he sought.

"Artie is going to keep Deacon at the tent overnight," Dick announced, strolling through the doorway. "He's doing just fine. The doc just wanted to take some X-rays to make certain nothing was broken and watch his vitals." The guy flashed Madelyn his patented *I'll let you cry on my shoulder, if you let me eat you out* half-smile half-frown. "I'm sure you want to see him. If you're ready, I'll drive you over."

Nathan had seen the damn charm work too many times to count. He fisted the kit and held his breath.

"Agent Brewer will take me. Thank you for trying to track down Dr. Laura. She usually runs her little clinic on the island Tuesdays and Thursdays. She must have left early today. And thank you for the update."

"Sure thing." Dick glanced at Nathan and nodded. "It looks like you're in good hands. So, I'll leave y'all to it. I need to talk to the tech about something."

"If this something keeps her from starting those tests right away, I'll send you back to Miami in a wooden box," Nathan warned.

"Would I ever stand in the way of justice?" The guy placed his hand on his chest. He had enough sense to clear out before Nathan could answer.

"So, I'm taking you to see Deacon?" He plucked two disinfectant wipes from the pack and set it on a neat pile of papers.

"Would you please?"

"As long as you know, my team is setting up a surveillance perimeter around your house and that I'm coming home with you tonight and to work with you tomorrow."

"Okay," she whispered.

"I was expecting more of a fight." He ripped a packet open and cradled the soft skin covering the back of her thigh.

"I'm not going to fight you anymore."

"You might want to after this." Nathan rubbed the pad on the worst of the abrasions. He didn't want to hurt her, but the thing needed to be cleaned to stave off infection. His gaze met hers. She didn't even bat a lash. "That doesn't hurt?"

She shrugged. "It doesn't feel good, but I've had...I have a high tolerance for pain."

"Why?"

Chapter Twenty-two

"We're here. Now, tell me why?" Irritation laced Nathan's voice, but he smoothed Deacon's fur with long, terribly gentle stokes.

The thrum of her heartbeat rang in her ears as loudly as it had when she'd seen Deacon hanging. Even more terrifying was the reason for her roaring pulse. Trust and the truth of her past didn't come easily. She'd nearly sacrificed a friend to keep it under wraps. She gripped the edge of the exam table, careful not to touch the leg of Nathan's jeans. His proximity. His touch. It ramped the vibration of every nerve ending.

"When you live with pain everyday it never hurts less." She laid her head on Deacon's chest. "But the threshold between tolerable and excruciating grows."

"Who hurt you?"

"It doesn't matter." Madelyn straightened. Nathan crossed his arms over his chest, so she placed her hand where he'd petted her dog and smiled at the reassuring beat under her palm. "He can't hurt me now. But this psycho killer has and can still. While we wait for the anesthesia Artie gave him to wear off, I'd like you to tell me everything you know about the Field-Dresser."

"You're going to have to tell me. Soon." He spread his feet like a drill sergeant ready to bark orders. Madelyn pinched her lips between her teeth in challenge.

Nathan pursed his lips and shook his head. "He is not a maniac; he is meticulous and controlled. He rapes and kills for the power, the control. By outside appearances he's a normal guy. More than likely he is someone you know."

Her pulse stuttered. Unable to speak, the gears of her mind ground slowly over the information. He was right. A sheen of sweat broke over her forehead. Both hands braced on the counter steadied her through the first wave of nausea. "Deacon would have only let a few people get that close to him. And Nichole wouldn't have ridden down the beach with someone she didn't trust."

He propped his elbow on his folded arm. The muscles bunched under the thin material of his pale blue shirt, stretching the fabric and her nerves into narrowly-bound strings. His fingers toyed with the cleft of his chin. "I have a theory about Deacon's attack."

"Come on, spill it. I have enough suspense in my life right now." *And enough to deal with that I don't need to add your handsome face to my list*, she silently added.

"I was working out the details..."

"The rough draft will do for now. Anything."

"We wondered why two women in the same town? Why the connection? Were all the victims somehow connected to him? They might be. We haven't been able to find the common link. But his move against Deacon is out of character. When I compare you to all the other second victims, the one thing that's different is your strength."

"He hurt my dog because I have muscles or because I didn't fall apart?"

His palm came up. "Summer Sutherland, the second victim from the first set of murders, didn't know she was the next victim. It probably wasn't his first kill, but it was his first using these methods and this pattern. Nancy Starks didn't have a sister. So, her friend Robin Young didn't know she was the next victim. But both women stopped going to work after the murders. They helped plan the wakes and funerals for their sister and friend. They surrounded themselves with family. They grieved openly. He thrived on their anguish."

Madelyn trapped that monster inside herself long ago. It gnashed and clawed at her insides, threatening to split her in two some days...like the other night. If only he could see the deep gashes on her heart, the holes in her soul. She pressed the heels of her palms against the cold table.

"It's not that I don't care," she whispered.

"Hey." His tone demanded her attention, but she kept her gaze trained on the rise and fall of Deacon's chest. She saw his hand a second before his forefinger nudged the bottom of her chin. The touch pierced her heart, but she tamped the sting of emotion. His decisive dark eyes softened. "I know you care."

The edge returned to his penetrating stare. "So does he." His touch fell away, but the heat of it stayed behind. "It's in your determination to see whoever killed Nichole brought to justice. It's in your dedication to your job. It's in your love for Deacon...who's coming around."

The amber eyes she'd grown to rely on more than her next breath gleamed in the bright tent lights. She blinked furiously. The horror of crying in front of the agent kept her in check. "Hey, bud." Her fingers rubbed snout to ears.

"You just don't show it in the way he needs it. He attacked the thing closest to you to illicit the reaction he desires."

"I won't let him win."

"We won't let him win," Nathan amended. "I know you're used to going it alone, but if we're going to stop him, we have to work together."

"I'll do whatever you tell me to do. I won't like it, but I can't put anyone else at risk because of my hang-ups."

Nathan blew out a breath and relaxed back onto his heels. "I honestly thought you'd die from your stubborn ways before you said those words."

"If he hadn't tried to kill my dog, I would have."

"So much for my powers of persuasion."

"It's not you. It's me."

"That hurt even worse." He placed a hand over his heart and groaned.

Despite it all a peal of laughter slipped between her lips. When he smiled back Madelyn covered her mouth. The rounds of her cheeks swelled under her touch. It felt good. The lightness beat back the dark for just a moment. "Thank you."

"I don't think anything's given me more pleasure than making you laugh." He plowed a hand through his hair and lifted both brows.

"Nichole would say, 'then you haven't been doing it right.'"

Their laughter grew boisterous. The mix of grief, relief, exhaustion, and hope filled the cloth walls.

Deacon snuffed, and then lurched. His attempt to stand on the slick metal sent his legs sprawling. All ninety pounds of him winged toward the floor.

"Woah." Nathan wrapped his arms around Deacon's body and hoisted. He settled the awkward weight in his grasp and smiled down at the dog. "I'm going to start charging you for my transportation services."

"What's all the racket?" Artie scuttled through the tent flap with a half-eaten sandwich hanging out of his mouth. "I swear, I can't leave you alone for a minute before you start tearing up the joint." He shook a finger at Nathan. "You're as bad as your partner."

"Dick?" Madelyn offered, unable to pass the opportunity to goad Nathan.

"He's not my partner," Nathan huffed.

"Dick's not his partner," Artie squawked atop the other man's words. "That boy may not know boundaries in the field, but at least he knows them in my lab. No, Special Agent Hunt traipses into my space like he pays rent and holds my equipment hostage until I finish the test he wants." The old man narrowed his bushy brows on Nathan. "Don't tell me he's rubbed off on you too."

"Never, sir. But ah, Deacon here would like to know the results of his test so he can go home tonight. You see, if he has to stay here overnight, I'm afraid he'd trash the place."

The smile on Madelyn's lips morphed into an all-out grin. She needed Deacon home tonight. The thought of leaving him made her short of breath. The thought of sleeping on the ground didn't hold much appeal either.

"The X-rays and tests showed no broken bones and no drugs in his system. But his neck will be sore for a week or more. I have some medicine to help with the inflammation and swelling. I guessed a bit on the dosage." Artie tossed his sandwich onto a file. "You'll need to keep a close eye on him through the night. If you notice any shortness of breath or vomiting, call me right away. It's been a long time since I made house calls and never for a dog, but it's the excitement that keeps me here."

"Thank you," Madelyn nearly squealed.

Artie smiled. "Now go on before Nathan wrecks the place."

Nathan pursed his lips. He adjusted his hold on Deacon and headed for the door. "Thanks, Artie."

Madelyn held the flaps and doors while Nathan situated her dog in the back seat of her Jeep.

"All right." He stepped back and offered his hand. "In you go."

"You're not going to make me sit in front?"

"As if I could ever make you do anything you didn't want to do. Besides, if he starts to hurl, I'll stop the car, but you'll have to make sure his head gets out the back window in time."

"You're crazy."

"You make me that way, Ms. Garrett." He plucked her from the ground, set her in the seat, and fastened her seatbelt while she stared at him, dumbstruck.

A few miles down the bumpy road Nathan cleared his throat. "I'd like you to name all the men you know that are 6' 3" or taller."

"I think you just won a prize for the most random question of the year." She rubbed the silk of Deacon's unscarred ear between her fingers.

"The murderer is a big guy. Artie and his people were able to narrow the numbers down based on the angles of the...because of the angles."

"Jim, Hanri, a bartender at Paradise, Chief, Ekene, Amadi, Mr. Stanley, my ninth grade teacher," and in sudden realization she adds, "and Glenn."

"Who's Glenn?"

"Someone from my past, but he's in California. Or, he was the last time I checked."

"When was that?"

"Five or six months ago."

"People are mobile."

"Yes, but why does it have to be someone I know? There are like two million tourists who come through these islands every year. Maybe one of them prefers offing pretty brunettes to snorkeling."

"You must think all the agents at the Bureau sit around all day twiddling their thumbs instead of swimming through seas of information looking for the tiniest clue that could help solve a case." Nathan rubbed the base of his skull.

"We have looked into those possibilities. We ran a cross-check of every airline, hotel, and cruise line database with the dates of the murders. Thirty people were in the islands for all the murders and most were over the age of seventy. Only one fit our physical description and he had rock solid alibis for not one, but three of the murders."

There was so much she could not compute. So much that did not make sense. She moved on to another concern. "Nichole was a strong woman trained in martial arts. I don't understand how anyone could've taken her and done all those horrible things without so much as a struggle."

"In terrible situations, especially when surprised, shock and fear paralyze people. Others focus on flight rather than fight. With either of those reactions the results are grim. His size alone would be difficult to overcome, and his method of abduction is another formidable obstacle. If he ever got his hands on you, which he won't, fighting would be your only chance. Now tell me this..." He continued, not giving her time to stew on the horrific scene in her head. "Who of the people you named could get close to Deacon?"

She ran through the list of possibilities and only four could get that close. "Amadi, Ekene, Chief, and Hanri."

"Not Glenn?"

"No, he's never met Deacon."

"Neither had I, and I got *extremely* close."

"Deacon can sense evil, that's why he hates Jim."

"You're not the only stubborn one in the car, Madelyn. Who is Glenn?"

"It's not relevant to this situation." She had tried to shift the topic and thought she had done a good job, but Nathan didn't miss a thing. The more reluctant she was to talk about her past the more gently and persistently he pushed.

"Why don't you let the professionals decide what is and isn't relevant to this investigation."

A growl rumbled in her throat. "He was my stepfather. I guess technically he still is, not that I claimed him a day in my life. But you have to let it go. He hasn't come to the islands to rape and murder women in an ultimate design to kill me."

"How can you be so sure?" Nathan's knowing eyes lit in the rearview mirror by the light of a passing car.

That gaze pinned her in the seat. It tempted her to free the weight that bowed her back and labored every breath. The weight that had doubled in the short time she'd known him. Because once he knew the truth he'd never look at her the way he had tonight.

If she couldn't face herself in the mirror, how could he?

"I told him if I ever saw his face again, I'd shove a knife into his belly...just like I did my mother's."

Chapter Twenty-three

Had the ground spit into a gaping chasm on the island road in front of him, Nathan wouldn't have been more astonished. He'd pried at her past for days and hypothesized about what could make a caring and vibrant young women hide from the world. Every scenario formed ice crystals in his veins, but none more than this revelation.

The words she and Chief exchanged played again in his mind.

"You may have seen a dead body at a funeral, but you haven't seen one carved up. It's a whole other deal."

"Actually, Chief, I have."

Nathan strangled the wheel, but otherwise showed none of the emotions cluttering his frontal lobe. Instinct overrode them all. His gaze flew to hers in the mirror. Damn the curving road. No passing cars lit the interior. The dim of night revealed only the outline of her forehead buried in quivering hands.

"Madelyn," he whispered.

"Don't." Her shielded face, along with her quiet sobs, distorted the word. "Don't say anything. Please." The dog shifted in the backseat, splaying his body atop Madelyn's lap. "You either," she cried.

He pulled into the driveway at the back of her small house and cut the engine. As though it were the crack of a starter pistol, Madelyn took off. She untapped her seatbelt, wiggled out from Deacon's weight, blew through the door, and bolted for the house.

"Fuck." Nathan wrestled with his seatbelt and yanked the keys from the ignition as her brunette hair disappeared into the house. The oxygen level in his body hit a rapid descent. He slammed the door, locked the dog inside the car, and churned the earth beneath his feet.

The interior hung in gloomy darkness just like the night. His hand slid across the smooth wall in search of a light switch. A *boom* at the back of the house had him running blind through the space. He hit the living area and the tiny string lights from the back patio illuminated the space enough to see through her open bedroom door.

Light slipped beneath the bathroom door. A cry came with it. Not a sob, but an anguished, terror filled bay.

Nathan tore open the door.

"Get—" A violent roll of Madelyn's stomach severed her protest. Her hands clenched the edge of the sink, while her bare back contracted. The shirts she'd been wearing lay in a small heap a few feet away.

He should turn and leave her to the business of dry heaving her emotions all over the bathroom, but he moved closer and closer still. Strands of dark, gentle waves curtained her face. He stepped behind her and swept the strands into his grip. His fingers grazed the chill on her skin. Yet the underside of her hair dripped with sweat. He yanked a washcloth from the shelf next to the sink and turned on the cool water.

After several heaves, Madelyn's head hung, limp, between her shoulders. He rung out the excess water and dabbed at the perspiration gathered at her nape. The knobs of her spine made an elegant line down her back. Petite, corded muscles splayed on either side of the sweeping channel with only the tanned lace of a bra interrupting the flow.

He forced his gaze away from the perfect set of dimples at the small of her back, just above the round of her bottom. If ever there wasn't a time...

"Please, go," she choked.

Chapter Twenty-four

The soothing washcloth settled over her nape. His sure fingers skimmed the cloth and a tiny fraction of her skin. The shocking tenderness flooded her eyes.

Please don't let him see me cry. Please don't let him hate me.

Her hair fell gently to her back and fanned across her shoulders. He retreated on silent steps. Only the *click* of the latch catching signaled his departure. The tears spattered the edge of the toilet and then puddled on the floor. Why did it hurt so much after all this time?

"Because you deserve it," she whispered.

Madelyn plucked herself off the floor, flushed the meager remnants of her lunch, undressed, and turned the shower on as hot and as forcefully as it would go. The water washed away the vomit and sweat, but the blood still stained her hands. No amount of good deeds would take it away. No amount of self-pity would make what she'd done acceptable. So, she shoved the hurt deep inside, scrubbed away the evidence, and got the hell out of the shower.

After blotting dry and applying moisturizer, she wanted nothing more than to dive under the covers and forget about her punch-in-the-gut confession. A few things stood in her way. Nathan wasn't leaving tonight. She needed to keep an eye on Deacon. Most importantly, she needed clothes.

Madelyn lived alone and had for her entire adult life. She'd been a nudist colony of one, plus a dog, all the way up until thirty minutes ago. With a huff and a tug she fastened the towel around her breasts and eased the door open a fraction of an inch.

"Here." Nathan thrust a pile of clothes through the door.

She stifled a scream and snatched the stack before he came any farther into the room. Not that she expected him to breach her privacy. Though, a pair of teal thongs crowned the heap. "Thank you," she squeaked.

Having little choice, she pushed the door closed with a hip and pulled on the panties and pink cotton boxers. But she considered the white cotton tank top clutched between her thumb and forefinger. She grimaced. If she wore the thing without a bra, he'd see the dark of her areolas and the peak of her suddenly stiff nipples. If she asked for a bra he'd snoop in her goodie drawer. She eyed the pile of discarded clothes and found the one she'd worn all day. The thing was as wet as if she'd taken a dip in the ocean.

"Damnit." Madelyn held the towel to her chest, hid behind the door, opened it a crack, and peered out.

Nathan leaned a hip on the end of her bed. His big arms crossed his chest and a devious smile quirked his lips. With a wiggle of his middle finger her matching teal bra shimmed against his side. "I wondered whether or not you'd ask for it. Especially, with the wonderland that is your bra drawer."

Madelyn's face flamed as though the comment had come with its own flame thrower. She slammed the door and planted her back on the cool wood.

"Hey." He knocked gently. "If it'll make you feel better, I'll let you look in my toy draw."

Her uproarious laughter snapped her embarrassment like a number two pencil. In the close confines of the bathroom it *pinged* off the tiles. The absurdity of the situation and his ridiculous comments added a level of hysteria to the giggle.

"I'll take that as a yes?"

She wiped her eyes and squinted through the crack of the door. "That was a yes, you're insane."

"If insanity makes you smile, I'll plead it." He winked and jangled the bra in front of her face.

"Looks like you have a lot of experience dressing women." She snuck out a hand and snatched the undergarment."

"I have more undressing them." He waggled his brows. Then the playfulness faded. A seductive glint lit his eyes. "But I have to say there's something sexy about knowing what you're wearing underneath your clothes. Something intimate about touching it before it touches your body."

Madelyn swallowed the lump in her throat and prayed it wasn't her tongue. Her lips parted and then closed. She didn't know how to flirt, but she wanted to and that was a major change in itself. The moment stalled.

"Think you can eat anything?" He took a step back and rubbed his palms over his pant legs.

"Maybe something small. I don't really know what I have."

"I'll take care of it." He pulled the door shut and his heavy steps receded.

Madelyn clutched the bra and tank to her chest to mute the flutter that dove and twirled in her belly and around her heart. His caring, fun-loving nature—especially after he should've written her off as a psycho—loosened something inside her held captive, bound, and chained for so very long.

It warmed her from the inside, made her want to run for shelter and twirl in circles all at the same time. Mostly, in one of the darkest times in her life, it gave her hope.

She slipped her arms into the straps and fastened the clasp. The firm cups held her breasts high. Her beaded nipples pressed against the fabric. A shot of desire rang out and reverberated through her.

For a moment Madelyn closed her eyes and imagined Nathan's hands cupping her breasts. The heat that had flamed her cheeks scorched her body as it scoured its way over her chest, across her belly, and gathered between her legs. The tingle of her breasts turned to an all-out ache. Her breath came in a rush and a gentle moan echoed off the tile.

Her eyes snapped open. This so wasn't the time. Madelyn chewed on her lower lip. Sure, if she let her hands wander, an orgasm would ease her tightly-wound coil of desire. But she'd nearly lost another friend to a maniac and she'd just lost her lunch. While a release was normally high on her list of priorities, a few other things had bumped it down a notch...maybe two. She huffed, shoved her arms and head into the tank, and hurried from the bathroom before she changed her mind.

"How are you feeling?" Nathan leaned against her tiny couch much like he had last night, only this time Deacon was stretched out with his back against the man's legs.

"Fine." She curled her legs beneath her and sat on the rug near Nathan's bare feet and Deacon's head. "How's he doing?"

"He's a tough guy." His big hand patted her dog's belly. "Until you scratch the right spot, and then he turns into a pile of goo."

Me too.

Madelyn forced a smile.

"You look a little flushed."

His saying it certainly didn't help the situation. She blushed to the roots. Her eyes darted around the room and settled on a plate with a toasted slice of her homemade bread and a small glass of clear bubbly liquid. "Is that for me?"

"If you can stomach it. If you don't think you can, you can sleep and try tomorrow."

"I can't sleep yet. I have some questions and —"

"They can hold until tomorrow. I've already pushed you farther than I should've tonight."

"Guess I'm not the only stubborn one around here." She cocked a brow.

Nathan granted her a crooked smile.

She stroked Deacon's head. "I need to know things to better protect myself and my dog."

"That's what you have me for." He lit her up with the full wattage of his grin.

"So, Amadi, Ekene, Chief, and Hanri are what, suspects in your eyes?"

"If you want me to answer that, take a bite of toast."

"What about you, have you eaten?"

"Always pushback with you." Nathan's disheveled hair flopped as he shook his head. "I ate, while you were in the shower."

She smirked and snagged the bread for a nibble. It didn't hit her stomach like an anvil. So, she took another. "Happy now?"

"Getting there." He just studied her, his gaze roving her face, arms, chest, and then legs. "That's better." She opened her mouth to protest. "Another bite," he ordered.

Madelyn snapped a large bite and set the toast on the plate. "Answer my questions, please," she begged around the hunk of deliciousness.

"Yes, they're all persons of interest. While I'm here, Agent Kepler is running background checks and combing through their pasts. Crimes like this seem random, but seldom are. There's usually a common thread. We just have to find it."

"I don't know the bartender that well, but he seems like such a nice guy. Ekene is just a big bratty kid. Sure Amadi has the skills and size to do these things, but he doesn't have the malice for it. He's so in control and Zen." She folded her arms over her chest. "And Chief is, well, Chief. He's all about protecting and serving. Besides, he was born, raised, and married here, and will likely die here an old man."

"There wasn't a marriage certificate in his file and he didn't mention a wife."

"I don't think they were married on the island. She's from Miami, I think. And she doesn't live here anymore. Hasn't since I've been here. The gossip is she left him and moved back to the States because she didn't like being stuck on an island."

"And what about you?"

"I love it. It's beautiful. Peaceful. Well, it was."

"It will be again. Now, how about another bite of toast."

"I think I'm good."

"Then to bed you go." He flicked his hand in the direction of her room.

"Excuse me?"

"You probably haven't had a good sleep in days. Now, go get some."

"I don't do orders."

A grin slowly formed on his lips. "I bet you would, if I gave the right ones."

The desire she'd tempered with talk of murder suspects flared from his jibe. She jumped up and stormed to her bedroom door before she wiped that smirk away with her pussy.

Goodness, that man. And that damn dog.

Did he follow her to the bedroom? No. He lifted his head, snuffed, and then lowered it next to Nathan's leg.

"Don't get your feelings hurt. We talked earlier. I told him I was going to keep an eye on him tonight, so you can get some rest."

She grabbed the edge of the door, ready to slam the thing.

"Door open tonight. Just in case. If you want to sleep naked, I won't peek."

Chapter Twenty-five

Her puffy eyes squinted open on a new day. Sunshine billowed through the window. She rubbed both fists against her eyes and stretched her legs toward the foot of the bed. Her toes peeped out at the other end of the covers.

Madelyn shot upright. She always tucked the end of her sheets under the mattress with military precision. But now the entirety of the bottom edge hung over the end of the bed or in a heap over her ankles. Her gaze shot left and right, looking for what? The killer, who'd menacingly untucked her cover?

A hollow dented the pillow next to her and the cover had been ruffled back. In the corner a medium sized duffle bag yawned wide. Patterned blue boxers hung from the side.

No way. He didn't.

She gasped and the delicious aroma of breakfast filled her lungs. Her stomach flipped, reminding her she'd gone to bed without dinner. But first she had some investigative work to do. She leaned into the pillow and inhaled. Nathan's decadent scent shot up her nose. She melted, her face crashing into the pillow.

That dirty, rotten, sneaky—

"You hungry?"

She rolled to the side to find his head peeking around the heavy wooden door. "Starving. Did you sleep in my bed last night?"

"You're a good snuggler. Way better than Deacon." He shrugged and vanished behind the door.

Madelyn launched off the bed and hurried to catch him. "You slept in my bed!"

"I couldn't find any bacon or sausage. So, we have eggs, toast, and fruit." He shoved a plate toward her and winked. "We might want to think about going to the store today. You have a good amount of vegetables and other fixings, but your meat supply is non-existent."

"I would hope so. I don't eat it." She smiled, awaiting his reaction.

"Oh, no." His eyes bugged and his upper lip curled.

"Oh yes."

"Is this some kind of payback for sleeping in your bed?"

Deacon lay in the middle of the walkway between the island and the refrigerator. She squatted and rubbed his head. "You traitorous mongrel," she cooed. "You could've given me a heads up." He only blinked his big amber eyes. Madelyn hugged his face in her hands, and then sat at a barstool and took several bites. "I can't believe you slept in my bed and I didn't know it. That's creepy."

"You were zonked. And honestly, I gave the couch a try. But only two thirds of me fit on it. I slept on the floor for a few hours, but woke to Deacon's butt in my face and a crick in my neck."

"Fine." She waved him off. "What exactly is the plan? And, are there agents watching the house? Because I didn't see any on the way in last night."

"If you saw them they wouldn't do us any good. They are there. Well, their surveillance equipment, taking in every inch surrounding your house." He snagged a banana out of the bowl and peeled it. "They're in a villa a little way up the beach, monitoring. If anything larger than an iguana moves out there we'll know about it. And the plan is to wait."

He gulped down a bite and practically swallowed it whole. "It's the hardest part of the job. The waiting game. Waiting for forensic analysis. Waiting for the bad guy to make a move or a mistake. Waiting sucks, but that's what we're going to do."

She finished her food and summarized. "So, I just hang around and be the bait."

He lifted his suit jacket and pointed to the gun tucked snuggly into its holster. "Bait with protection."

She'd slept later than usual and missed her morning run and gym time. "Did you turn off my alarm?"

"Can't go to the gym right now, so I figured I'd let you sleep a little longer."

"Why can't I go...never mind."

"I'll take those." He grabbed her empty plate, put his banana peel on top, and scooped up her glass. "You don't have much time to shower and get to work."

"School," she croaked. The grisly scene flashed in her mind.

"You'll get through it. I'll help you."

Chapter Twenty-six

Unexpected. Madelyn Garrett was the most interesting puzzle ever created. If given a million other words to describe her, killer would've never blipped on his radar. From his beat cop days to his years with the bureau, Nathan had locked up more murderers than should exist. Not one of them had her compassion. Not one had her principles. Not one of them had her sweet vulnerability. Not one of them had her wistful eyes. Not one of them had her smile.

Plenty of them had scars though, scars from abuse doled out by the very people meant to protect them. Parents' harsh words maimed the innocence of the child. Their hands hardened them to love and peace. Their assault broke the frayed string that bound them to virtue.

Madelyn had scars. The wounds—whatever kind—inflicted by her mother and stepfather still caused pain. She used that to build a barrier between herself and anyone with the potential to inflict more harm. But she didn't let it turn her into a monster. No monster could light up a room full of children the way she did. No monster could light him up the way she did.

A lanky kid, maroon shorts grazing his calves, rushed into the classroom. "Ms. Garrett, how's Deacon? Do they know who—" The boy skidded to a halt. His fist tightened on the notebooks in one arm, while his other flew to the seat of his britches to keep them from hitting the floor. "Why are you here again?" He balked, narrowing two light brown eyes on Nathan.

"Outside until you're dressed properly, Suada," Madelyn snapped before Nathan opened his mouth to answer. "And the next time you step into our workspace trying to flash your drawers, I'll hook your belt loops over your ears."

"Yes, ma'am." He backpedalled the way he came and hung his head a bit, properly scolded.

The guitar rift from Van Halen's *Hot for Teacher* strummed through his brain. He shifted uncomfortably in the wooden chair in which she'd ordered him to sit. Watching her traipse around the classroom in a wrap dress that hit all the right places might be more difficult to endure than the interrogation evasion tactics class he'd had at Quantico.

A small tidal wave of adolescents poured into the room over the next few minutes, all with similar concerns. Madelyn ordered them to their seats and Nathan took the opportunity to shift his back from the crowd. He wanted to see their faces as they asked their questions and be able to see out the closed window, just in case.

"I want you to know Deacon was cleared to go home last night and is doing well. He's sore and tired, but he'll be back to his old self in no time. We don't yet know who was behind the attack...and that's all I can say about the investigation. If you saw something, remembered something that you think is relevant, Special Agent Brewer will speak with you after you've finished your work for the day."

She made it to the front of the classroom, turned toward her students, and softened her hard-nosed exterior with an empathetic smile. "I know we've all been through a lot over the past week, but we can't let it stop us from living our lives. We have things to learn, places to go, dreams to conquer." Her lips hardened into a line. "I want group one to work on your Hamlet essays. Group two, you finish up the BVI history timeline. Group three, get your Algebra workbooks out and complete pages sixty-seven and sixty-eight."

Two steps brought her even with a female student's desk. Her gaze cut quickly to the girl and then back to the class. "This is not code for chat with your friends. We have work to do. We'll rotate in thirty minutes. Any questions?" Hands shot up around the room. "About an assignment?"

One by one the hands lowered, except for one. "Yes, Suada?"

"If we don't finish, will your boyfriend shoot us?" The boy lost it at the end of his apparently hilarious question. His open mouth disappeared behind his hand and he doubled over so forcefully he nearly cracked his head on his desk. The classroom followed suit, their shoulders shaking and mouths curving into severe grins.

The question wasn't particularly witty, but Nathan found himself fighting the urge to join in. His eyes must have given him away. When Madelyn's gaze landed on him her eyes grew about two sizes and she popped both hands onto her hips.

"Put your desk next to his and find out." Madelyn's straight face brooked no argument and showed no amusement. That sobered the masses.

In the space of a minute the room went from straight rows to clusters. Kids argued softly over the villains in Hamlet or a history factoid, while others scribbled quietly on pages. And a dark faced, bright-teethed boy eyed his jacket warily in between equations that made Nathan's head ache.

Madelyn made the rounds, helping one student after another. Sauda's eyes followed her for a minute. Nathan was about to tell the kid to quit staring at her butt—that was his job—when the kid turned toward him conspiratorially. "Are you Ms. Garrett's boyfriend?"

"Why do you ask?" He could have gone the *this isn't any of your business route*, but he wanted to see where this was going.

"It's just," Sauda shrugged, "she's not married...and she's never had a boyfriend." The kid whispered as though too much noise would rouse a pack of guard dogs.

No boyfriend, the entire time she'd lived here. That surprised him. With the collection of goodies in her drawer, he'd assumed she had lovers, at least on occasion. He hadn't expected a relationship, but in this small town people would have assumed a fuck-buddy was a boyfriend.

"Sauda, working, not talking," Madelyn called from the front of the room.

"Her back was to you, how'd she know you were talking?" Nathan practically mouthed.

"Agent Brewer, you too," she added.

Nathan folded his arms and huffed, but scanned the perimeter outside each window. So she used all those toys on herself. Man. Heaviness gathered in his balls. His cock surged to attention. What he wouldn't give to show her how much better it could be with a partner.

"Most of the men are scared of her," the boy whispered.

He arched a brow. When the boy looked away to find Madelyn in the classroom Nathan discreetly adjusted himself in his pants. Crown him king of inappropriate timing.

"My father was at Paradise Bar one night and he told me that she broke this guy's arm because he grabbed her...uh, you know...behind." Sauda's head bobbed and a palm was up as though he preached the gospel.

"I only sprained it." Madelyn braced two hands on Nathan's desk. "Why don't you go sit behind my desk."

Nathan stood, walked around the desk, grabbed her upper arm, and brought his lips a whisper away from her ear. "Do you want me to stay after class too?"

Her skin flashed hot under his touch while her mouth formed a beautiful O. A grin morphed the shock. "Yeah, I'll introduce you to Melody."

"Is Melody your WE-Vibe?" he breathed.

Madelyn pressed her lips between her teeth and turned a pretty shade of pink. After a few breaths, she found her composure. She stepped from his grasp. "Class, Agent Brewer isn't scared of Melody."

'Ooh's' and 'oh no's' erupted. He narrowed a look at her.

"Bottom left desk drawer. You'll know her when you see her." Madelyn placed one hand on her hip and scooted him along with the other.

The way the students followed his every move, he half expected a giant anaconda to spring from the drawer and swallow him whole. He pulled back the drawer and stared at Melody.

"Go ahead. Pull her out," she encouraged.

It took both hands to maneuver the thing out of the depths. He dropped it on to her desk. The *thud* echoed in the room. And the kids looked ready to bolt.

"She has a five page minimum. The offender has to complete as many pages as it takes for them to promise never to do what he or she got in trouble for doing ever again. If they break that promise the next step is fifty pages. Melody works like a charm." Madelyn beamed.

"I've seen smaller New York City phone books," Nathan awed.

"That's the idea." She winked.

"I'll be quiet. I swear." He placed his hand over his heart and lifted the other to the sky.

"What do you think, guys? Make an example of him or let this be his one free pass?" Madelyn turned to the clumps of students.

The girls opted to give him a pass. The guys elected to keep his trigger finger busy. Luckily, there were more girls in the class than boys.

"Looks like you're off the hook for now," Madelyn said.

Nathan tucked the gargantuan book away and meandered around the room. A few minutes into the second group rotation movement outside the window caught Nathan's eye. Two wide green leaves of a short tree lolled...in the breeze? None of the branches around it shifted. He stopped walking and studied the landscape.

Situated on the west side of the building, it would have been a great place for the killer to hide before making a move. His gaze bore into the foliage. The shadows of the vegetation stained dark amidst the blazing daylight. He adjusted his line of sight to that of a six-foot five-inch man.

And found the whites of two eyes staring back at him.

Nathan's hand slid over the cool grip of his Sig. The figure bolted. Leaves and branches shook and shimmied in his wake. Nathan left the gun in its holster, flipped the lock on the window, and shoved it wide. "Lock the window behind me."

"What are you doing?" Madelyn's voice trailed after him through the window, but he didn't stop to explain.

He reached for the radio clipped to his belt and barked into it. "Suspect on foot, moving west away from the school." Nathan cleared the gravel and plunged headlong into the thicket.

The guy drove through the woods like a bulldozer, marking a clear trail for Nathan to follow. He stretched the limits of his tailored pants and fancy shoes, cutting through the brush and churning up dead leaves and dirt. The fleeing suspect's thunderous footfalls grew louder.

Nathan blinked through the perspiration slipping down his forehead. His arms swung faster. He gained ground on the monster. He gained ground on Amadi.

On his arms and legs chiseled muscles bulged under midnight skin. His close-cropped hair glistened in the sunlight reflecting off the beaded sweat. He moved fluidly through the undergrowth, but his height and bulk could only condense so much.

Stretching and digging deep, Nathan closed the distance. Only a handful of feet stood between him and answers. He didn't want to shoot the guy. Not until he got answers anyway. So, he pushed harder.

Amadi jumped over a wet patch of earth. Nathan followed too closely to see the puddle in time and didn't give a flying fuck if he got his shoes muddy. All he cared about was plowing this guy into the ground.

His foot hit the puddle and found nothing beneath it.

One section of a rotten log gave way, along with the ground around it. His entire leg plummeted into nothingness. Every ounce of momentum he generated met with the immovable planet in a catastrophic explosion of pain in his ribs.

On impact, the radio flew from his fingers. It landed some thirty yards away. Amadi's frame shrunk with the distance he put between them. Nathan's lungs refused the oxygen he struggled to deliver with every busted gasp. Still, he shoved both legs into the hole to boost himself out.

Nothing solid revealed itself. He kicked wide. He stretched deeper. Yet, he found no bottom, no side, no back of the chasm.

Nathan dug his fingers into the soggy ground, drove the toes of his shoes into the crumbly earth and pulled. He crawled out of the hole like a subterranean animal, and then collapsed onto his back. One by one molecules of air returned to his lungs, along with the knowledge that he knew who the killer was, and had let him escape.

Chapter Twenty-seven

"Stop being a baby," Artie chided.

"Stop poking my ribs." Nathan shot back.

"Dead people are so much easier to work with," the old man huffed.

Madelyn stood with her arms crossed in the middle of her otherwise empty classroom, waiting to find out what the hell had happened in the woods.

Artie rocked back in her desk chair and wiggled his jaw side to side. "Shirt up. I'm going to need a better look."

"I said I'm fine," Nathan reminded.

"And I said I'd like answers," Madelyn yipped. "If I'm not getting answers, you're not getting out of this exam."

"I'll tell you. I'm just waiting for confirmation on something first," Nathan explained.

"Then you can let Artie examine you while we wait." She settled him with a glare.

The old man didn't wait for Nathan's compliance. He yanked Nathan's shirt from his pants and hoisted it into the air.

"Hey, watch my gun." Nathan twisted his torso and every link of fibrous muscle contracted into a gorgeous set of abs stained with a vibrant bruise from one oblique to the other. Breath hissed between his teeth.

Artie slapped Nathan's hand away from the holster. "I've seen plenty of guns in my day, kid. And there aren't many worth getting excited over."

Madelyn would have stifled a giggle, if she weren't so angry at Nathan for holding back. Of course, she held back plenty...but that was personal. This was business. Business was the entire reason he stepped into her life in the first place.

The medical examiner prodded the purple and red areas as though playing in finger paint. Nathan's lips and jaw clamped tight, and his face paled. "All right, get dressed so no one gets a peek at your gun." The guy stood and waltzed to the door.

"You can't jab around like that and not tell me what you found." Nathan shoved his shirttail in his pants, winced, and then continued the task with gentler stokes.

"Oh," Artie turned toward them and rubbed the back of his neck. "It's the whole undead thing. Sorry. I don't think they're broken."

"You don't *think* they're broken," Madelyn repeated.

"There could definitely be a hairline fracture or two, but there's no obvious break." Artie curled his upper lip in an Elvis-ish gesture. "But it doesn't matter. If I tell him to take it easy for a few weeks, he'll ignore me...kind of like a corpse." He scratched his grey hair. "Oh, and I stopped by your house earlier, nearly got shot by your team of bandits, and then checked on Deacon. He's a better patient than that one." His thumb hiked toward Nathan. "And he's doing just fine."

"I can't thank you enough," Madelyn said.

"Your smile is thanks enough. Now, you kids be safe. We don't want that ninja warrior guy to dress you up like a Thanksgiving turkey." He waved and headed out the door.

Madelyn struggled to stay upright. Her legs suddenly lost all bone density and worked about as well as taffy. She grabbed the edge of her desk. "Tell me what happened out there. Now."

Nathan's arm wrapped around her middle. His sturdy side steadied her back and he bore most of her weight. They sidestepped to a chair and he lowered her into it. He moved back to the desk and leaned on the edge in front of her. Their gazes locked.

"No."

"No?"

"I'm waiting for a call. When I know, I'll tell you."

"But you know what happened out there," she snapped.

"I know what happened, but I don't know why and I don't want to jump to conclusions. I'm having a hard enough time not doing that already."

The opening classroom door broke their stalemate. Special Agent Kepler strolled in, his hair standing on ends. "He's not at his house, his mother's, cousin's, or the gym. Not a lot, but a little bit of stuff has been cleared out. Underwear drawer. That sort of thing. But hey, on the bright side, they canceled school for two weeks for child safety issues."

"Amadi or Ekene?" Madelyn demanded, ignoring his good news.

"Amadi. You haven't told her?" Dick's gaze swung to Nathan.

"There's nothing to tell because we don't have him in custody, yet. And we haven't questioned him." Nathan snarled.

"Not nothing. The guy's our prime suspect with the skills, the size, and frequent travel itinerary to be our killer. Plus, he was hanging around the woods the day after her dog was attacked by the killer, who hung out in those woods to make a statement." Dick sucked in a long breath.

The first wave of shock rolled past and her brain began to tick again. Sure he had all the markers, but he didn't have the heart for it. Madelyn stood. "He didn't do it."

"What?" Dick looked at her as though she'd been sewn together without a brain.

"Don't argue with her," Nathan warned.

"He can argue with me if he wants." Madelyn swung the full force of her fury into a glare. "At least he's talking to me."

"He's only going to piss you off," Nathan explained.

"You've already accomplished that." She pointed to her face.

"Why exactly?" Nathan stood. "Because I wouldn't tell you or because it's looking an awful lot like your instructor is a twisted guy?"

"I'm gonna go and let you two...work this out," Dick said as he backtracked to the door.

Madelyn didn't pay him any attention. She had her glare set on Nathan. "I know he didn't do it."

"How well do you really know him, Madelyn?"

"Better than I know you."

Veins in Nathan's neck bulged and his fists clenched at his sides. He stepped toward her, but she refused to back down. She refused to be scared. But really he didn't scare her.

"Better than you knew your mom?" Nathan asked.

Her brain skidded and spun from the completely unexpected question and his surprising anger. Maybe he scared her. Not that she feared he'd beat her, but he could hurt her. He poked the tender spots no one else could. He pushed her to confront the uncomfortable questions, the painful memories.

"I knew her well enough to know she'd betray me for a fancy house and social status."

"And because of that you think I'll deceive you?"

"No. I won't let you."

He took a step toward her, and then another. "Deceit isn't something you allow or forbid. It's something another person chooses to do to you. What matters is how you react to that deceit. Shutting yourself off from the world lets them win." His face hovered inches from hers. "So, are you defending Amadi because you believe he's innocent or because he's another person you trusted who potentially betrayed you?"

The words landed so close to the truth she jerked from their impact. Big, fat tears stung her eyes, but she couldn't cry. To cry would be to admit defeat. To admit she had no control over her life. To admit her heart was shattered again. Nowhere near as much as before, but still...

"Fuck you," she blustered.

Nathan's shoulders dropped. The anger faded from his narrowed eyes, but their intensity didn't soften one bit. He shoved his fists into his pockets. His expelled breath coasted over her exposed neck. A trail of gooseflesh lay in its wake.

"When you trust me... When you really let go... You'll enjoy it."

"I told you, trust doesn't come easily."

"But it *will* come—and so will you."

He sucked the anger right out of her and replaced it with desire. Hot, melting desire that made her weak. Without the anger life became dangerously close to being more than she could handle. Everything hurt so damn much, even her yearning for his touch.

"I want to go home. I need to see my dog."

"Let's go." Nathan pulled his hand from a pocket and offered it.

She stared at it for too many seconds. Taking it would open the door to trust. Refusing it would prove her mother still had a strangle-hold on her life. His hand became so much more than an offer for help. It became a step toward revival or damnation. And she wasn't sure which she deserved.

Madelyn hoped he'd drop his hand and step aside, so she wouldn't have to choose. But his hand and gaze remained steadfast.

"Has anyone told you you're stubborn?" she whispered.

"I hear it's highly contagious." He smiled.

Something inside her broke free. Her hand shook as she flattened her fist and reached across the fissure of the past and present, of hell and healing. Calluses ridged his palm. Hot fingers encased her hand and made the burden bearable for the first time.

Chapter Twenty-eight

The tough-as-titanium woman placed her hand in his as though she were as fragile as fine China. A primal need to shield her from harm thrashed its way to life, annihilating every reserve he'd clung to over the past few days. Some things weren't worth fighting. Fighting the need to possess Madelyn was like wrestling a hurricane. He battened down and dug in the best he could. When that didn't work he ran like hell. But one gust knocked him flat on his ass. One wave swept away the world he'd known. And he was done fighting the one woman who could rearrange his priorities.

Hand on the grip of his gun and the other wrapped around something far more dangerous, Nathan led the way to her Jeep. They rode in silence for a while. The echoes of their argument rang in his ears. He'd pushed her, but no further than she could handle. But now her head sagged against the leather rest. "I'm—"

"Don't you dare say you're sorry," she interrupted.

Still tough.

"I was going to say, I'm thinking steak for dinner."

"I guess it's a good thing you're a terrible liar."

"It's no lie that having a whole cow spit roasted and served on a platter has crossed my mind a time or fifty in the last few days."

"Gross."

"Delicious."

"You can eat whatever you want, in my house or out. I want a shower and bed."

"Good luck getting rid of me."

"The craving will get you sooner or later."

"A different craving takes precedence." Nathan caught her gaze for the first time since he'd released her hand and closed the car door.

"You're on the job. Isn't there a policy against *that*?"

"There's a whole handbook against it. Not to mention my own policies, which have held firm all the way up until you bullied your way into my life." He gave her a sideways grin and turned back to the road.

"Bullied?"

"Yep. You refused to leave. You refused a protection detail and a free vacation in Miami. You got me."

"Can I renegotiate my terms? Miami sounds nice."

"If you really want to, yes. I'll have you on a plane tonight." He didn't want her to go, but he wanted her safe more.

"What was it you said? Good luck getting rid of me?" She looped her tote over her shoulder and prepared to exit the Jeep.

"How about you wait and let me go in first this time?"

"If you insist."

"I do." He killed the engine and waited for her to join him. "Stay behind me."

"I thought your people were watching this place 24/7."

"They are."

"But you don't trust them?"

"People make mistakes."

"Some bigger than others," she said wistfully.

He grabbed her hand and pulled her into the house. Shock of shocks, she didn't jerk away. Deacon greeted him with a muzzle to the crotch.

"Should I leave you two alone?" Madelyn whispered.

Nathan poked her gently in the ribs and addressed the dog. "Buddy, we're going to need to set up some personal boundaries. But if a bad guy shows up, that's the perfect spot to bite. Now come on, let's go find a bad guy." They walked room to room, clearing the space. Deacon gave up in the living room and flounced onto his bed.

"It's just you and me." Madelyn's quiet voice bounced off the tiles and smacked him in the nuts.

Yes, it was just the two of them in the bathroom with nothing but time to pass until they caught the serial killer. His hand slid from the gun and he turned. Her hand hid her sweet mouth from view.

"I didn't mean...it's just you and me. I meant...there's no boogie man lying in wait." Her cheeks flushed that unmistakable shade of pink that set off the lightly toasted tan of her skin.

"Mmm-hmm." He took the hand from her mouth and glided his up her naked arm.

Her breath hitched. Long, dark lashes veiled her gaze, which followed the trail of his fingers. He'd happily chance a shot to the balls to kiss her, but she wasn't ready yet. He lifted the bag from her shoulder.

"You have a nice bath." Mounting every bit of strength he possessed, he turned and walked out the door.

He fixed a couple of wraps with enough vegetables to make a hundred kids weep, choked one down, and then checked with Dick. The, 'No progress' text worked a growl from his throat and called Deacon into the kitchen. "Hey, big guy. You need to use it?"

The dog chuffed.

"All right, don't run away, 'cause I'm in no shape to catch you." Fucking great. If he was in no shape to catch a dog, how the hell did he expect to catch a goddamned serial killer? "Run if you want, I'll catch your ass...eventually." He'd taken off the suit coat in the middle of the brush to help him breathe. It hadn't worked one bit. And he'd forgotten it there in all the hoopla. So, he rolled the grass-stained sleeves to just below his elbows and nodded at the dog, who scooted out the door before him.

Deacon trotted from the base of the mountain to the rolling surf, cataloging smells and looking for the perfect place to handle his business. A text vibrated Nathan's phone. He snatched it from his back pocket and glared at the readout.

Miss me yet?

If it hadn't been for the area code of the unfamiliar number, he'd have required a trace. Instead he smiled and called the number. The line picked up and before the person on the other end said a word he answered the question. "Hell yes. When can you get here?"

His partner's laugh boomed through the speaker. "He's that bad, huh?"

"I've contemplated feeding him to the sharks once or twice."

"Why didn't you?"

It was his turn to laugh, for a second. That shit hurt. He stifled a groan. "The woman—"

"The Dresser's next victim?"

"Next target," Nathan corrected. "Yeah, she put Dick in his spot—which is under a rock at least fifty yards away from her—day one, minute one."

"I think I'm in love," Hunt chuckled.

"You're always in love."

"It's lust. Always in lust, and it's fun. You should try it sometime."

"So, whose number is this?"

"Tammy's."

"Who the hell is Tammy, and are you even out of the hospital yet?"

"She's my evening nurse. And they're talking about releasing me into the wild in three long days. But...I've found sufficient entertainment until then."

"Some things never change."

"Yeah, like you working yourself into the ground," he shot back. "You know, if you took a vacation or didn't work until the janitors kick you out every night, when you came back there'd still be plenty of jackasses to put in jail."

"Sure, but what about the families they torment in the meantime?"

"I get it man, but if you work yourself into the dirt you won't do anyone any good."

Finished exploring, Deacon ambled to him. "I gotta go."

"Get this asshole and don't get dead," Hunt ordered.

"You get some rest and don't screw yourself into an early grave."

"What a way to go though."

Nathan ended the call and stared at the house, pictured Madelyn stripped and waiting on the bed. "What a way to go." Ignoring his aching ribs, he jogged to the front door with Deacon on his heels. He locked up and eased through the kitchen. Her bedroom door stood open, as did the bathroom door.

Well, he found her on the bed. Only not in the manner he'd fantasized about. Long airy breaths that leaned toward the territory of snores breezed through her open lips. Her hair was heaped in a damp, tangled mass on the pillow he'd used the night before. She lay atop the comforter, curled on her side in a tight ball.

He stood there staring at her for far too long, wondering what she'd feel like cuddled up to him. As much grief as he'd given her this morning about snuggling, he'd stayed on his side of the bed and she'd stayed on hers. Because if he touched her, really touched her, he wouldn't be able to stop.

Nathan ducked into the bathroom, scrubbed off his failed chase under a heavy spray, and dressed in boxers. He moved her from the edge of the bed to the wall side as he'd done the night before, neglecting every soft curve he came in contact with and every heady scent that wafted off her. His screaming side helped him redirect his thoughts. That, and the fact that the killer still lurked in the shadows.

Sleep came quickly, but the distant rumbling of thunder woke him before the sun. He looked at the clock. It read 2 a.m. He let the storm lull him, but wouldn't sleep until it passed.

Chapter Twenty-nine

The slap and vibrating rumble of thunder jarred Madelyn from sleep. At least she guessed it was thunder. Large droplets of rain pelted the metal roof. It created a symphony of tinny clatter that usually soothed her straight to sleep. Given the current situation though, it quickened her pulse and jittered her nerves.

She sat and rubbed the sleep from her eyes. It didn't help the dark room come into focus. Her hand slicked over a slimy hint of drool at the corner of her mouth. Wonderful. A sexy man occupied half—over half—of her bed and she drooled like a dog. The association made her think about Deacon. Little by little, she eased over Nathan's heavy legs and slipped from the bed.

Thunder cracked and shook the ground under her feet. She tiptoed to the window and peeked out the curtain into the intermittent blackness. Water poured off the roof's edge in a constant stream. Sheets of sideways rain battered the villa. Lightning bolts crawled across the sky like demon fingers searching for souls.

One soul down. Nearly two. One to go.

Madelyn turned to Deacon's bed nestled on the floor between the bureau and the bathroom door. His patterned fur gleamed in a gentle flash of lightning. She walked over to him and eased down to the floor. "Hey, bud." Her words barely rippled the quiet, but he nuzzled her hand. She stroked a hand down his side. He settled deeper into the fluffy bed while the torment of what happened to Deacon nestled further into her brain, joining forces with the misery of Nichole's horrible death.

Anger. Regret. Fear. Frustration. The distorted emotions coalesced. They compiled with the past. Madelyn's chest tightened. The weight of it all pressed against her ribs, threatening to crack them under the tension. Her muscles strained against the urge to break apart. She buried her head in her hands and grappled for breath.

She wasn't strong enough. A sob broke free.

Before Madelyn could smother the daunting sound he was there. Not Deacon, but Nathan. His firm grip pulled her against the hard heat of his chest. His arms encompassed her shaking shoulders.

Her will to fight vanished and she sank into his comfort, borrowing his strength just for a minute. The hurt and remorse, the sorrow and loss escaped in fat tears and jagged cries. Her stomach muscles cramped from the violence of her lament. Wetness matted her hair to her face.

When her tears ran dry he held her still. Their chests rose and fell. Their breaths mingled. His heart thudded in her ear. Stubble grazed her forehead. His lips followed in a heartbreakingly gentle kiss.

She lifted up from the brace of his chest. Without a word he grabbed her hand and led her back to the bed. He paused at the side and lifted the hem of her tear soaked shirt. As he pulled it over her head the cool night air chilled her damp skin. Her nipples beaded in plain view because of the electric sky.

Nathan's gaze remained on her face. He used the edge of her shirt and wiped away the tear stains on her face and chest. After tossing the tank top toward the hamper, his hot touch turned her to the bed and gave a nudge. She climbed onto the mattress and he followed close behind. His arm coiled around her waist. Her exposed back met his naked front. He entwined their hands and nestled them in the valley just above her breasts.

With his body bracing hers, sleep welcomed her back.

Madelyn woke first. Or probably more accurately, he feigned sleep and let her get up first. She dashed to the dresser, grabbed a shirt, and ran for the bathroom. After taking care of the essentials, like combing her tangled mess of hair, brushing her teeth, and rubbing some moisturizer on her puffy eyes, she hurried to the kitchen to make breakfast, not even pausing long enough to see if his eyes were open.

She yanked out the blender, grabbed an assortment of fruits, veggies, nuts, and seeds, and spread everything out on the island.

"You're energetic this morning." Nathan rubbed a hand over his bruised abdomen and slid her a calculating smile.

She jerked her gaze away and considered a bag of raw almonds. "Are you allergic to anything?"

"Avoidance. Interesting." He dragged out both words.

"Not avoidance," she insisted, avoiding a glance at his side of the room. "I need to know for breakfast."

"I'm allergic to murderers, rapists, and thieves. Irritation settles in my trigger finger and it doesn't let up until I've cuffed them or shot them."

She looked at him. "Wouldn't that make you a murderer?"

"I said shoot. I didn't say kill. I prefer them alive and in pain, so they can serve their time stripped of their freedoms."

Madelyn filled the blender, covered it, and hit the button.

"Oh, I think I'll catch a burger in town or something." Nathan hollered over the noise. His nose scrunched and his head swung back and forth.

When the mix was smooth she turned off the machine and flashed him a grin as devious as the one he'd given her. "I'm making this special. Just for you."

"You really shouldn't have."

"Don't puss out on me now. I have a maniac after me. I can't go to the gym. And school is out for two weeks. I need you in tip-top shape and this is just the thing to get you there. It's packed with chlorophyll, anti-oxidants, and natural vitamins."

"What activity do you have in mind?" His thick brows waggled.

"Running's probably not a good idea today. Kayaking and snorkeling are probably out too. How about sailing?"

He pursed his lips and shrugged. "I was thinking sex, but I guess sailing would be okay."

Chapter Thirty

"You have your own yacht?"

Deacon blew past them and hopped onto the boat, showing the first sign of spunk she'd seen since the incident.

"She was a gift."

"From who, the Sultan of Brunei?"

Madelyn nudged him with her hip and pointed to the gold scrawl on the back of the navy ship.

Nathan's dark gaze followed her finger. "Lady Catherine." He read the ship's name aloud. "Lady Catherine?"

"My grandmother."

"Y'all were close. I can see it in your smile."

"She raised me...until I was eleven. She died when I was nineteen."

He watched her intently, maybe waiting for her to elaborate. She strained to hold onto the falling arch of her mouth. "Have you ever sailed before?"

"A fifteen-foot Vanguard off the coast of Georgia with my cousins, but nothing like this."

The bubbling anxiety fizzled out and she stepped onto the teak deck. Her hand ran over the smooth composite of the boom. "I'll show you the rigging, but it's not much different than that. How long ago was it?"

She suddenly realized she didn't know anything about him except that he worked for the FBI and lived in Miami, and he liked steak.

"Twelve years." He stepped onboard, adjusted the bag he carried for her, and then bracketed his hands on the boom. She was trapped by his intense stare more than his body. "It's just like riding a bicycle, right?"

"Sex?" she gasped.

"Sailing." He grinned and stepped into the cockpit.

Madelyn shook off the embarrassment and uncovered the mainsail. "Do you have any siblings?"

"Nope. But I'm pretty close with my cousins, even though we grew up in different states."

"How many cousins?"

"Just two. Ava and Ford."

"Older? Younger?"

"Yes, counselor. Ava's older by a few years and Ford is younger by a few months."

Madelyn tossed the cover at him. He dodged the damn thing easily. She stepped into the cockpit, but stayed on the bench seat, making her a couple of inches taller than Nathan. "You're staying in my house, sleeping in my bed, and I don't know anything about you."

"You know about as much about me as I know about you." His finger slid under the hem of her top and danced along the edge of her shorts, tickling the skin of her belly. Her eyes closed at the exquisite pleasure the pad of his finger persuaded. "I figure we can get to know each other a little better today." His touch fell away and her eyes popped open. He winked. "You know by...talking."

She planted both hands on his shoulders and pressed him out of her way. "Tease."

"Not teasing. I want you to talk to me. I want to know you more than I've wanted to know pretty much anything. And I'm a curious guy."

Deacon stood at the front of the ship and barked once, twice, three times. Nathan went rigid until she laughed. "That's dog speak for get a move on. He likes to chase dolphins." The coded padlock clicked under her fingers and then released. One at a time she slid out the teak guards and stored them. "Why don't you go put our stuff below deck. I'll get us sailing and we'll see about the rest."

The cobalt sky hung above them, expansive, yet crowded by cotton candy clouds. Wind billowed the sail. They clipped through the teal water for the better part of two hours. Their faces arched to the sun. Sea-spray stifled the worst of the heat.

A small steady gust keeled the ship, pulling the cable railing toward the surf. Absolute euphoria lightened Madelyn's frame. She gripped the wheel and whooped. Deacon yowled.

"Two little daredevils." Nathan's strong legs braced against the opposite side of the bench seating.

"It's the freedom," she hollered. "Nothing compares."

"You mean, nothing yet," he corrected.

All of the sudden her damp hair and the cool breeze did nothing to stifle the heat that washed over her. "Nothing yet," she mouthed. Deacon barked in rapid-fire succession, making her jump. Her gaze swung opposite Nathan to where her dog bounced on his front feet in the crook of the cockpit and stretched toward the cresting water. "Dolphins." She nodded at the rolling backs of the bow of the ship.

Nathan's pearly whites flashed wide and the dimple at his chin deepened. A pod of three kept alternating time with them for a quarter mile, and then set out on the blue. "That was awesome."

Seeing him so relaxed and excited, and knowing she'd given that to him, made her agree. "It was. Are you hungry?"

"Always. What's on the menu?"

"There's a tiny island not far from here. It's not more than a pile of sand and some shrubs. We'll drop sail in a minute and the current will carry us in. Have you dropped an anchor before?"

"Is that a euphemism?" He smirked, and then held up a hand. "I have. Just holler when you're ready."

Boy, her bathing suit bottoms were soaked through and she'd never been so ready. But having sex with Nathan would mean something she wasn't ready for.

"You weren't kidding about small. Is it on a map?"

"Yep, but it's only a spec."

"Do you come here a lot?"

"All the time. Deacon likes to chase the fish. I read or just sit and contemplate the big questions in life."

"Which questions are those?"

"What is the purpose of life? What do I want to be when I grow up? Why do men leave the toilet seat up?"

A deep chuckle left Nathan's throat. He dolled her an unapologetic smirk. "It's in our genetic code."

She lowered the sails in preparation. Given the word, Nathan released the hunk of metal from the bow. Madelyn moved to the stern letting the ladder down into the water and unlatched the safety cords above it.

Hopping down through the hatch she retrieved the watertight bag she had prepared at home. She checked the anchor line and then launched the bright yellow bag out into the blue. Then she wiggled out of her strapless cover, revealing a simple yet lethal black string-bikini as she dove in to meet the bag.

Chapter Thirty-one

Nathan, a trained observer, didn't gawk, but also didn't miss one inch of her lean, yet voluptuous figure before the water distorted the details. The only parts he didn't see were the small—but important ones—covered by scraps of material. His mind explored the possibilities.

"Heaven help her. She doesn't have a chance." He knew his touches and flirtations affected her from the flush in her cheeks and the look in her eyes. And he wasn't the type to give up.

Coming up for air she turned back to the boat. "FBI, can you swim?"

"Are you kidding?" He tugged the polo from his torso and tossed it to the deck, leaving only khaki shorts hanging low on his hips. He removed the gun and holster from his hip and scaled the mast.

"What the hell are you doing?"

"Proving a point."

"You're insane. I get it," she squealed.

Reaching the spreader midway up the queen's mast, he took a running leap, and completed a forward double summersault into the blue. He slipped smoothly into the lukewarm sea. Still, the ripples of dispersing water rankled his abdomen. Showing off while battered sure as shit wasn't his brightest idea. But the look of excitement on her pretty face when he jumped paid for every ache.

He popped up inches from her disapproving scowl. "Your ribs!"

"Wanna kiss 'em and make 'em better? I've always had a naughty nurse fan—" She lunged at him and braced both hands on either side of his shoulders. Salty seawater covered his head.

Nathan popped up closer this time. He hooked her knees and wrapped them around his torso. The tread of his legs and the slow steady sway of his arms and hers kept them afloat, but the zap of skin-to-skin contact threatened to pull him under. Currents and waves flirted with intimate flesh. The conductive properties of water amplified the power of her draw.

Madelyn's treading slowed. The curve of her breasts and the black triangles covering them rose and fell in time with her accelerated breaths. "I..."

He stopped breathing all together waiting for the words to come out of her mouth. *I want to kiss you. I'm falling in love with you. I could come right now. I don't think we should do this.* Possibilities and expectation drove him mad.

"I need to get the bag to shore," she said in a rush. Her legs unwound from his middle.

"Chicken." He taunted with a smile.

She shoved him under again. When he came up she sidestroked furiously for the shore, pushing the watertight bag with her lead arm. He dug in. Water frothed and bubbled around him.

Madelyn's squeal and giggles drifted back. Nathan let out a whistle for Deacon and the dog launched off the edge of the boat. He hit the surface and it rippled like an actual cannon ball had landed in his place. They raced for shore.

Nathan snagged the bag about ten meters from the break and had their lunch nearly prepared by the time she and Deacon made landfall.

"Always have to prove a point, don't you," she said, collapsing back on the beach blanket he'd laid out.

"Maybe." He tossed her a bottle of water and sat next to her.

Waves lapped at their feet. Two boats, no more than specks, dotted across the horizon while they ate in companionable silence. After he stored the container, Madelyn laid down, stretching her lithe body in the sunlight.

Nathan hadn't pushed her. Hell he'd only known her a few days, but his crazy yearning to know her pressed the matter. "Can I ask you a question?"

"Yes, you can ask. But the answer is no."

He arched a brow.

She cupped a hand over her eyes and tilted her head toward him. "No, I won't sleep with you."

"Sure you will, but that wasn't my question."

Her eyes rolled heavenward, but she didn't look away.

After a minute passed, he began again. "Do you honestly believe you don't deserve to be happy?"

"I...what?" She scrambled off her back. "I never said that I... I'm happy." Her knees tucked under her bottom and she pointed them in his direction. "Or at least I was before last week. You don't know what you're talking about?"

"I know you punish yourself. I know you didn't want your mother dead."

"Didn't I? I'd wished her dead so many times, I lost count."

"Wishing someone dead and killing them are two very different things."

"And I did both. So…" She snatched up the metal water bottle, unscrewed the cap, and then twisted it back on without taking a drink.

"Did she hurt you?"

"She still does." Her knuckles whitened as she attempted to strangle the metal. "Every damn day."

"What happened?"

"Everyone has a past, Nathan. I like to leave mine there."

"But you don't. It's always with you, buffering you from humanity."

"I'm engaged with my community."

"Yeah, a group of people. Mostly kids. But get you alone or even in an intimate group and you draw so deeply inside yourself no one can touch you."

"And you don't?" She slammed the bottle onto the fabric and pointed an accusing finger at him. "I've seen your mask too."

"We all have them."

"People don't want to know where their food comes from, they just want it there. The truth of it is ugly enough to twist their stomach, to make them look at their favorite burger with disgust and never eat it again. Same thing here. You don't want to know."

"You don't want me to know." Nathan countered more loudly than he'd intended. She blinked at his sharp tone. He took a breath and forced himself to calm. "You're afraid I'll look at you with disgust and never want to touch you again. Or worse, that I'll pity you. Am I afraid you'll look at me like I'm a terrified seven-year-old when you find out I was forced to watch my mother be beaten and gang raped?"

Madelyn's cheeks matched the color of the white sand. Her fingers interlaced and she shoved them between her thighs. But no gasp or cry of horror escaped her lips.

"Fuck yes," he said in answer to his own question. "But I'd have told you, if you'd asked. Because I trust you." He pulled his knees up and rested his forearms on them. "Trust isn't a grand gesture. It's a small, nearly insignificant, thing to the rest of the world, but to the person who deserves your trust...it's everything."

"I didn't think you would tell me. So, I didn't ask." She twisted toward the surf, hiked her knees up, and propped her arms atop them mirroring his pose. "I'm asking now. Is that why catching the bad guys is so important to you?"

"When I started out it was the only reason. Then as I did the job the reasons—the fuck-head pieces of shit of the world—kept piling up."

"Tell me about it?" Her whisper was almost caught in the wind and carried to the corners of the world.

"I grew up in a poor neighborhood in Miami and saw things no one should. Prostitutes on the street corners. Gang-bangers in the open. Drugs down any alley. It was all I knew, and we managed all right. We kept our heads down and kept walking. But one night my mom and I stopped at the corner store for milk and bread. When we came back to the car the men were waiting. The whole time it was happening she reassured me. She told me everything was going to be okay. She told me to look away and think of the summers I spent in Georgia. She told me to think of good things while she went through hell."

Tears welled in Madelyn's eyes, but they didn't fall. "You were both going through hell."

"Yes," he agreed. "I kept thinking they were going to kill my mother and there wasn't anything I could do to stop it. Shortly after the incident my father left. The coward couldn't handle her trauma. What a weak bastard." Nathan grunted in disgust.

"What about your mom? How did she recover?"

"My mom is amazing. She didn't break or fade away. The opposite actually. She went back to school, finished her degree, and became a therapist. Her practice is in the same parking lot as the old gas station where it happened. She councils rape and trauma victims, travels the world speaking on the subject." He dusted some sand off his leg and breathed for the first time since he'd started talking.

"I focused all my effort on becoming an agent. I spent the last eight years putting bad guys behind bars. And the one thing I have learned is that there are always more bad guys."

"Nathan, there are good guys too, and good things. You have to remember that."

He turned to her and peered directly into her soul. "I know there are."

Chapter Thirty-two

"I want to be strong like your mom."

"You are strong, Madelyn. A little too strong. You don't have to have it together all the time. Trust me, there were plenty of ugly days in our house." He gave a wry chuckle and his chin dimple flexed, stealing another piece of her heart. "There are still ugly days...especially when I try and convince her to move to the Georgia suburbs and open up shop near my uncle."

"You're scared she'll get hurt."

"I'm scared something will happen to her, and then I'll be that helpless boy again."

The tears came slowly and steadily, slipping down her cheeks and onto her legs. She refused to wipe them away or hide them from his stare. "That's the worst...the inability to make it stop."

Deacon quit digging in the surf. He ambled over and lay his wet back against each of them. Neither spoke for a while. She soaked up Deacon's strength and Nathan's support, and stared at the tiny grains of sand.

"My mom never wanted a child, but she screwed around enough that when she got pregnant at seventeen she didn't know whose sperm had done the deed. When I was a few weeks old she stole cash from my grandfather's safe and ran. She never called, never let them know where she was, or if she was okay. Momma Catherine told me Papps couldn't handle the worry. He died of a massive heart attack on my sixth birthday."

She chanced a look at Nathan, but he didn't study her like a Rorschach blot. He stared off into the blue, intent on her words.

"Things were hard for a few years. My grandfather owned an investments company and had done all the financials since they'd gotten married. She hadn't gone to college and hadn't had a job outside the home since she'd been a teenager. I'd wake up most mornings and find her asleep at his desk using stock portfolios and ledgers as her pillows."

Madelyn smiled and wiped at her tears. "A wealthy banker tried to force her to sell the business, but she showed an amazing knack for numbers. She bought his bank on my ninth birthday. Those years were the best. Just the two of us taking on the world.

"My mom showed up one Friday. We assumed she wanted money. Shock of the century, but she wanted me. She'd become a model in LA and married some rich record mogul. I didn't want to go. Momma Catherine didn't want me to go. She tried to pay her off, to get her to leave, but she was insistent, and the lawyer told my grandmother she didn't have a chance of custody."

"Even though she'd taken care of you and was your mother for all intents?"

"It wasn't that simple. My grandmother hoped her daughter had finally come to her senses. She didn't want to fight over me. I started school the next Monday eighteen hundred miles away from everything I knew with two strangers. I was scared and upset, but despite my best instincts, I was interested, excited to find out who my mother was, and what it would be like to have a father. Stupid."

His finger looped around hers. She turned to find his gaze heavy on her for the first time since she'd started talking. "Not stupid."

"Trusting," she countered with a hitched brow.

"Young and hopeful."

She nodded. "As it turned out, she didn't want me...he did."

Nathan's eyes darkened to midnight.

"Not like that. He had my mom for that."

"Plenty of men have women, but it doesn't stop them from..." He growled a curse.

"He liked to show his dominance with mind games and his fists. When she showed up for shoots with bruises she lost jobs and value in his eyes. So, he used me as his personal punching bag. He used her to get off."

"And she allowed it." He didn't ask. So she didn't answer the obvious.

"Sunday before school we went shopping. She bought a whole new wardrobe, but insisted on pants and long sleeves. I thought she'd joined some church that required it, but tossed the notion because she dressed like a floozy. Thankful to have any clothes to my name, I dismissed it.

"I'd been there for five days the first time he hit me. Everything had been going so well. We ate at the table like a real family, talked about our day, and then he got a call about some deal falling through. He hung up and by the time the phone hit the receiver I was on the floor clutching my chest."

She traced a finger over the meat just below her collarbone. "His fat diamond ring left an ugly stamp. If it hadn't been for that, I'd have thought I hallucinated myself onto my side crying into the carpet." She gave an ugly laugh. "I remember sitting in the corner of the bedroom that night waiting for an argument to erupt. I waited to hear my mom defend me and dare him ever to lay a finger on me again. There were grunts and shouts, but none in rage, and not like I'd ever heard before. Then there was quiet. I waited for her to come sneak me out. I waited until the sun came up and it was time to get ready for school.

"At first I was too shocked to say anything to a teacher, and then I was too terrified. He caught me trying to call my grandmother one night. He told me, if I ever left or tried to lie about my life there, my mother would die of a broken heart. He said, 'She'll throw herself off the roof and shatter into a million pieces because you left.' So, I kept quiet."

"How long?" Nathan's voice ground like sandpaper on concrete.

"Four years. No matter what he did, I never fought back. But then I turned sixteen. My peers started driving, started experiencing freedom. I knew I couldn't endure for much longer. I knew it was me or him, suicide or murder. I'd sit in class and daydream scenarios of how I'd fight back...one day. I never thought I'd have the guts to go through with it. And I thought, if I tried, he'd overpower me and I'd die in the process.

"Self-defense. They called it self-defense, but I meant to ram the knife into his belly that night." The brilliant day plunged to darkness and she was back in the cold kitchen. One hand gripped the handle of the industrial-sized freezer to bridle his advance, while the other reached blindly for the icy handle of the butcher's knife. Remembered adrenaline hijacked her heart and sped it back through that horrible night.

Nathan's arms slipped around her. In one fluid motion he lifted her onto his lap and cocooned her in his corded arms. He tucked her head in the lee of his scruffy chin. His scent and his hold grounded her in the here and now. She wrapped both arms around his middle and held on for dear life.

"I screamed with everything I had, 'I'm going to kill you, you son of a bitch.' My mom's shrill voice filled the kitchen. She screamed, 'No.' He pushed the freezer door so hard it pinned me to the counter. I thought that was it, I was going to die, and something snapped. I arched the knife wildly, blindly around the corner. He yelled, and the pressure let up, but only for a second. I started to slide out from between the two, and then the weight forced the door back again. It slammed into my forehead. I caught myself on the counter. The knife shifted in my grip. I reared back and stabbed around the door."

The resistance of the blade sliding into flesh and muscle still tingled her palm. Madelyn's entire body shuddered. "I hate that I can still feel it in my hand. I can still feel her blood coating my fingers."

"I wake up some nights," Nathan's voice rumbled in her ear, "and I still hear their grunts. I still hear the horrible things they said to my mom."

"Will the memories ever go away?" she asked.

"No. Will they fade? I hope so."

Madelyn levered back to see Nathan's face. Her cheek nuzzled the sun-heated skin of his shoulder. Strands of her hair caught on his stubble. His hand slipped up her neck and splayed over her jaw. The light touch chased away the worst of her remembered fears. He smoothed the locks down her back. Then he urged her on with an easy nudge of his chin. And the strangest thing happened...the burden of telling the story lightened.

"She hadn't defended me—her flesh and blood —a day in her life. But she protected a grown man— an abusive, egotistical, maniac—from her battered daughter and died doing it. When I came around the door and realized what I'd done, Glenn was gone. I called the police. Things were so crazy for so long. I've never answered so many questions in all my life. I'd never been so scared and conflicted. Yes, he couldn't hurt me anymore, but I'd taken a life...my mother's life."

"What happened to Aldrich?"

"They eventually found him at a high class brothel. He tried to claim he hadn't been home that night, but the evidence was there on his face and in the blood all over the house. I'd flayed open his cheek. My grandmother came out for the funeral and trial. They charged him with abuse and capital murder. My scars and old fractures along with testimony from the school district counselor and a few teachers, and the crime scene gave them all the evidence they needed to put him away for life."

"That's why you were so sure it wasn't him committing these crimes."

"Yes."

"And your grandmother passed away..."

"I moved back in with her after the trial. We had a couple of hard years, and then she had a massive heart attack. Clogged arteries due to years of good eating. That's what the doctor said anyway. I think my mother and I broke her heart."

"Not you."

"Either way. That's my story."

"Thank you." Madelyn stared at his supple lips as they formed the words.

"For what?"

"Trusting me."

She should thank him for making her talk about it. She should tell him that she hadn't felt such peace in her entire life. She should warn him to run away because little by little she was falling in love with him. But one sentence shouted over all the others, and it was the one her mind and body agreed upon.

"Nathan, make love to me."

His fingers bit into her hip, and then her world shifted. Thrust from the shadow of his neck, she squinted at the brilliant, streaming light. Uneven sand cooled her back. She spun from the abrupt switch. Top to bottom. A lump, too juvenile and chaste to have existed in her hedonistic body, made swallowing impossible. Deacon scrambled up from the blanket and trotted off.

Somehow her body coiled around his as though it were an intrusive species of vine. Her legs wrapped behind his thighs while her bottom pillowed his crotch. He levered over her, blocking the sun with his chest. His face crowded close, much like it had the last time he had her flat on her back in the sand. Only this time, he didn't wear a mask.

He held himself inches away. His eager breaths heated her cheeks. Or maybe the sight of him, barely contained, all bulging muscles and bedroom eyes did that. His hand plowed into the hair at her nape. Her lips arched toward his mouth. An eager moan slipped between them.

"I'll make love to you. I'll fuck you. I'll make you forget the day of the week. The year. Hell, Madelyn." His mouth quirked and his lips may as well have been on her clit for the potent effect they had on her aching lady bits. "If I really put my mind to it and some of your gadgets, I'll make you forget the century. But, I think we need to start with a kiss."

"A kiss?" she gulped.

He skated a finger over her lower lip, persuading her mouth open. "You make it sound so innocent."

Saliva pooled on her tongue. Her breaths came faster.

The calloused pad skidded across the top bow of her lip. "So mundane."

Wet heat slipped over the edge of her bottom lip. Her lids, which had fallen to seduction, exploded open. He eased back and spread the moisture over her mouth. The pliant skin shifted under his more ardent touch.

"Every great love. Every great lay. They start with a kiss." He dropped his mouth where the barest heat of his lips brushed her. "Don't think for one second that this is harmless."

Her patience evaporated in the heat of their intimacy. Madelyn latched onto his shoulders and pressed into his kiss. At least, she tried. The hair at her nape grew taught.

"You have no idea how much I want to tear these ribbons from your body and bury myself inside you," he growled. "No matter how much it hurts, I won't rush this." His teeth nipped lips. Madelyn ground her ass into his lap and moaned. "It seems you have no qualms about it though."

"I did," she moaned. "Just can't find...a single one right now."

Nathan lunged into the kiss. Sweet contact thieved her breath. His chest flattened her breasts and the hard ridge of his dick pushed against her bottom. Supple but firm, his lips maneuvered the bow of her mouth. Her lips molded to his, inviting and caving to his need, to her need.

His chin nudged hers. Madelyn's lips parted wider. The tang of citrus bit her tongue as his eagerly caressed it. Her fingers explored the slopes and edges of his back, and then plunged into his hair. Their mouths danced a seductive tango that left her drunk.

Before long his hips rolled in time with hers. Each decadent surge brushed the throbbing tip of her clit down his arrogant length.

Yes. Yes. Yes.

He sucked her bottom lip into his mouth for the barest of seconds and popped it out. Tension gathered in her core. "More. Please, Nathan. I want more."

"I said a kiss, and that's all you're getting, Madelyn." His words punched her in the gut, but his fingers eased the pain. His fingers promised more. They pressed against her throat and over her abdomen. His palm flattened onto her hip, snuck under the string of her bikini, and tugged at the material. "But a kiss given in the right way, in just the right spot, should take you where you want to go."

"Yes," she breathed against his mouth.

"Damn, I'm going to enjoy taking you there."

Nathan guided the tiny bottoms off her round butt. The material seared a path down her legs and fell away. He shifted her ass to the corner of the blanket. Before she could blink, his weight settled in the crook of her thighs.

What a difference a few days could make.

She arched, grinding her swollen flesh onto his crotch. The rough khakis chaffed her naked labia, but didn't stop her thrusts. His barring grip did though.

"You are magnificently stubborn." His gaze tightened.

Madelyn opened her mouth to protest, but
Nathan opened his and clamped it around her
hidden nipple. She bowed deeper off the sand. The
silk of his short hair rumpled in her fists. Imposing
suction knotted the ever-expanding tension that
had traveled from her center to every extremity.

The ties at her back and neck gave way.
Nathan fisted the triangles and tossed them to the
side. His knees pushed beneath her thighs and his
hands moved to her back just below her shoulder
blades. He held her up as if in offering and feasted
on the descended red nubs.

Helpless to fight the pleasure he poured on in
tidal waves, she relaxed into the praise of his
mouth. Arms spread wide, she gripped the sand in
one and the blanket in the other and rode straight
down the barrel.

"What was that? Did you have an argument to
make?"

She wanted to launch a snappy comeback,
but her brain was busy following the progress of his
hands. They molded down her abdomen, over her
hips, and then braced on either of her spread legs,
inches from her exposed intimates.

"Hmmm." The muscles in his jaw contracted.
He shifted his hips back and leaned so close to her
pointed clit she braced for his electric touch. But he
hovered there, exploring her with his hot eyes. "I
knew you were beautiful, but this is a little too close
to perfection."

"It's just a pussy, Nathan."

"It's not just your pretty cunt, Madelyn. It's
you. Look at you, spread wide, on display, not a shy
bone in your body. You're here with me every step,
ready, and willing to give yourself to me. And not
because I'll make a good prop for your Christmas

cards. But because you see me and you let me see you."

He started with maddening tenderness, placing not-so-innocent kisses on the lips of her sex. When her hips shifted restlessly his hold on her thighs pinned her to the ground. His mouth eased lower. Her belly convulsed. The anticipation ratcheting higher and higher. His lips pressed against her entrance, and then sealed there.

He schooled her in the most intimate art of French kissing. His tongue pierced her vagina with rhythmic thrusts and deviant twists. If his hands didn't hold her in place, she'd rocket into space. His near-onyx hair bobbed between her legs. Veins and muscles coursed his steady arms.

Madelyn cupped her breasts and moaned against the maddening sensation. She wanted to buck and grind into his touch.

"Fuck me," he mumbled onto her flesh.

"Yes. Yes."

Nathan's eyes sparkled. He leaned in and bracketed her pulsating clit with his mouth. While she watched, transfixed, he jacked her erect bundle of skin and nerves. He used firm lips and a forceful suction that curled her off the blanket. Madelyn braced both hands behind her back and panted. Her incoherent noises caught on the breeze and scattered over the water.

Her toes curled. Her fingers sank into the sand. The pad of his tongue flattened and swirled around her clit. Every nerve ending in her body celebrated his expertise by exploding. The force rippled through her, incinerating everything in its path. Her ability to speak included. She collapsed half on and half off the beach blanket and worked harder than normal to breathe.

Nathan lapped up the last of her orgasm, and then closed her legs so that she curled onto her side. The unusual sensation of her swollen sex pressed between her thighs reinvigorated her spent libido. He placed a kiss on the round of her hip and stood.

A massive erection ballooned the front of his pants. Madelyn swallowed the saliva that pooled at the sight. Nathan's hands laced behind his nape, causing every muscle in his torso to flex. His gaze drank her in. His chest rose and fell in measured breaths.

"Nathan, what's wrong?"

"Nothing." He licked his lips and his eyes clamped shut as though in ecstasy or misery.

"Then come here."

"We should get back." Nathan scrubbed a hand over his face and took another step away.

"You're not getting off this island without getting off."

His eyes opened, appearing like tiny coal-burning furnaces, but his head shook back and forth. "I don't have a condom."

"And you think intercourse is the only way to do that?" She eased onto her knees, and then stood on noodle legs. With a sweep of her lower back and brush of her hands the sand cascaded to the beach. She took a step forward.

"I know it's not. But with what happened..."

"The thought of a woman on her knees with your hot cock in her mouth doesn't turn you on," she supplied.

"Fuck." His hands balled into fists at his sides. "I wish it wouldn't." His head lulled. "I just won't ask a woman to subjugate herself for my pleasure."

"How have you kept them from throwing themselves at your feet? Do you go for the snub-nosed conservative type?"

"They go for me. I don't pursue women."

"So you call all your sly comments and devilish tongue not pursuing a woman?"

"You're different."

More than she should, Madelyn hoped his whisper was true. "Most women would go for a door opening, cooking, cleaning, employed, good-ole boy who won't make them suck cock." She nodded and took another step. "I can see it. Plus you look like a fucking great Southern edition of GQ. But let me tell you something you and all those other women don't know."

Madelyn collapsed on her knees in front of him and ran her hands over his tight thighs to his fly. The button slipped between the fabric. His fly screamed open. She pulled down his shorts and boxers in one easy motion, and then looked him in the eyes. "This is the most erotic and most powerful position for the fairer sex."

Her gaze dropped to clear pre-cum smeared over a narrow head. She licked her lips and canted her head to better see the wide shaft that bulged his dusky skin.

"So you've never had a blow-job?"

"Fuck. No. And if you don't quit looking at my junk like that, I think I'm going to come before you touch me."

A grin the size of the Big Bad Wolf's spread her lips. "This is going to be so fun."

"For you?"

"Oh, yeah."

"It's going to be torture for me. I don't want to hurt you. It's not like my dick is a good fit for your sweet mouth."

"Sweet, huh?" Madelyn latched onto his lean hips, wet her lips, and then pressed them against the head of his cock. She used the slick tang of his lust to lubricate his thick column. Ballooned veins ribbed his length. A sigh of ecstasy rumbled in her throat as she pressed him deeper.

His tip brushed her tonsils and he groaned. The heady sensation of authority over this virile and heartbreakingly sweet man's pleasure made her nipples stiff. He was always eager to prove a point, but now it was her turn. She slid to his curved head, and then slowly sank back to mid-shaft. Her jaw relaxed. Her gaze reached for his, desperate to see his reaction.

Madelyn swallowed him inch by delectable inch, but had to stop short from his base. The man didn't joke about the fit. She pulled back before her eyes watered and he called the whole thing off. Though—judging by the flare of his pelvic muscles, the clench of his fists, and the look of cannibalism in his eyes—he might be too far gone to care. Satisfaction prodded her to the edge. She pumped him deep for long enough that Nathan's fingers plunged into her hair and he muffled a string of obscenities.

Her skin prickled. Nothing existed but their need. His need for release. Her need to give it to him.

She backed off, firmed her lips, hollowed her cheek, and sucked. The lips of her sex dampened. Nathan's control broke. His hips rocked in time with her working mouth.

"Good fuc—"

Her increased pace stopped his exclamation, but she figured the two words fit perfectly. A warning shot warmed her mouth. Greedily, she took it all and got more. After she sucked him dry, she stood, wanton, and wildly willing to forgo protection to get him inside her. "Just a kiss, right?"

Nathan used his grip on her hair and pulled her in for a ferocious kiss. Their sweat and scents mingled in an erotic cologne that did little for her intellect and everything for her libido.

He pushed her back to arm's length. "Get in the water before I wrap your legs around me and bury my dick inside you."

"That's not really incentive to go."

The line of his brow smoothed. "Are you on the pill?"

Well that took the wind right out of her sails. "No. I haven't had to be."

"Ever?"

She shrugged.

"Are you a virgin?"

"No, but my most major sexual relationship has been with myself."

"Really?" He wiggled a brow.

"I've had sex with men. A couple. To make sure I wasn't...broken."

"There's nothing broken about you, Madelyn. Stubborn? Yes. Cautious? Yes. But those aren't bad traits. Well..." His lips pursed and waggled.

"Hey!" She protested with a step in his direction.

His hands shot out as though she bore the plague. "I'm usually a self-controlled guy, but with you..." His gaze honed on hers. "Unless you're ready to welcome a strapping baby boy in nine months and marry me months before that, get your ass to the boat."

She stumbled back, but his words took her much further aback. Like Canada back. A wedding and a family had never been on her horizon. Were they on his? And if they were, how did she feel about that? This? Them? Was there even a them to think about?

A wave brushed her calves, and then her thighs.

"The faster we get back, the faster I can get inside you. You get the boat ready. I'll wrangle Deacon and grab our stuff."

Madelyn dove into the sea and let the current play with her until her lungs burned. Heaven knew the tumult of it couldn't compare to the emotions Nathan wrought inside her. Joy. Surprise. Peace. Ecstasy. Fear. Love.

Chapter Thirty-three

Nathan downshifted in the turn, and nearly snapped the ball right off of the shifter. He wanted to blow past the junker of a car that had gotten in front of them a mile back. Madelyn's giggle filled the open topped car.

"What happened to not rushing this?"

"We're not in the middle of the ocean and about as far away from condoms as a man can get. Plus..." He dared a glance at her long legs sticking out of the bottom of her thin cover-up. "Damnit, woman. I know you're naked under there and exactly what all that real estate looks like. And tastes like."

Her legs shifted and shuffled in the seat.

What the hell was he doing almost literally screwing with a case? At the very least he could get lumped into the same category as Dick. At the worst his straying focus could get Madelyn hurt. Try as he might, he couldn't think of her as a case, as a potential victim.

"I'm not going anywhere," she whispered. "Not as long as I can help it."

"You're not going anywhere." The thought of losing her at all clawed at his guts. The thought of losing her to the Field-Dresser turned his blood to ice.

Nathan wheeled the Jeep onto her foliage crowded driveway, rolled slowly along, and scanned the density for anything out of the ordinary. He stopped the car short of its destination.

In the back seat Deacon stood and yipped.

"What's wrong?" Madelyn straightened in the seat.

"Amadi's here."

"Where?"

"Edge of the woods. Left of where you park."

"I don't see him."

"Neither does my team. The sneaky bastard." He reached into the console and handed Madelyn the gun he'd given her the other night. "Stay here. No matter what, don't get out. Do you understand?"

Her gaze bounced back and forth between him and the wood line. She drew a shaky breath and nodded.

This guy had size and years of lethal fighting skill on his side. Nathan had a gun. He wouldn't hesitate to use it to protect Madelyn. He exited the Jeep and squared his shoulders.

The shadow in the tree line shifted. Amadi Chiduben emerged from the foliage with both palms up. Though the guy was all right for the profile, from another angle he was all wrong. The fact that his skin was blacker than night and that most serial killers were Caucasian didn't play into it. His eyes did. A psychopath's face could change, show expressions of joy and sadness, but true emotions never hit their eyes.

Even from half a football field away clear anguish pulled at the man's face and clouded his amber gaze. Nathan stopped two yards from him—a distance the giant could cover in a blink—and settled his palm over his Glock.

"What do you want?"

"I am sorry for unsettling you yesterday. When Madelyn didn't show up to the gym I needed to know she was okay."

"Why not call?"

"She doesn't have a phone."

He didn't know she had a phone, because up until a few days ago she hadn't. "Why snoop around the woods like a suspect?"

"I grew up in these woods. I heard the killer had stalked Deacon in the brush and I thought...I don't know. Maybe I could find a clue."

"A clue?" He'd heard a lot of lame excuses in his day and this one took the cake, which meant it was probably close to the truth. People lied better than that. Especially when given time to fabricate it. "What aren't you telling me?"

The man's huge chest inflated slowly and he huffed a breath. "It's a long story, but I think it will help you figure out who's killing these women."

Nathan cocked his head. "I'm all ears."

"It will make me look more guilty than I already do."

"Must be one hell of a story."

"Nathan," Madelyn called from the Jeep.

"I want to hear this story of yours. So, don't go away. And...you can put your hands down."

"You're not going to shoot me?"

"Not unless you pull a weapon, run away, or run at me."

He returned to the car, keeping Amadi in his line of sight until he chanced a glance at Madelyn.

She thrust a phone into his hands. "I grabbed your phone from the bag to call for help, if we needed it, and saw you have about four missed calls."

"Where's your phone?"

She shrugged. "Inside, maybe."

"If you don't have it on you, it does you no good."

"Says the man who left his phone in the car."

"You distracted me...too much."

The device vibrated against Nathan's palm. Dick's number flashed on the readout. He answered the call and put it to his ear.

"Don't shoot him," Dick said.

"Why not?"

"When Trisha Sutherland was killed he was in a tournament in Shanghai. Won the whole damn thing. Then went to the Henan province to live with Shaolin Monks."

"You're kidding?"

"Nope. You might want to stand a little farther back. I think this guy could kill you with a hard stare."

"What about the other murders?"

"Teaching until eight-forty-five the night Starks went missing, which makes it pretty unlikely he island hopped, took her, tortured her, and then hung her in time to get back for a god-awfully early morning class."

"Which he taught?"

"Yep. And none of the people I interviewed thought anything was out of the ordinary those days."

"Not that they could remember, at least."

"His girlfriend at the time of Starks and Young's murders said they had a very romantic night on the beach and back at his place when Young went missing. And everything else checks out clean. The cousin does too, only opposite. He paid for the kid to go to the Shanghai tournament the following year. He got creamed. He taught while Amadi was gone, and there were a bunch more women on his alibi roster."

"The bartender is looking pretty sketchy. Lots of odd jobs and small time crimes."

"I want you to look into Adrian Tau's wife. See if you can find her."

"How about we trade places and you look into it?"

Nathan disconnected the phone.

"What'd he say?" Madelyn asked, her face scrunched with concern.

"Amadi's not our guy." When the smile grew too big for her face, he added, "But that doesn't mean I trust him."

"So, now what?"

"We go listen to his story."

"What story?"

"I have no idea."

Chapter Thirty-four

"Are the cuffs really necessary?" Madelyn scoffed.

"He can cuff himself or I can hold a gun on him the whole time." Nathan patted his side arm. "You pick."

"Fine." She released the cuffs and watched Nathan walk to Amadi and toss over the manacles. When they entered the house she pulled the Jeep into its normal spot, grabbed the waterproof bag, and hustled Deacon in through the back door. She needed underclothes before dealing with company.

Slightly more presentable, she practically ran into the kitchen where Amadi made her dining table look like a children's toy and her big dog sitting on his lap look like a puppy. "Deacon, have some manners. I'm so sorry about that, and those." She stared at the cuffs. Her pup huffed off to his bed in the corner.

The man's brilliant smile lit the room. "I'm not. I'm glad he's doing okay. And this," he held up the handcuffs, "means you're finally letting someone look out for your best interests. As long as they're not permanent, I'm okay."

"A drink? Food? Can I get you guys anything?" She sounded jumpy to her own ears and hated it.

"Water would be great," Nathan whispered from just a few steps behind her.

She rushed through the kitchen, grabbing cups and filling them. When she sat down a sheen of sweat had formed between her breasts.

"How are you, Madelyn?" Amadi asked.

"Good considering my world has been turned upside down." She tugged at the edge of her cover-up. "I have grieved for my friend, but now I'm focused on justice for her."

Nathan pulled out the chair for Madelyn to sit with the table between her and Amadi, while he pulled a stool from the bar and perched on the edge, blocking any access Amadi might have to her. Her heart hiccupped at the protective gesture. "So, what do you need to get off your chest?"

Amadi's bound hands sat atop the table. He rubbed his thumbs together and stared at them. "My father was a poor builder, but he was a great man. He taught me what it is to respect yourself, so that you can respect others. Even more than I've trained to be the best, I've trained to be the best man like my father was. While I could fight just about anyone and win, I've never been in a true fight. I've never hit someone outside the ring. I help people find the best of themselves.

"So, when I meditated on the southern mountains of the island four years ago I refused to believe what I saw with my own two eyes. Because I look for the best in people. That area of the mountains isn't populated. It's stripped of man's sounds and nature takes over. Back then, I would go there once a month to be alone with my thoughts. But on that day I was not alone on the mountain."

Madelyn's pulse kicked up a notch.

Amadi lifted his head and stared at Nathan. "Grunts pulled me from peace. Curious, I moved closer to the noise. Concealed by the woods I watched as an ox-like man trudged his way up the incline. He labored because he carried something large over his shoulders.

"I left, immediately unsettled at the sight, and never returned to my mountain retreat. I pushed the image out of my mind. Just a farmer burying one of his fallen stock. I told myself it was nothing and of no consequence, but now I fear it is of grave consequence." He bowed his head in disgust.

Nathan's orders began, "Describe what he was carrying."

"It was long and draped over his shoulder. A fallen soldier was the first thing that came to mind. It was covered in a dark blanket. The tips weren't pulled tight, which is why I refused to believe what I know now that it was."

She pushed away the glass of water, afraid she'd meet it again if she drank anymore.

"Did you see the man's face?"

"No. He was moving away from me, farther south."

"Skin color?"

"White."

"Why didn't you mention this sooner? Years ago?"

"Denial, I guess. Murders, things like this, don't happen here."

Nathan fired a barrage of questions and Amadi answered them all. They went over every detail of that day until Madelyn's head spun. She stood.

"Are you okay?" both men asked in unison.

"I need to busy myself before I go crazy." Though she had no appetite the thought of feeding people eased the quivering inside. "I'm going to cook something." She piddled while they went over everything and more again.

"Can I help with anything?" Amadi asked some forty minutes later.

"You can eat some of this feast I've concocted." She gestured to the vegetable fajitas, rice, beans, and salad cluttering her counter. Nathan stood in the threshold of the living room with the phone to his ear, peered at the spread, and smiled.

"It looks great, but I don't think I can eat right about now."

"I'm so sorry about all this."

"Don't be. It's not your fault."

"He took your fancy bracelets off."

"Let's hope for good." Amadi's long fingers rubbed at his wrists. "I can't help but think that if they find a body and I'm the one who told them about it, then I'll be the one they lock up for it."

Madelyn extended her hand across the island and covered part of his with her own. "No matter how well the truth is buried, no matter how secure the locks, it always finds a way to escape. Reality is relentless and so are we."

Amadi folded her hands between his and bowed.

"It's taken care of. You'll meet them at the tent at dawn, take them to the site, and help with the search." Nathan announced.

"I will," her friend agreed.

"Sure you won't stay for dinner? I have enough to feed at least the two of you," Madelyn offered.

"Man, y'all grow abnormally large around here." Nathan raised his chin to look Amadi in the eyes. "I'm not short, but if I stay here much longer I might develop a complex."

"It's all in the genes," Amadi told him. "You know most of our ancestors were slaves in the cane fields."

"I've learned a thing or two in Ms. Garrett's class." Nathan nodded.

"You all stay safe." Amadi gave one last bow, and then left.

"I want eyes on him all night," Nathan said into the walkie-talkie he pulled from his pocket. "Just in case."

"Do you really think what he saw on the mountain has anything to do with our current situation?"

"We'll know soon. The team will begin searching the area at first light."

"Do you feel like eating?" She waved her fingers at all the food.

"Am I breathing?" he said in answer. "But you have to eat some too."

"A little."

They stood at the bar and picked from the platters for a while, both quiet and deep in thought. The drive to get each other naked had taken a backseat to reality. Just like she'd told Amadi, it didn't take long for the truth to creep up.

Nathan covered the containers, shoved them in the fridge, and then grabbed her hand. "I want to hold you."

"Isn't that the girl's line?" she joked.

"Probably, but I'm secure in my manhood. How about you?"

"Oh I'm very secure in your manhood."

Chapter Thirty-five

"Why don't you pursue women?" The angel whispered into his ear. He sighed and pulled her closer. His lips found flesh and feasted. His angel giggled. "You may as well stop that. I haven't had a shower and I have morning breath...bad. I can't believe you let me go to sleep in my clothes."

"Me either," he mumbled. His hands skated up her thigh and beneath her wrap...cover...thingie. "I'll rectify that mistake right away, ma'am."

"No you will not." She shoved at his hands. "In case you missed the first part, I haven't had a shower since you got me all hot and sweaty on the beach."

"Mmmm, a dirty girl." Nathan opened his eyes to the mid-day light pouring into the room and the woman who lit it up. He could seriously wake to that face every day and not get tired of it.

She snuggled close, fusing her body to his, and hiding her head beneath his neck. His arms tightened around her and she breathed him in. "If you stink, I stink," he warned.

"I like your smell." The words muffled against his shoulder. "So," she levered back. "Why didn't you pursue women?"

"Women tend to want commitment."

"Commitment phobe?"

"No. It's just... I'm committed to my job and that doesn't leave room for other commitments."

"Oh."

"Now I sound like an ass." He rolled them over and propped her on his chest where he could see her expressive face. "What about you?"

"What about me?"

"Ever wanted a husband, kids, the whole thing?"

"Just because I'm a woman, I must want all that, huh?"

"I didn't say that. I'm asking."

Her pointed lips shifted from one side to the other like she was measuring how much to say. "I've honestly never thought about it. I figured with my background I'd never trust anyone enough to have the whole thing." She shrugged one shoulder. "I get why your job is so important to you."

"It's not just that. What I do is dangerous. My partner almost died on our last assignment. I couldn't do that to a family, make them live with that fear. Every time I left the house they'd wonder if I was coming back. And I couldn't give up what I live for. Putting bad guys away is all I've wanted for so long."

Frown lines curved the edges where her smile had been only moments ago and he wanted to take back every word. But he wouldn't lie to her. Not even to spare her feelings.

"Why'd you ask...the thing..." She gnawed on the side of her cheek for a second. "You know the thing about the baby...when we were on the beach?"

"I understand the possible consequences of having unsafe sex. I've never bent my rule on that. But looking at you, being with you... It just came out. And I would have gone all in to be with you. Does that scare you as much as it terrifies me?"

"Hell yes." She nodded so vehemently her hair danced about her head.

"I think it's time for a cold shower. A really cold shower."

"You can have it. I'll use the hot water. Thank you."

He smothered her with a lip-lock, and then slipped from the bed. He was a professional. He had protected beautiful women before. What was it about her? He had to get control and stay focused on the case. If he didn't stay focused they could both get hurt or worse.

The strident tone of his cell pulled him out of his internal lecture. He retrieved it from his pocket, hit the button, and held the phone to his ear. In seconds he replaced the phone and made it back to Madelyn.

He grabbed her with one hand and placed a finger from the other over her mouth, warning her to keep quiet. Her wide eyes blinked in reply. Sliding it off her lips, he placed it on the butt of his gun, which he'd snuggled last night. He pulled her to the bathroom and tucked her into the corner.

"Stay here. I'll be right back." Deacon ran to his side, tail arching wildly through the air, curious to know what game they were playing. "You stay put too."

Madelyn's grip clamped onto his arm. "What is going on?"

"Someone's approaching the house. I'm going to check it out."

Her ornery jaw tightened along with her grasp.

"You'll be fine."

"I'm not worried about me," she bellowed in a whisper.

He placed his hand over hers and pried it off. "You damn well should be! This isn't a game. He means to kill you in the worst way possible. The last thing you need to worry about is me. I'll be fine." Her eyes rounded, but he turned away. He exited via the patio doors and rushed around the side of the house.

Nathan eased his body to the sand and removed the gun from its holster. He moved silently down the wall until he reached the front corner. Peering around, he found a male figure stood on the front stoop.

"Hands on your head. Knees on the ground," Nathan barked.

"Holy shit, Agent Brewer, it's me, Sauda, from Ms. Madelyn's class! Don't shoot me!" The kid's hands flailed in the air.

Nathan holstered his gun. "I wasn't going to shoot you." He knocked on the front door. "It's me and Sauda." The boy used every second until she came to the door to regain the color that had drained from his face.

"Sauda, I hope he didn't scare you," she said, stepping out of the house.

"No, Ms. Madelyn, he didn't." The young man swiped his brow.

Never one to kick a man while he was down, Nathan let the lie pass with a smile.

"What do you need, Sauda?" Madelyn asked.

"Oh yeah." He wiped his likely-sweaty palms on his shorts. "We were getting together a game, and wanted to see if you two would play."

Madelyn looked at Nathan for approval.

"Sure," he answered. "We'll be down in a few minutes." Nathan waved the kid off and turned to Madelyn. His smile faded, replaced by a glare so intense it moved her back into the house. Nathan's teeth threatened to crack under the pressure of his jaw. She wasn't one to back away, not until today.

He closed the door so hard the walls rattled. His anger backed her into the wall. When she had nowhere else to go he closed the gap between them. He grabbed the tops of her arms and lowered his eyes to hers. There was only fleeting air between them in a combustible blend of heat and anger.

His rough voice broke the silence. "Don't ever put yourself in danger because you're worried about me. It could get you killed. I am here to protect you. Do not worry about me."

She tried to wiggle free, but he held tight. "But —"

"You're the one in danger. I am here to protect you. Don't worry about me."

He ignored the tears and hurt in her eyes as he released her. She fled the kitchen. The bathroom door closed and the water turned on, drowning out her soft sobs. He couldn't comfort her like he wanted to. He couldn't hold her and love her like he wanted to. It was the only way to keep her safe.

Chapter Thirty-six

Nathan played well. Even the opposing team's best player Mendel, a college player, could not keep up with his footwork. The sand didn't slow him down. She loved to watch him work the ball, orchestrate his teammates for passes, and push them toward victory. Even if he pissed her off.

She sat under the palms with Deacon while the newest soccer star gave out strategies and pointers to the lot of boys and girls huddled around begging for his secrets. She couldn't hear the details, but tons of 'yes sir's' littered the air. They looked up to him, and she knew why, because she did too.

The crowd finally dispersed and they headed back to the villa.

In that moment, walking side by side in the sand, she fell in love with him. Her mind dared not believe what her heart felt, but she couldn't deny it. Rough and angry or smooth and kind, she loved him.

Hard and fast she fell. She wanted him. Not for one night. She wanted him forever.

The notion made her weak in the knees. She rubbed her palms together. What the hell was she thinking? She didn't know how to act. She'd never been in love. So, she aspired for normalcy. "Thanks for taking time with the kids."

"It wasn't anything."

"I know it meant a lot to them."

"They're good kids. I enjoyed talking to them."

She felt a little embarrassed, but went ahead with the comment that had been floating in her head. "You've got some moves."

"And you haven't seen my best ones."

Her face heated. While she quietly walked on, her mind reeled with the possibilities.

Madelyn could not stop thinking about him making love to her. Instantly she was back on the beach with Nathan's firm, hot body on top of her, but this time there were no clothes or contraceptive worries to hinder them. She imagined his hands both generous and demanding over her naked body, coaxing her to do the most intimate things.

Nathan's voice jarred her from her phantasm, before she got good and started. "State champs three years in high school and two in college. I had really great coaches who taught me a lot."

Madelyn could not make her mouth move to comment. And when he turned a slight grin in her direction she knew he could read her mind and all its inappropriate thoughts.

"Are you hot?"

The mortification must have lit her like a Christmas tree. "Pardon me?" she squeaked.

"Are you overheated? You're redder than a clown's nose."

Madelyn knew she had to recover for sanity's sake. Taking a few clearing breaths she made her attempt. "It is a hot day today and that last game took it out of me, but I'm fine."

Only part of it was a lie.

She hurried into the house and disappeared into the bathroom, totally ready for that cold shower Nathan had talked about earlier. Thirty minutes later she was cool and clean and no less in love with the man then when she'd hopped into the shower. She stared into the mirror. "How'd you let this happen?"

The woman with wet hair plastered to her head didn't have an answer. So she dried her hair, hoping the woman with dry hair might have the answer. That chick didn't have a damn clue either.

"You can't love someone you just met," she chastised.

"Madelyn?" Nathan's voice rumbled from the other side of the door.

Her skin leapt off her skeletal system, and then snapped back into place like a gigantic rubber band. Oh God, had he heard her?

The doorknob twisted and she sprang for the towel she'd shed while under the unforgiving heat of her hair dryer. She yanked it in front of her as though he hadn't already seen everything she had to offer. But that was lust, exhilarating and joyous. Love was worrisome and not an option. He'd said it himself. She'd said it…before he'd shown up and jarred her world.

He stepped into the room and closed the door behind him. Like he wasn't the whole reason she'd closed it in the first place. She nearly smiled at that, but strain around his eyes and the rumpled mess of his hair stopped her.

His hands disappeared into his pockets. "I was an asshole earlier. I just…"

I just love you and it scares me. She finished the thought for him in her head.

"It's my job to make sure you're safe," he finished.

Boom! That hurt.

It must have shown on her face because he stepped forward and pulled his hands out of his pockets.

"Stop," she said throwing up a hand. "I understand. It's okay."

A lie with a drinking problem.

He grimaced, but stopped. "Whatever else is happening between us... Your safety is what's most important right now."

"A maniac with a thing for brunettes and gutting them like a game animal is a big problem." And amazingly it seemed small in comparison to the shattering of her heart. "Anything else?" She wrenched the towel in her grip to keep from crying.

"Dick called. They found a body hanging on the south side of the island, forty yards from Amadi's spot, up an old goat trail."

"Who was it?"

"It had been there for four years in the elements. Part of it was obscured by vines, while the lower portion had been scavenged."

"Scavenged?" Her stomach twisted.

"Stolen or partially consumed by animals."

"Holy shit. Was it the same killer?"

"The method and materials, as far as they can tell, are the same"

"What does this mean for the case? And do you think there's another one hanging around?"

"We don't know yet. Dick's going to keep searching and the techs are taking evidence from the scene. The body's back at the lab. It could be his first victim. It could be he started here and now he's returning home."

"So it's possible I don't know the killer?"

"Anything is possible." He swallowed so hard his Adam's apple bobbed.

Her chest constricted. "Anything?"

He sucked in a long breath and Madelyn held hers.

His phone split the silence with all the grace of a hatchet. She inhaled and readjusted the towel to cover her ass, while he answered the call.

"Yes, sir." Nathan took a step back, and then another. 'I have to take this,' he mouthed.

While he hurried to the makeshift office he'd set-up on the kitchen island, she made use of the privacy and stood in front of her bureau. What the hell did one wear when something you never knew could exist died?

Her eyes fell on the skinny strip of vermillion covered in plastic at the far side. Half the island had been invited to Sylvy's grand opening. Teacher clothes didn't exactly go with Harvey Thompson's ultra fancy restaurant. Since she and Nichole had planned to attend she'd splurged on the simply sexy, banded dress. But Jim had pitched a fit and they didn't go to the party.

Madelyn waggled her mouth. She pushed the hangers aside and studied the artistry. Inspiration struck. She grabbed the dress, a pair of slinky black panties, and her phone, and then hurried back to the bathroom.

It took some pleading and quite a bit of make-up, but fifteen minutes later Madelyn propped her shoulder against her bedroom doorframe. Nathan leaned over a map on the kitchen table. Both his hands braced on the edge and he rolled a pencil between his teeth.

Why did he have to be so adorable and hot at the same time?

"Hey," he said without looking up. "I'm sorry about tha…" He stood at attention. The pencil dropped from his mouth. He caught it deftly, and then tossed it onto the table. But it kept the momentum and rolled off the end. "You look amazing." His gaze caressed her from peep-toe stilettos to the simple diamonds in her lobes. "And overdressed for the back patio."

"We have reservations."

"Oh?"

"To be accurate, I have a four-top reserved at Sylvy's in forty-five minutes. Amadi and Ekene will be here in twenty to pick me up. I'd like you to join us."

His arms folded over his broad chest and considered her for a long minute. "Why the sudden urge to go out?"

Because I don't want to be alone with you all night and...

"A celebration of Nichole's life, before the funeral."

"You'll be extremely exposed."

"No more than yesterday."

He coughed. "That's not what I meant and you know it."

"If I'm going to die in a week, then I'm going to live while I can."

His bare feet pounded across the room, rattling the window panes. She didn't flinch. Worse, her panties dampened. He stopped inches from her sandals and she had to tilt her head back to look into his eyes.

"You're not going to die in a week or a month or a year."

"You can't promise that. No one can. And I'm okay with that."

His cheeks hollowed as though he'd retort, but he kept his mouth shut. He huffed, stepped around her, said something like, "I need more ammo," and stalked to the bathroom.

Chapter Thirty-seven

"You have got to be kidding me."

Madelyn chuckled behind her hand. He'd swear she'd organized this evening specifically to torture him. Amadi purged himself from a car that looked more like a Skittle than something that carried people.

The big guy expanded like an accordion and finally reached his full height. "If I can fit in this thing, you'll be fine." He turned to Madelyn, "Are you ready, dear?"

She stifled the laughter only long enough to squeak, "Yes." She sobered a little. "I can't thank you enough for agreeing to this. I mean, getting three men into suits on short notice is a big deal. But you guys look so handsome." Her gaze met his. "Nathan, are you ready?"

Ekene's knees smashed into the dashboard and the back seat looked big enough to fit one toddler...maybe. He put an arm around Madelyn and her giggles died. "We'll meet y'all there."

"Suit yourself," Amadi grinned.

Ekene cranked down the window. "Chicken."

Nathan scratched the sand with his fancy shoes and pecked the air. "Bwok bwak brrr-awk!"

Madelyn's side quavered under his hand and the musical sound of her laughter tickled his ears.

Her laugh chipped away at the resolve on which he'd built his life.

"We'll see you there." Nathan steered her to the Jeep and opened the door. Slowly her laughter faded and she looked at him with the same dreamy-eyed, flushed-faced expression she had on their way back from the soccer game. The instinct to kiss her senseless gnawed at him. Instead, he offered her a hand.

She hardly breathed during the ride. Maybe it was the dress. The thing clung to every dip and curve of her body and made breathing hard for him. Why not her too? His gaze skirted time and again to the swell of her cleavage at the sharp V of the front. If that wasn't enough, when he helped her out of the car, the deep U of the back twisted his tongue into his throat.

The restaurant boasted white tablecloths, waiters in black pants and vests, and a large wooden dance floor with a four-piece string ensemble. Every pair of eyes that had balls attached to their other ends—and even some that didn't—followed every move Madelyn made. He couldn't blame them for looking. She was a gorgeous woman and that dress accentuated every one of her bountiful positives. Still, he found himself anchoring her to his side as they followed the hostess.

The young woman in a classic black dress ushered them to their table at the edge of the dance floor surrounded by other tables on all side. Tiny hairs on the back of Nathan's neck stood on end.

"Here we are," the hostess said.

"I'm sorry to trouble you. We'll need a table in the corner, please." He flashed her his most dapper smile.

Her lashes batted so much he thought she might have a lash in her eye. "I'm terribly sorry, but we're booked full tonight. It was all I could do to get you a table at all on such short notice."

Nathan scanned the area and found just the table they needed in the back corner.

"We've got all the angles covered," Amadi whispered in his ear.

That was exactly the issue. He didn't want to have to rely on the two guys to protect Madelyn. It was his job, his priority, and he didn't trust them, not completely. Cleared or not.

"This is wonderful." Madelyn beamed. "Thank you."

"If you would, give me just a minute." Nathan slipped through the maze of tables until he came to the one he needed. "Excuse me, ladies." Four striking mid-forties blondes perked. "Seeing as you've yet to get settled, I was wondering if you'd like a prime table by the dance floor?" He pointed to the table in question.

"If you promise me a dance," one said.

"I'd love to, but I'm on duty." Nathan put a hand in his pocket and flashed his holster. "My friends would be more than happy to oblige you, I'm sure."

"Come on, Diana." The woman sitting in the corner stood with a grin and tucked her purse under her arm. "I've always wanted to see if what they say about black men is true."

The other women erupted into laughter. The eager woman met Nathan's gaze and balanced. "You know, that they're good dancers."

"Right." Nathan smiled and made his way back to Madelyn.

"Did you sacrifice your body as a peace offering?" she asked.

His grin deepened. A jealous streak looked damn good on her. "Nope. Theirs."

Ekene bobbed his head and strutted toward the women.

"For the good of the team, I'll deal. But for future reference, I like my women darker and thicker." Amadi straightened his tie and headed for the frothy blondes.

"Noted." Nathan placed his hand on the small of Madelyn's back and ushered her to the table. After situating her in the corner, he ordered a bottle of red. He studied the opulent room, its exits, its guests. "Your boyfriend is here."

"My boyfriend?" Madelyn's chin rose from the menu she'd quietly studied since they'd sat. Old Man Malik waved a sun-dried hand at Madelyn and winked.

"I wouldn't have pegged him for this kind of place." She blew the guy a kiss.

"It's not his, but it's hers." A dolled-up gal plucked from the pages of an old Hollywood magazine swatted his shoulder.

"Oh, how sweet."

"Sweet? Blow him another kiss and she might deck him."

"She wouldn't." Smile lines deepened on either side of her face and her cheeks rounded. "She might."

"Women are jealous creatures."

"And men aren't?"

"Some are."

"And you're not?" Her shoulders straightened and the long elegant line of her neck distracted him. "Nathan?"

He loved to hear his name on her lips. "Never have been."

The waiter filled all four glasses.

"Perfect timing," Amadi said, taking the seat across from Nathan. He grabbed the glass and tipped it up.

"I didn't think you drank," Madelyn scoffed. "I was planning on stealing your glass."

"Don't usually," Amadi clarified, "but after that I needed it. If the grabby one had gotten any bolder, I'd have to buy her dinner."

"Looks like Diana might be buying Ekene's dinner tonight," Nathan said.

"And dessert," Madelyn added. She raised her glass. "To good times and good friends, both here and away."

Ekene joined them for appetizers. "Nathan, I heard you were one hell of a soccer player."

The subject of sports and the size of the steak he ordered got them through the meal and on to another bottle of wine. Madelyn had talked as much as any of the guys about the World Cup and Cristiano Ronaldo's 'moves.' But now she quietly contemplated her glass as though it had asked her a quantum physics question.

The words sat on his tongue, but he couldn't make them come out. If he asked her to dance, she'd yank the rug out from beneath him. As it was only his toes and the will to balance that kept him from careening.

Amadi eyed Madelyn, and then Nathan. The nosey giant bulged his eyes out of his head discreetly prodding Nathan to dance with her. He folded his arms over his chest and tipped his head. The man's eyes rolled to the sky. Then he stood and extended his hand to Madelyn. "Would you be so kind?"

Her sad gaze hopped from her cup, to Amadi's hand, to Nathan. His heart twisted inside his chest, but he didn't let it show. She stood with her head held high and swiveled heads all the way to the dance floor.

Nathan tried to track all the eyes that followed her. Chances were good the killer was watching. He carefully considered each member of the crowd. He tried to remain calm, but his efforts became more and more futile as Madelyn's dance partners devolved. Ekene hopped next in line followed by Old Man Malik. Madelyn swatted the coot's hand at least three times when it inched too far south.

"No, sir, you can't!" the hostess hollered. Jim Gallow pushed past her, wearing a sleeveless shirt and a murderous sneer.

Nathan sprang from the chair.

Ekene called behind him, "What's going on?"

He cut through the tables. A couple grabbed their martinis and screamed. Nathan vaulted the railing and landed on the dance floor.

"You loud-mouth bitch!" Jim slurred.

Madelyn turned toward the bellow. Her mouth gaped for a split second before she clamped it shut and stepped in front of Old Man Malik.

The crash of shattering glass stalled the music. Jim shoved another waiter out of his way to the dance floor.

"This isn't the time or place to air your grievances, Gallow." Two steps onto the wood, Nathan cut him off.

"Who the fuck are you?" the man blustered.

"My friends call me Brewer. You can call me Special Agent Brewer."

"You're the asshole stirring up trouble for me." His meaty fist shook.

"Seems you do that all on your own," Nathan explained. "Now, let's step outside and let these nice people get back to their—"

Nathan saw the punch coming probably before Gallow knew he was going to throw it. He just hated making a bigger mess in the ritzy place.

Chapter Thirty-eight

Madelyn chanced a glance at Amadi. The ninja champion of the world hung back with the crowd. She wanted to scream at him to help Nathan with the jackass that towered half a foot over him and outweighed him by a good sixty pounds.

Nathan's calm, commanding voice went silent. Madelyn snapped her head around. An inhale caught in her throat.

Jim's heavy fist sailed toward Nathan's skull.

Every muscle in Madelyn's neck clenched. A centered punch from a man that size could shatter bones. And Nathan didn't move an inch.

Until he did.

His right foot dropped back. Jim lurched forward. The angry fist sheered past Nathan's nose. The edge of his flat-handed strike met Jim's exposed neck.

David and Goliath. Jack and the giant. Size wasn't everything after all.

Jim's face turned a royal shade of red. His hands flew to his throat. He staggered. The leg of a chair caught his leg and he crashed onto a tabletop. High pitched screams erupted. A plate of rock shrimp and rice toppled to the floor, splattering all over a beautiful pair of black pumps.

Nathan attacked so quickly and with such accuracy the fight was over before it had begun.

Amadi chose that moment to break away from the gawking throng and move to Nathan's side. They exchanged words, and then Amadi snatched Jim by the wrist, twisted it behind his back, and ushered him toward the door.

Jim wrestled against the hold. "I didn't kill her! I loved her!"

Madelyn owned every bit of resentment and anger toward the man. "Really?" Her voice rang out, loud and violent. "What about the time you beat her so badly she couldn't see for a week? Is that how you showed her your love, Jim?"

She lunged forward, but sturdy hands encircled her upper arms. Nathan's face blocked her view of Jim.

"Come on," Nathan drawled. "I know you want to dance with me."

Well, of course she did, but her adrenaline pegged out, making romance an impossibility. Not that Nathan wanted anything to do with her in that category. Apparently, one taste was all he'd needed.

"I'm not in the mood." She shoved against his chest.

"I could get you there." Nathan slid his whole hand down her arm to the curve of her palm and wrapped her hand in an easy grip. His other hand grazed the left side of her breast, coasted over her ribs, and settled on the small strip of material between her bare back and her fabric molded bottom.

Before she could speak, he moved to a beat all his own. On instinct Madelyn grabbed his shoulder with her left hand and held on as he turned her around the dance floor. One of the violinists hadn't gone to rubberneck with the others. He picked up his instrument and pulled the sweetest sounds across the strings.

"How can you dance after you nearly got your head knocked off?" she puzzled.

"Hardly. He was too drunk to fight Old Man Malik. Don't tell me you thought he'd take me. It'll break my heart." He clutched her hand to his chest. "To answer your question, I know what's important. Wasting time on Jim Gallow isn't worth either of our time."

He spun her with ease, and then pulled her in so close her belly brushed the cold metal of his belt buckle. The erotic image of the leather slipping between her fingertips transformed her anger into lust.

The exquisite burn of his finger between her shoulder blades cauterized the open wound on her heart. Though temporary and superficial, she'd take however much of him she could get for as long as she could get it. If that made her desperate, who the hell cared? As Nichole's death had shown her, life was too fucking short.

"It worked," she whispered.

"What worked?"

Madelyn curled her arms around Nathan's neck and leaned into him. His smoothly shaven cheek caressed hers and her lips brushed the shell of his ear. "I'm in the mood."

Chapter Thirty-nine

"May I cut in?"

Nathan saw Adrian Tau swagger in like he owned the place. He saw the man talk with the hostess. He saw the man amble up to the dance floor. He saw something in those dull blue eyes that sounded alarms, locked down the gates, and made him pull Madelyn that much tighter against him.

So, when the man asked to cut in, his answer was hell the fuck no. But he couldn't tip a hand that he wasn't sure he even had.

"Chief." Nathan kept an arm around Madelyn and stepped forward. He offered the man his hand. "Take it you heard about the chaos. I must say, that's an awfully fast response time."

The man crushed Nathan's hand with an easy smile. Nathan crushed his back and smiled wider.

"We live on an island, Mr. Brewer." Tau pointed his fat finger between himself and Madelyn. "News travels fast and it doesn't take long to get from one point to the other." His gaze settled on Madelyn. "I'm sorry Jim bothered you again, and I'm sorry the Bureau is too blind to see the killer when he's standing right in front of him."

"So you're admitting you're the "Field-Dresser?" Nathan asked.

"What?" Madelyn flitted her hand in the air and giggled. "No, he was talking about Jim."

"She's a smart girl," Tau said.

"But," Madelyn corrected with a stop sign for a hand, "I don't think Jim is the killer any longer, Chief."

"I see he's gone and hypnotized you." Tau glared at Nathan's hand latched around her.

"No." Madelyn shook her head.

She tried to side step and put some distance between them, but Nathan held tight. His unease grew by the second.

"The attack on Deacon changed my mind," she clarified. "He never would have let Jim get close enough to hurt him."

"Ah." Tau bobbed his head. "I never thought of that. Okay, smart lady, how about a dance?" The man flourished a ham-sized hand.

"I thought you were here for Jim." Nathan said.

"You handled him. They're cleaning the place up. I don't think he'll be a problem for anyone else tonight," the man explained.

"Nathan, it's all right. One dance with Chief, and then we'll go." She patted his hand.

He had no choice but to let her go. His jaw clamped so hard his teeth ached, but he smiled and nodded. Amadi caught his eye on the way back to the table. His gaze told Nathan he knew something was wrong. While Nathan's back faced Madelyn and Tau, the guy's amber eyes never left the couple.

"Want to tell me what's got your back up?"

"Nope."

"Fair enough."

Nathan sat facing the dance floor and wished he could read lips. At this distance all he could see was body language and to the casual observer everything looked on the up and up. Tau's hand stayed firmly on the fabric of Madelyn's dress without wandering north or south. She seemed in good spirits, smiling and cruising easily over the floor.

Ekene chuckled. "Oh man, you got too much ile in you."

"What?" Nathan asked without moving his gaze.

Ekene stood and pointed to the group of busty blondes Nathan talked to earlier in the night. He turned toward them, but cocked his head back. "I'm going to take care of my ile right now."

Nathan groaned and flashed a half-cocked smirk.

Amadi rested his forearms on the table. "I know what's going on."

"Oh yeah?" Nathan asked.

"Nathan, I like you. You are an honest man. And I can see how you feel about Madelyn. But, friend, if you hurt her you'll disappear and they'll never find your body."

Nathan thought he had been playing it smooth, but Amadi mirrored what he'd been trying to deny. He was in deep. He wanted Madelyn not just tonight, but every night, and every morning. He wanted her body, her mind, and her soul to consume him.

So many questions remained, but he'd answered one. Why did she affect him so much? He loved her. But the biggest question remained...could he afford to do anything about it?

The now-full string quartet completed their song with a drawn out low note. Madelyn stepped away from Tau and dipped her head. The man gave a stilted bow. His swollen belly got in the way. She turned to leave, but his arms stretched wide in invitation for a hug. A moment of awkwardness ensued.

A crowd of people stood from their table and blocked his view. Nathan tossed the napkin he'd literally tied in knots onto the table. He stood, nearly ramming his chair into the gentleman's behind him. When he still couldn't see Madelyn he stepped onto the chair.

"Nathan?" Amadi said with a string of unease in his voice. He ignored the question, hell bent on finding her in the crowd.

He reached the full height. Still he couldn't find their heads over the others. His heart swelled and contracted, sponging up all the blood in his body, and then shooting it through his veins. Nathan poised to make his second fast break for the dance floor for the night.

Then Tau's head popped up from obscurity. A congenial smile arched his splotchy face. The crowd shifted. Madelyn straightened from Tau's arms. She'd gone in for the hug after all. She turned. Her gaze found him—on the chair like an idiot. Concern hooded her eyes, instead of embarrassment.

Nathan's veins constricted once again. He locked on Tau. The man's smile had slipped from pleasant to severe. Those crazy blue eyes narrowed on Madelyn's back. Tau's hand reached. Two fingers brushed the tips of her straightened hair.

The simple gesture sealed Nathan's intuition with melted steel and rivets.

Tau's gaze met Nathan's. His easy smile returned with a crooked slant. Then he turned and strolled for the door. Nathan hopped from the chair.

"Stay with her," he ordered.

"Yeah, man," Amadi agreed.

He weaved around waiters, dodged tables, and made it outside in time to see Tau slip into his car idling at the curb. The bastard flashed him that mocking grin. He put the car into drive without breaking eye contact. The wheels rolled forward. Still, Tau maintained the look. At the last possible second, Tau turned his head and maneuvered the lot's exit.

Nathan snatched the phone from his pocket and called Dick. "I want someone on Adrian Tau around the clock."

"What? It's not like we have unlimited funds or people," Dick countered. "What makes you say that?"

"I want inside his house and his bank accounts," Nathan continued.

"I want a harem of supermodels. But I'm not rich and my cock isn't two feet long. Do you have any evidence?"

"Fucking no. But I know he did it."

"How?"

"It's in his eyes and...and he brushed the tips of Madelyn's hair."

"You're just pissed he has a crush on your girl," Dick chuckled.

"It wasn't that he did it. It was the way he did it. Have you gotten anything on his wife?"

"So far, nothing. No bank accounts. No taxes paid in the US or the BVI in the last four years."

"Doesn't that seem suspect to you?"

"Sure it does. I have a call in to the mother, but the lady works on a boat and they won't be back in for two days."

"Did you at least find an old picture of her? What color is her hair?"

A pause weighted the line. "Brunette."

"You're telling me a missing wife with brunette hair isn't enough?"

"Not yet, it's not."

"Keep eyes on him. I don't care if you have to take surveillance off Madelyn's. I know this is the guy."

"The bartender is looking good, Brewer. No alibis. A record of assault."

"Women or men?"

"Both."

"What's going on?" Madelyn asked breathlessly.

"Let me know as soon as you have a word on that body." Nathan clicked off. He hated not being involved in the investigation. It was where he worked best, but he couldn't leave Madelyn's protection to anyone else. Even if it was for the best.

"Madelyn," Amadi called after her.

Nathan wheeled on Amadi. "Seriously? You couldn't keep her inside?"

"Not unless you wanted another knock-down-drag-out in there." Amadi hiked a finger toward the restaurant.

"You can't just order me around. Stay here. Do this." Madelyn stabbed him with her finger.

"Sure I can," Nathan said.

"Excuse me?" Her hands popped onto her perfectly arched hips.

Amadi grimaced. "I'll just go back—"

"Take this, will you and get dinner?" Nathan handed him a credit card.

"Dinner was my treat." Madelyn scoffed.

Amadi snagged the card and retreated.

Nathan stepped close, wrapped an arm around her waist, shoved the other into her hair, and sealed their lips together. He kissed her fight away. The tangle of their mouths carried on longer than he'd planned. But once he touched her, it was hard to stop. Finally, he pulled back. "I'll do whatever it takes to keep you safe."

"Even if it means taking away the freedom I've worked so hard for?"

Madelyn's whispered words pierced him deep. He didn't want to answer because he knew how much it would hurt her...and how much he could lose.

"Adrian Tau is the killer."

****

Madelyn tossed her tiny purse onto the island. She licked her full lips, shoved two fingers in her mouth, and stabbed the silence with a sharp whistle.

Deacon pranced through the door and rubbed his sandy face on Nathan's pants. "Thanks," he whispered. He brushed the sand out the door, and then closed it behind him. The dog stood in his path to Madelyn with his tail thrashing and his front paws dancing. Nathan tossed his coat onto a stool. He rolled his sleeves, leaned over, and scrubbed Deacon's square head.

"Talk to me," Madelyn pleaded.

"Based on the last twenty minutes you spent as a mute, I didn't figure you were in the mood to talk."

She stared at him, and then at her hands. After everything, she didn't trust him. It pried his heart open with an old-school can-opener. He couldn't expect her to walk over hot coals for him. Not when he hadn't promised to be there for her on the other side.

The dagum dog flopped to the tile and rolled onto his back, directing Nathan's scratches to his belly. Neither of them were going to make this easy. He dropped to one knee and rubbed Deacon's belly.

"I was assimilating to the news," she whispered. "It's hard to think about all the times

Nichole and I were around him. We were so close to evil and we didn't know. Never suspected."

Nathan centered his gaze on her crooked mouth and scrunched lips. "You mean, you believe me?"

Madelyn's head jerked upright. A wrinkle formed between her brows. "I trust you, Nathan. I trust your instincts, even better than I trust my own." She tucked her lower lip between her teeth and bit down. Her hands plowed through her hair. Then she scrubbed them down her arms. Once. Twice.

Suddenly she clawed at her skin.

"Madelyn?"

She didn't look. Her eyes were swollen with fear and revulsion, and locked on her arms. Nathan stepped over Deacon and crossed to her. Fat tears ran down her face. Red scratches marred her arms.

"Stop."

"I let him touch me." A serrated cry escaped her lips. And still, she clawed at her skin.

Nathan clamped his hands around her wrists. She tensed against his hold. Her breaths blew quickly over his neck, but she didn't weep. Her jaw set and her chest heaved.

The thought of Tau's hands on Madelyn made his trigger finger itch. And damned though he was, it made his cock swell with the need to make her his. He needed to erase the memories and the scent of every other man and replaced them with his own.

"Let me touch you." The words were so desperate they came harsh and low.

Mascara slipped down her cheek with another tear.

"Touch me," she begged.

Nathan scooped her into his arms and walked to the bathroom. He set her down, adjusted the

water to a full hot stream, and then emptied his
pockets...mostly. One by one, their shoes landed
with a thud. He pulled back the curtain and picked
up Madelyn again.

One of her arms encircled his neck, while the
other clutched the front of his shirt and his
loosened tie. Nathan stepped into the claw-foot tub.
Water splashed onto the burnt orange dress,
coursed down her legs, and hit the floor. He sat in
front of the spray and closed them in together.

With an easy touch he turned her around to
face him. He tilted her chin up. Water soaked her
hair. He gathered the strands stuck to her chest and
slicked them behind her shoulders.

"Close your eyes."

When her lashes hit her cheek he pressed her
forehead into the flow. The narrow spray trickled
across her lids, over the bridge of her nose, and
down her exposed neck. It pooled in her cleavage
and the tightly knit fabric.

Nathan ran his thumbs across her eyes. A
muddy mix of beauty products cascaded over her
face and stained his fingers. He rubbed the arch of
her brows. He massaged the slope of her
cheekbones and the curve of her jaw. Her lips
parted and water trickled down the edge of her
mouth. He repeated the process until all traces of
make-up fled her face, and then pulled her face
from the beating spray.

"Open your eyes."

Her shadowy orbs lit on him and the emotions
they projected nearly brought him to his knees. He
grabbed the soap and worked lather into his hands.
With firm strokes starting at her arms, Nathan
washed away all traces of Adrian Tau. His fingers
slipped between hers and held them as he had when

they'd danced. His other hand slid up her back and he pulled her close.

"Whose hands do you feel now?"

"Yours."

"Whose hands do you want to feel?"

"Yours."

The groove of her spine hugged his finger all the way to the hot-red fabric of her dress. He seized the zipper and tugged. One tooth at a time, the pull revealed a wide-strapped lacy black thong. Nathan groaned. The enticement did its job and broke his easy pace.

He released her and stepped back.

She tugged his tie and his head followed, colliding with her eager mouth. The bite of wine tumbled across his tongue. He drank it in, drank her in, and then pushed back before he lost himself completely.

"How much did you have to drink tonight?"

Her onyx lashes fluttered several times. She licked the bottom of her lip as if savoring him. His balls throbbed. But fuck him sideways, he wouldn't take advantage of an intoxicated woman. Even if the sight of her intoxicated him.

"I had enough to convince myself that this is just sex and that I'm okay with the just part."

His wet clothes molded to his body, defining every bump and line, and making his arousal blatant. Her gaze dropped to his crotch. Madelyn used the point of her index finger and traced up one side of his shaft, over his head, grazing just the tip, and then down the other side. He tensed to keep from pressing his cock into her hand.

"I didn't drink enough that I'll regret it in the morning, if that's what you're worried about."

"Just sex. Like our kiss was just a kiss?" he asked skeptically.

"Just like that."

Which meant it was a hell of a lot more, but neither of them was willing to say as much.

"Just like that." He wrenched the sleeves off her shoulders and peeled the dress off her body.

The fabric plopped to the floor of the tub, leaving only the crest of her mons hidden behind airy lace. Her dusky nipples flushed pink.

Nathan grabbed the back of her neck to keep her steady. His other hand rasped her tight buds. He plucked and tormented them to red tips. Madelyn's head lulled in his hand. Her breaths flew through her parted lips. He stepped closer and let his fingers follow the water down her body.

The scrape of fingernails on fabric grated in the small confines.

"Oh." Madleyn's knees buckled and she dipped.

His knee came up. His arm clamped her back. Her sweet thighs straddled his. Nathan pulled her up, slid her down, and then jerked her up again. Shoved from her daze, Madleyn fisted his shirt. She moaned and pressed against his leg. Her hips rolled.

He sank the fingers of his free hand into the flesh of her ass. In a brutal rhythm he helped her toward the brink.

An animalistic growl rumbled in her throat. "Fuck me. Now. Please. I want you inside me."

"Come first," he ordered.

Her hands flew to his tie, tugging and nearly chocking him. "I want you inside me when I come."

"I will be. But we have all night."

"Now. Please don't make me wait."

Fuck, shouldn't he be the one begging to get inside her, not the other way around. And why was he arguing?

He set her down, whipped off his tie, and went to work on his pants while she managed the buttons of his shirt. Nathan shucked his sopping shirt, dug the condom out of his pocket, and lost the pants. Madelyn launched herself at him before he was fully sheathed.

A stupid smile split his mouth and he crushed it to her. Water poured onto their faces. He adjusted his grip on her bottom. She'd lost the panties somewhere in the frenzy.

Her heels dug into his back. She levered herself over him. Nathan adjusted and found her hot, slick opening. Gravity and her doggedness nearly completed the act.

"We can say this is just sex, but I won't act like it is." He held her the barest inch off his cock. "Look at me, Madelyn. Be with me."

She lifted her gaze. He lowered her onto his shaft. Deliberately. Her hands tangled in his hair. She pulled him forward and kissed him hard. Her hips rocked in small circles, stealing his sanity a little at a time.

"Yes," he mumbled against her mouth. "That's it. Fuck me. Feel me. I feel you. So deep. So damn tight."

Her breasts jostled against his chest. Her ass cheeks slapped his balls, while her pussy stroked him higher and higher. But her eyes... Her throaty breaths... He thrust against her, pressing his hip onto her clit with every blow.

A cry poured from her lips. His head stung from the hold she had on his hair. It pushed him on. The tempo rose. Her cry rang in a crescendo. His balls constricted and he came with her, pumping out the last of their pleasure.

She slumped against him. Nathan stumbled back. Water slushed around his ankles. He panted.

He blinked and finally realized their clothes clogged the drain.

Gathering his wits, he turned off the water, kicked their clothes to the back of the tub, and stepped out. He wrapped a towel around Madelyn's shoulders. When he disengaged their bodies she whimpered.

"You won't be rid of me for long." He set her on the ground, cleaned himself, and then scooped her to his chest. "Nap or round two?"

Chapter Forty

Madelyn went from the most intimate experience of her life to Nichole's funeral. Talk about highs and lows. A strange haze hung over the morning sun. It added a layer of humidity to their hell.

Nichole's mother, a short, generously curvaceous woman, clutched the lapel of her husband's tan suit and sobbed uncontrollably. The woman's weeping brown gaze centered on the pewter urn holding her daughter's ashes. Her aunt held firm to his other arm and cried the same broken tune.

Bless the man, but he stood tall, though the burden of grief paled his sun-leathered complexion. His gaze stabbed across the low-set marble mausoleum on which the urn sat, only to land on Jim. The hate exchange seemed a two-sided coin. Seething anger radiated off Nichole's widow in waves. Only a small-framed Methodist preacher at the head and the large FBI agent at the foot barred an escalation on their ancestral burial ground.

Madelyn gripped Nathan's hand and fed from his unflappable calm. It gave her the footing she needed to ignore the contentious climate and the seas of attendants behind them. She focused on her final goodbye to her good friend. Pain lanced deep and carved out a piece of her heart. They would never again make memories together, but she could only be grateful for the ones she'd been given. In a real sense, Nichole had saved her the way she'd wanted to save her friend.

When the ceremony concluded, Nichole's mother leaned down and scooped the silver vessel into her arms with the same tender care of a new mother. Madelyn's throat constricted. The woman shuffled forward as though the last week had crippled her. Madelyn had known this was coming, yet there'd been no way to prepare for it. Tears burned her eyes. She swallowed and blinked them back.

"I didn't agree with many of my daughter's decisions for her life, and I don't agree with her wishes after her death. But I respect her enough to grant her this." She hung her head low and kissed the top of the urn. Her tears splashed onto the lid and rolled down the side. "I don't want it back after it's done. I have my memories. I don't want an empty jar to remind me of my Nichole."

Madelyn started to speak, and then stopped. She shoved back the threatening wail. She sucked a shaky breath. Nathan released her hand and placed his hand on her nape, giving Madelyn the strength to reply. "I thought you'd come with me. Your family is welcome."

Nichole's father tucked his wife under his arm. "Thank you. But the ceremony was for us. The scattering..." One fat tear fell from his eye. "I'm sorry, but we can't."

"I understand," Madelyn breathed.

The pair handed over their daughter's remains, and then left with the same broken gait. She held her head high and sucked back the moisture choking her. Something about Jim caught her eye. She tried to turn away, but like other tragic scenes she was caught in the pique and couldn't look away. His handsome features drew into horrid lines of genuine grief. He had the sad, dazed eyes of a lost dog. The crowd dissipated, but he stayed rooted to the spot, staring at the spot that had held Nichole's ashes through the ceremony, like he might never leave.

Nathan brushed the back of her hand with his thumb. "I have a message from Pippa, the crime scene tech," he whispered. "I know this is terrible timing, but I need to call her. Don't let me rush you. We can stay as long as you want."

"I'll drive while you talk. I need to get out of here."

Madelyn clutched the urn to her chest. Whether or not Jim had killed Nichole, he hadn't deserved the love she'd given him. Maybe that was the thing about love. It wasn't always neat and easy. It wasn't always reciprocated or even appreciated, but that didn't change the constancy of true love.

She watched the road, the urn strapped into the back seat, and Nathan in equal measure. She may regret things in life, but loving him would never be one of them.

"The son-of-a-bi..." Nathan's gaze slid to the back seat. "The killer didn't slip up and leave us anything new at the scene outside your classroom." He tossed the phone onto his lap.

"That's too bad," she said.

Nathan looked out the window. The farther they rode the lower his shoulders slumped.

"Bitch. Fucking bastard. Ass-hat. Piece-of-shit," Madelyn announced.

That swung his gaze around and earned her two high brows.

"Nichole cussed like a long-shoreman. So, you don't have to tone it down on account of her ashes.

She'd hate to know she ruined a good man bashing."

"I'm sorry I didn't get to meet her." A chuckle shook his frame.

"Or maybe not." Madelyn tapped the front of her lips with her index finger. "She'd have had us in a chapel with a preacher in no time."

"Like I said." He winked. "I'm sorry I didn't get to meet her."

Chapter Forty-one

Nathan held her in Lady Catherine's cockpit. She nuzzled into him as they rocked with the gentle ocean. Minutes turned to hours. The rumble of his stomach, the cramp in his leg, and the numbness in his butt from the lack of padding on the ship's teak bench threatened his quiet resolve. Luckily he'd been water-boarded, electrocuted, and beaten as part of an extra-special Bureau training and knew real pain. He did not say a word, just let the emotions pour out of her.

The ashes had been scattered by the wind and current far beyond view before she emerged from the shelter of his arms. She wiped away the last of the tears on her face and let out an unexpected giggle.

"Do you think it's ruined," she asked pointing at his mascara-blotted shirt.

"Tears dry and mascara washes. No worries."

She looked past him onto the horizon. Pink and yellow hues framed her beautiful, splotchy face. "Is it okay if we stay here tonight? I'm not ready to leave."

"I don't suppose anyone can sneak up on us out here. I'll let Dick know. But what are we going to eat? I'm starving."

"I'm shocked." She smiled and stood. "I happen to keep a stocked freezer and fridge for my overnight excursions. How's grilled cassava and white fish with grilled pineapple for dessert?"

"Too good to be true. I'll get the grill going."

They prepped, grilled, and ate in the serenity of the ocean. Madelyn took the plates below and swatted his hand for trying to help. He guessed she needed something to keep her busy.

Nathan sampled his beer and glared at the final scrap of daylight. He had always had careful rule over his emotions. But now—with her life in danger and the killer free because of a technicality—he couldn't seem to rein them. And different scenarios of him taking the law into his own hands and ending Adrian Tau's life seduced him.

"What's wrong?" Madelyn stood paralyzed half in and half out of the main hatch. Fear widened eyes overtook her face, which turned ghostly white.

He turned his head in search of the cause of her concern. His rage transformed into self-loathing. She was scared of him.

Chapter Forty-two

Madelyn wouldn't say she was scared of Nathan in that moment. Wary was what she'd call it, for her own comfort. She'd never seen his emotions turn so quickly or so brutally. Even without a word or a movement she could see that he was a mortal threat to any adversary.

Scared or not she had to know what caused the shift. Mustering up an ounce of courage she spoke, "What's wrong?"

In a near-snarl he discharged his fear. "He's out there. He's getting ready to carry out his plan, for you, and the only thing I can do is wait." His expression did not change as he continued. "It's fast approaching. Whatever his plan is...he'll do it soon."

Her fear was gone. His concern was real. He only hid it better than she did. Quickly, she ended the distance between them.

"It will be fine. You and your team will stop him." *Then you can go back to your life and leave me in pieces.*

Nathan cussed under his breath. He pulled her close and tilted her chin up until their gazes met. His hand caressed the length of her face. "If anything happens to you... I don't know what I would do."

Madelyn struggled to lighten the mood. His care and concern made her love him. It hurt like a mother, too. "Look, your work here will be done soon. You'll be done with me one way or the other. And you'll go back to Miami and get on with your life."

He huffed out a breath. "Then let me hold you while I can."

She dove into him and curled into the safety of his arms. The sun fell off the earth and darkness corrupted the exquisite beauty. The stars sparkled like glitter in the sky. Madelyn nudged the crook of his neck with her nose.

The whiskers of his day-old beard grazed the skin of her forehead. The bulge of his deltoid nudged the back of her neck. The scent of him washed over her fears and distress.

Her worries melted into desire. Yearning heat pooled in her mouth. She remembered his taste. It moved down, slowly simmering in her chest. Her breasts swelled to fine points. Lower still, it shifted, resting in the juncture of her thighs. And suddenly it wouldn't be contained.

She took Nathan's hand and led him down the ladder stairs of the galley. Before his feet hit the solid wood floor she lunged, attacking his mouth with hers. She pinned him against the wooden steps.

Nathan ignited her passion and now he'd have to deal with the consequences. He tried to wrap his arms around her, but she wouldn't allow it. She clasped his hands, shoved them over his head, and held them there. Their tongues battled.

Her lips explored his lips, his jaw line, the muscular ridges of his neck. She had to pace herself and make the most of the time she had with him. In an act of sheer will and determination, she planted her hands on his concrete chest and peeled herself off. Stepping back a few feet, she flashed him a devilish grin.

Madelyn slipped her fingers into the edge of her shorts. Inch by inch, she worked the material down. Her hands run over her hips and back, and then over her ample cheeks. As she reached the curves of her thighs gravity did the rest. Nathan's gaze scoured her body.

She pressed her palms close to the silky skin above her breasts and pushed them over the cliffs of her shoulders. Madelyn savored his hungry eyes and took her time coasting the material down the length of her body. Bare and burning with desire, she stepped toward him.

Her fingers inched under his shirt, and then glided over his rippled abdomen. She reached the ridge of his chest and pressed on, moving over the plateau and around the back to the muscles of his shoulders. She lifted the shirt up over his head. Her covetous eyes roved his dips and plane, and then snagged on his grin.

"You like that?"

"I like that you're not afraid of your own sexuality. Or mine." He grabbed the top of the railing and his biceps flexed.

"Mine can be fun, but I like yours better"

Madelyn curled her fingers into the edge of his jeans, and then released the button and zipper blocking her progress. She slipped her hand down his body. His erection filled her palm. Satin skin caressed her fingers. She stroked his steely length and massaged his tip, enjoying the feel of him for a while.

A deep groan rumbled in his throat and pushed her over the edge. Her restraint snapped. All she wanted was to feel him inside her and all over her.

With a yank his pants hit the floor. She climbed the ladder until the head of his dick lined up with her greedy flesh. Her thighs clamped around his torso. She arched back in search of his slick head, but found herself hoisted into the air. Her arms flailed. Then a sexy-as-sin view of his ass cheeks—dimples and all—filled her view.

Nathan moved through the cabin into the bedroom. He tossed her onto the fluffy white linens. "You've had your fun. Now it's my turn."

"Oh yeah?"

"Fuck yeah. Look in your bag."

Madelyn's heart zipped across her chest. She kept him in sight while she leaned to the shelf that ran the perimeter of the queen sized bed. Her zipper yawned and a slender black case came into view. Her heart ran circles until it got dizzy and fell over.

"I've never used my toys in front of anyone."

"Don't worry." He plucked the case from her bag and evicted her Crave Duet. "You won't be using it. I'll be using it on you."

He braced a knee on the mattress and prowled toward her like a wolf. Her insides quivered. When he yanked her by the knees she shrieked and giggled. His thighs brushed the insides of hers.

"You had a first with me. It's only fair I get to have a first with you."

He held the silver end of the sleek device between his thumb and forefinger. Slowly he turned it this way and that, examining the narrow silicone prongs.

"You're taunting me."

"And you like it."

Boy did she. Her body tingled. The anticipation and his sadistic grin curled her toes.

He pressed the on button. "Now, where to put this?"

He settled the long, smooth edge at the bend of her knee. The whispered touch tickled, but still sent an easy course of need snapping up her leg. She rustled them against his firm, hairy legs. His eyes narrowed. His hand drifted, dragging the low vibration over her skin to just above her kneecap.

The brunt of his lightly-haired chest pressed her into the mattress. His mouth clamped onto her nipple. She arched into him. The vibration rose up her leg.

"Yes. Oh, Nathan. Yes."

A pop filled the room as he released her breast. "Hmmm, maybe it goes here?" He dragged the tip over her chest, in the valley, and then across her mound. The two prongs pressed in on either side of her distended nipple. Pleasure rippled through her body. She moaned shamelessly.

He depressed a button on the other end and the pulse zipped to life. "Forgive me, but it's my first time."

"Right," she panted.

"Really, it is." He grinned and flicked her other nipple with his rough fingers. "Your collection had so much to choose from. I almost went with the small pointy things, but there were a few different sizes and I didn't want them to get lost."

Her face heated about ten degrees. He'd found her plugs. Nathan slid the edge of the vibrator along her abdomen, and then flirted with the rim of her belly button. Her stomach danced.

"Let's face it, I know just what to do with your phallic shaped tools. But this one..." He pointed the end up like he could stab her with the fork end and ran the barest tip over the flushed lips of her pussy. Her head fell back onto the pillowed cover. She cried out through a wide mouth.

When she was alone, this device got the job done sweetly, given a bit of time. With Nathan in the driver's seat it rushed her to the precipice of orgasm before it had even touched her clit.

"Yep," he groaned against her ear. "This one is a mystery to me." He kissed her lobe, and then sat up. His knees parted her legs and he kneeled between them. With firm hands, he spread her.

The jut of his cock rose between her stretched legs. She pushed her hips off the bed to slick him with her wetness, to taunt him like he taunted her, but he only extorted her exposed flesh. The full length of the flat side zapped the top of her mons, and then expertly pushed down. He trapped her erect clit between the soft prongs. Her nerve ending sizzled and snapped.

"So, I'll just have to see what I can figure out," he growled.

Madelyn gripped the covers and braced for the impending orgasm. Her eyes closed against the onslaught of pleasure. So close. She rose higher and higher. The vibrations died. Her eyes popped open.

"I found the off switch." A smirk corrupted his face. "But don't worry. I'm not done with you."

"I hope you're never done with me." She whimpered, but Nathan cut it off with the head of his dick. He swirled his bare silk in her cream. His smooth tip titillated. Her hips undulated, needing more.

Nathan's playfulness fell away, leaving him as exposed as she'd ever seen him. A crazy mixture of joy, fear, elation, and terror shone brightly on his features. She'd seen that look before, on her own face, when she thought about how much she loved him.

No. The pheromones and hormones and Nathan's sexy body beguiled her intellect. Madelyn closed her eyes. She tried to focus on the here and now, on his touch, on his attention. Tomorrow didn't matter.

"Madelyn, I'll never be done with you."

Her heart caught, but she didn't open her eyes. If she did and this turned out to be a dream, she'd cry.

The head of his cock pressed inside her. She blinked him into view. His eyes were trained on her. They had more impact than a fatal gunshot. He held her gaze and pushed in the barest inch.

"Nathan," she gasped, "you forgot…" She tried to ease back and reach for her purse that held a full box of condoms.

His hands barred her hips and her escape. "I don't forget things like that."

She levered onto her elbows thinking she'd missed him rolling one on, but found his beautiful dick unsheathed, except for the bit nestled inside her body.

"Tell me you don't love me, that you don't want this—us—to be more, and I'll stop. I'll put on a condom and finish what I started."

"I can't," she breathed.

"Why not? It is because it feels too damn goo—"

"Because I love you," she blurted. "Because I can't bear the thought of you leaving. Because I see a future with you, a future I never knew I wanted."

So this was what jumping out of an airplane felt like. The rush mingled with fear, but the freedom overpowered it all. No matter what happened, she couldn't regret this.

Nathan dropped the vibrator, leaned forward, and rested his forehead against hers. "I—"

"Don't," she whispered.

"Don't what?"

"Don't say anything. I know it doesn't change anything for you. I didn't even mean to say it, but... It's how I feel. No matter what, I'm happy to know I can feel this way."

His dimple creased on unspoken words.

Madelyn's throat constricted. She wanted to hear him say he loved her more than anything. But she didn't want to persuade it out of him. Or worse, she didn't want to hear him let her off easily. Her feelings were out in the universe. What he did with them was his business.

The brush of his lips over her eased the pain. His big palms cupped her face and she met his kiss with a tenderness that matched what he gave. Pressure of his teeth on her lower lip escalated the contact. He arched her head back and grazed his bite over her chin. She undulated beneath him.

He rocked into her, pressing in and withdrawing with maddening patience. His hands locked around the back of her shoulders. Trapped beneath anyone else, panic would have seized her. Being trapped by Nathan's sinewy body zinged her clit more than the vibrator could.

She held fast to the bulge of his lats and let everything else go. The head of his dick kneaded her G spot. His width pressed into her already sensitive flesh. He ground her tender nub with each drive. But the barely fastened restraint tensing his muscles and the look of awe in his deep eyes set her free.

Her scream ricocheted off the walls. His shout followed. But not from his climax. No, he unleashed his control. His pace ramped. His force doubled.

"Fuck, Madelyn, I never thought I wanted to hear those words, but out of your mouth... You've unhinged me."

A fine sheen of sweat slicked his body. Madelyn braced her heels on his hard bottom and joined in the furor of their passion.

Sweat dripped off his chin and onto her breasts. She surged against him over and over. The quiver of orgasm started in her toes. It shot up her legs and sang to every extremity. She cried out.

Nathan pulled out and fisted his red cock. His neck strained. Awareness glazed with lust. He came hot on her belly and breasts. When he finished she pulled him down atop her, wanting him close forever.

Chapter Forty-three

The sweat beaded and dripped off of their bodies. Their lungs heaved air in and out. They moved together in steady rhythm.

"I can't believe you have the stamina for this after last night," Nathan said.

"If you can't handle it, just say the word and we can stop." Madelyn giggled and picked up the pace.

A playful sting licked her bottom. She yelped. Then Nathan blew past her with that devious smile curving his cheeks. His long legs ate up the wet sand. Madelyn dodged the froth of a receding wave, and then—like a true sap—stretched her stride so her feet landed in the imprint of his tennis shoes.

Deacon galloped alongside her. A comforting sense of normalcy lightened her steps. "We'll be all right won't we, bud?"

He barked in answer and she took it as a, "Hell yes."

"Good," she breathed.

Before long the gym came into view. It struck her with all the heft of one of her stepfather's fists. Her feet ground to a halt in the middle of the street. She rubbed a hand over her chest. Not so normal. Nichole wouldn't be there.

Nathan skidded to a stop and hurried to her side. "Hey, if you're not ready, we can go back or

just run. Though, I vote for going back. I really want
to try those beads on yo—"

She shoved his shoulder, but his tactic
worked. A grin toyed with her mouth. He could have
reiterated all the reasons he thought this gym
excursion was a bad idea, which he'd done in
earnest all morning. Instead, he helped soothe the
ache. "You're going to run out of playthings by
tomorrow, if you keep it up."

"No way, the internet is an amazing place." He
winked and grabbed her hand. "So, what do you
say?"

Madelyn turned his hand and spread out his
fingers. She brushed her thumb over the rough
bumps, and then placed a kiss in the center of his
palm. "If I don't go now, it'll only get harder, and I
won't let him rule my life like that. So, let's go work
out."

He made a ridiculous version of a duck face.

"Then," she added, "when we take a shower,
I'll do that thing you like so much."

"I'll follow you anywhere, sex goddess."

"Come on." She entered the gym with a smile
on her face.

"Madelyn." Amadi stood from the pretzel of a
meditative position with grace a man his size
shouldn't possess. He crossed to her and bowed.
"I'm happy to have you back."

"I'm glad to be here." She bowed.

"Nathan." Amadi stuck out his hand. "Glad to
see you're alive. I thought Madelyn would take you
out the other night."

Her lover chuckled and slid her those devious
eyes. A surge of embarrassment crept up her face
because she could just hear him say, 'The other
night? She nearly killed me *last* night.' Thankfully,
he just shook Amadi's hand.

"So, are you going to get in the ring or take it easy today?" her coach asked.

"Y'all get started. I'm going to take a look around," Nathan said.

"He's not going to show his face around here," Madelyn protested.

"That's what I'm afraid of," he answered.

"Here's the key." Amadi tossed a small key ring to Nathan. "You can lock the back door, if that will help."

"I will. Thanks. Any other doors besides the front?" Nathan shoved the key into his pocket and she caught sight of the gun strapped to his waist.

"No." Amadi said.

"All right." Nathan looked at her. "I want you sweaty by the time I get back." He winked, and then headed toward the back of the building. When her gaze finally left Nathan's backside she looked at Amadi. One of his brows quirked toward the rafters.

"Not a word from you," she warned.

"What? I was only going to suggest yoga."

"Oh goodness," she huffed. The boys only did yoga before a major competition to get centered or before a big date to get limber.

Well, he hadn't been kidding. She and Amadi twisted and stretched through nature. Suns. Trees. Dogs. Pigeons. Eagles. Cats. Cranes. By the time Nathan came back in from his security sweep, she'd been drenched with sweat. Luckily, he didn't come close enough to catch a whiff. He sparred with Ekene and a few other guys.

"You've got it bad and I haven't seen you with it...ever."

Madelyn whipped her neck around and eyed Amadi. He sat across from her with his back straight, both legs tucked near his bottom, and both hands resting palm up on his knees. "You're supposed to be meditating quietly."

"So are you, but with your neck craned like that and your mind racing a thousand miles a minute you may as well give it up."

"I don't have it bad," she protested. "Agent Brewer is working. He has to be with me all the time until the Field-Dresser is caught."

Amadi shook his head. "It's not the fact that he is with you. It is how he is with you, and how you are with him. It is something real, whether either of you want to admit it or not."

"It's his job."

He threw up his hands. "Fine." Amadi hopped up and inclined his head toward the ring. "Come on. I want to see you two spar. That's always the true test of love."

"You're crazy. I'm going to the ladies room. And then I'll watch you two spar."

Before he could say a word, she hurried down the hall. She shoved the door open with more force than necessary. It nearly slapped into the wall, but she leaped forward and caught it. So, maybe she was a little upset Nathan hadn't declared his love during the night.

Madelyn closed the door gingerly and made her way to the sink, ignoring the two stalls to her right. She didn't have to pee, only escape Amadi's knowing stare. The faucet squeaked under her hand. She cupped several handfuls of water and splashed them onto her face.

A sharp sting—like the biggest mosquito in all the islands—jabbed into her arm. She wheeled around and collided with a wall of immovable flesh. The water thick in her lashes obstructed her view. Her gut twisted, answering the question her mind had yet to form.

She blinked wildly. A hand sealed over her mouth. One huge arm banded around her arms and chest. Her back hit the softness of a potbelly. The ground gave way. Her legs flailed in search of purchase. She thrashed. At least, she tried. An odd weight settled into her muscles. The edges of the mirror blurred.

In the clear center Adrian Tau nuzzled his face into her hair. His eyes were different. Detached. Deranged. She inhaled to scream, but everything went blurry to black.

Chapter Forty-four

"Give me a minute." Nathan wiped the sweat from his brow and stepped back.

"It was just getting interesting," a bull-dog looking guy said from the ropes.

"Ah, if I beat him now it wouldn't be fair now would it?" Ekene grabbed his sides and huffed. "Madelyn's got him distracted."

Hell yeah she had, twisting and contorting her lithe limbs in all those interesting shapes. But now her absence rankled more than anything.

"Can't say I blame him," another fighter added.

Good thing Nathan had more important things to deal with. Nathan headed for the bathroom. He'd seen her head that way three minutes ago. It wasn't an unreasonably long time to be in the bathroom—especially for a girl—but he was on edge. The clock ticked on the Hangman's timeline and on the identification of the newly discovered body.

He needed that body to prove Adrian Tau was the killer. Unless he was wrong. The identification could just lead to another dead end and more questions. Which was why when his phone rang he stopped in his tracks. The readout showed Artie's number. *The results.*

He looked at the bathroom door, and then at his phone. He'd heard Amadi giving her a hard time. She was probably just getting over embarrassment. He decided to give her a minute or two more and take the call. Besides, she would want to know the results as much as he did. He answered the phone and put it to his ear.

"Give me good news, Artie."

"We have an identification for the body." Artie's frantic tone pricked every hair on his body. "Her name was Kira Tau."

"Thanks."

Nathan ended the call. His fingers hovered over the number, ready to call Dick and work out the tactics for taking 'Chief,' a.k.a. Adrian Tau into custody. But, as far as he was concerned, Madelyn had been in the bathroom for far too long. He wanted to kick the door in. Instead, he strode to it and knocked forcibly.

"Madelyn?"

She didn't answer in the two seconds he waited. He pushed through the door. Oh well, if she was still taking care of business. He had to make sure she was okay.

His stomach churned and his blood vaporized inside his skin at the sight. The room was vacant. He checked the stalls and shower, without relief. She was gone.

He leaped, grabbed onto the ledge of the high windowsill, and pulled himself up. Shallow ruts gouged the gravel behind the gym and his heart along with it.

Nathan dialed Dick. The tone rang in his ear. Once. Twice.

Deacon trotted into the bathroom. The short hairs along his spine stood on end. He sniffed the counter, the floor, and then sniffed his way to the window. He raised his front feet onto the wall and growled.

"I know, boy."

Dick answer, "Special Ag—"

"I thought you had Tau at his house," he roared.

"He is," Dick defended.

"Then how the fuck did he take Madelyn?"

"I thought you were with her?"

Fuck him. He should have been.

"She went to the bathroom at the gym. I didn't think... Goddammnit."

"It's an island. He can only get so far."

"Artie called. The body you found is Tau's wife. We have cause. Get in his house and find out where he's taken her."

"I'm on it. What are you going to do?"

"Fuck if I know, but something."

Nathan shoved the phone in his pocket and turned on a pin. He burst out the door and down the hall. Deacon stayed hot on his heels.

Amadi must have seen the raging horror on his face. The guy matched his stride. "What's wrong?"

"Chief is the Field-Dresser. He has Madelyn. His wife was the first body, the one you saw."

His fists clutched. He hated himself for letting her out of his sight. Now the bloodthirsty killer had her. Nathan shoved it all out of his mind. He had to focus. If he wanted to have any chance of seeing Madelyn again—alive—he had to think.

He was so out of the loop on the investigation. Hell if he knew where to start. Hopelessness sucked at his feet. He kicked it off.

Amadi had lived on the island his entire life. Maybe he could help. "Does Tau have any close friends, someone who would do anything for him?"

Amadi shook his head. "He seemed a nice enough guy, but he kept to himself."

"What about his spare time, is there a place he hangs out a lot?"

Again Amadi shook his head. Deacon paced frantically back and forth.

Nathan dragged a hand through his hair.

A resounding click marked each minute as it past.

Son of a bitch! Think!

"What about his family?"

"Dead or moved off the island." Amadi shrugged.

"Is there any significant place linked to his past where he might take her? It might be some place out of the way, forgotten."

The big guy's eyes brightened.

Finally, a break.

"Yes, his mother had a house at the base of the mountain where the latest body was found. It's on the west side of the trail back in the woods."

Before Amadi finished his directions Nathan was headed for the door. "Watch Deacon for me."

He flew through the front door and leaped over the steps to the asphalt below. His feet stopped at the first vehicle he came to. He tugged on the handle. The sleek sports car's door didn't budge. Next to it a tan truck's windows were down. He rounded to it, opened the door, and found the keys on the floorboard. With little thought he turned the engine to life and ripped out of the parking lot.

Every second counted.

Chapter Forty-five

Madelyn didn't dare open her eyes. Wooziness rocked her like a rough sea. One hint of light and she'd vomit for sure. Her hip throbbed as though it had taken the burn of some serious force. A twinge in her shoulder wrestled for her attention too. What the hell had happened?

Remaining still, she tried to recall her last memory. Her slushy brain didn't cooperate. Visions of hugging a toilet bowl danced in her head.

Damn.

Her breaths came steadily and she focused on that. In and out. Nice and calm. The worst of the nausea dissipated. Adrian Tau's menacing face flashed in her clearing mind.

She needed to figure out what was going on. With an extreme amount of focus, one lid opened a crack. Dirt and bits of leaves collected in the deep grooves of a vehicle floor mat.

Madelyn slammed her eyes shut. If she was in the front seat of a car, the driver couldn't be far away. The truck stopped. Her mind projected all sorts of horror scenes from her past onto her closed lids. She reeled the thoughts in. She wasn't a little girl any longer, and she wasn't helpless.

Nathan had told her to fight. She could fight. She would fight.

The door across from her opened. Clothes rustled and the seat squeaked right by her head. Then the door slammed shut.

The realization that he'd been so close to her turned her marrow to ice. Gravel crunched as he circled the vehicle. The door creaked open behind her back.

He was coming for her.

Don't panic. Don't panic.

If she wanted to survive she had to control her emotions. She grappled for calm. He inched her off the truck seat and onto his shoulder. The air fled her lungs and shoved her stomach into her ribs.

She hung across him like a rag doll, swaying with his motion. With her head to his back, she chanced a look around. Her eyes actually worked. Survival mode took over. She looked for landmarks, escape routes, and weapons.

A house straight out of a ripper movie dangled upside down. Its wooded over windows, stripped paint, and dangling back and forth taunted her. Outside would be her best bet of escape. Once inside she would be trapped with him.

Before she went wild, Madelyn tested her legs to see if they'd respond to a command. Now that she concentrated a tightness restricted her ankles and wrists.

She had no choice but to play possum.

They entered the dark and dust laden shack. A rat the size of a child's football scurried into the far corner. The furry creature was the least of her worries. When the room pivoted Madelyn closed her eyes.

She sought calm in the knowledge of the Field-Dresser's ways. She knew he took his time with his victims. Not that she looked forward to that time. But time meant opportunity.

Her side met the floor with a dull thud. It took all her strength not to cry out or flinch. Her head pounded. Her knee and hip screamed. Yet she remained limp. Tau's footsteps retreated to the door.

"Hold on, sweet thing. I'm going to get my bag and then the real fun begins."

She tried not to stiffen at the sound of his voice or the message it carried. She must have done a good job because the door closed with a bang. A metal on metal scrape reverberated from the other side of the door.

A bolt?

Fear clogged her throat. She needed to look around, but it could be a trick. The last thing she wanted was to open her eyes and see him standing over her. She was helpless restrained like she was. Gathering every bit of courage inside her, Madelyn opened her eyes.

He was gone for the moment. She sat and tugged at the ankle bindings. The ropes nearly cut into her skin. Her nails dug into the tightly knitted fabric. Sweat—or maybe tears—slipped off her nose. It took a hundred years to free her left ankle.

In reality it had been less than a minute when the bolt screeched through the empty house. It was too late to play possum now. She clawed at the rope and freed her other leg from the binding.

Tau's sinister form appeared in the doorway. Madelyn sprung to her feet. Cinched rope bound her hands in front of her. But she wouldn't make this easy for him.

She craned her neck to meet his haunting stare. In the doorway he towered like a building. His width blocked the light from the morning sun. His eerie stare looked nothing like the kind man she had known as Chief Adrian Tau. He was gone. In his place was a seething, dead-eyed alien. She didn't consider reasoning with him. And she wouldn't beg him to release her, no matter what. That is what he wanted. Pleading. Crying. Begging.

Boards covered all the windows in the small kitchenette. She wouldn't take a chance getting trapped in the hallway and she had no idea where it led.

Madelyn squared up to the Field-Dresser and stood her ground. She read his body, waiting for the slightest tell.

As she had anticipated, he came straight in to grab her. Fluidly, she swung left, planting her foot to the side. Madelyn powered her right knee up and slammed it into his side.

A snap echoed off the peeling wallpaper. His arm swung wide. She jumped out of his reach. From the grimace on his face she'd taken out a rib or two.

"You stupid bitch! Oh, I'm going to enjoy gutting you more than fucking you. I'll make you scream and beg." His nostrils flared as his intake of breath increased. He cocked his head and stared at her with vacant eyes.

Her resolve quivered, then it bounced back. She was getting to him. Madelyn tried to move left again to work her way past him to the door. He moved in to counter. His heavy fist aimed for her jaw.

She stepped into his space, dodging his fist, and rammed the point of her elbow into his solar plexus. He grunted, but didn't even stagger.

The monster charged full on. He caught her around the waist and battered her back into the wall. The flimsy thing looked like they should have crashed right through, but it held firm.

Wind swooshed from her lungs. Shooting stars zipped by. Still, she dug deep and rebounded.

Taking advantage of the closeness, she drove down onto his spinal column just below his head. His knees buckled on impact.

The instant he went down he came right up. His head rammed into her jaw.

Darkness.

Chapter Forty-six

"Just stop and wait for us. We're five minutes behind you," Dick begged.

"I'm not waiting," he barked into the phone. "You have a lock on the location?"

"Yes."

"Whatever you do, don't come in there sirens blazing. I want it smooth and silent."

"What about you?"

"It's Tau you should be worried about. Not me."

The whites of his knuckles gleamed as he gripped the life out of the steering wheel. He wished it were Tau's neck. Nathan would kill him. It was only a matter of time.

Madelyn had just come into his life and had turned it on its head. He liked it. He liked her. He liked getting to know her, exploring life with her. And damnit, he wasn't ready to give her up. He'd never be ready.

It took a lifetime to get to the mountain's base, he was sure of it. With his maniacal driving it had taken eight minutes. A half-mile away from the hut Nathan ditched the truck and sprinted. He wouldn't give himself away.

When the frayed wood and rusted tin of the shack came into view he slowed. He moved silently through the trees. From the look of the rusted out nail holes and splitting wood the place had been abandoned a long time ago. Nathan made his way to the back of the house.

He couldn't hear anything. No animals moving in the forest, no wind blowing above, and no screams emanating from Madelyn's throat. Nathan was not a God-fearing man, but at that moment he offered up a Hail Mary. He knew the lack of screams meant she was still unconscious or she was dead in the bastard's haste. Nathan knew they all screamed, faces contorted in horror, and his heart sank into the abyss.

Chapter Forty-seven

The muscles in Madelyn's neck ached as though they'd been serrated by a knife. And her skin was the only thing holding her jaw and skull together. She winced with every little jostle. The motion of her blood pumping with each pulse sounded like crashing symbols. She couldn't have been out long. But it was too long to benefit her escape.

Her body lay sprawled over an old wooden table. The dust from it lofted in the air. Her wrists were no longer tied in front of her but bound to the table's legs, which made her arms stretch open up over her head. Her legs were bound to opposing table legs, spread wide.

"I wanted you because you were pretty and sweet. You reminded me of my mother, Madelyn." He stood over her. His crotch lined perfectly in the crook of her legs. An ugly smile curved the one side of his mouth. "Your pretty brown hair lays nice and straight down your back—just like hers—with a little curl."

The clashing of her pulse intensified. Awareness of what he was about to do hit her like a locomotive. He was going to ravage and rape her—just like he had done to Nichole and all the others. It didn't matter that her sweated-through workout clothes clung to her body.

"But you're not sweet, are you?" he hollered. "You're a bitch. You think you're smart enough to stop me? You think you're strong enough to take me?"

Madelyn yanked on the ropes. They didn't give, not one little bit. She couldn't stop what was about to happen. But she could make sure he didn't enjoy it.

She would challenge him. She would be brave. And frankly, a little bit nuts. But she would be the opposite of what he wanted. Maybe she could drive him to the third act sooner. It was worth a try.

Madelyn stared into Adrian Tau's stone cold face. She clenched her teeth and poured her hatred through her gaze.

"I'm going to carve some sweetness into you. See if I can't persuade you to play along." He reached into the canvas duffle bag and pulled out a long blade. "This one isn't my favorite to work with, but it suits my purposes all the same."

The metal flashed inches from her face, reflecting the little bit of light in the room. Her distorted features reflected back. Why did she look so afraid?

"You will scream and you will beg." Anger laced his laugh. "Beg for your life, bitch."

She wouldn't.

He lowered the knife. The point scraped the top layer of skin over her collarbone. It flayed the fabric across her breast and across her stomach. Down it went on her left thigh—lighter now—to the bottom of her athletic shorts.

She gulped.

The knife gleamed as he twisted it and jabbed into the flesh of her leg.

Madelyn clamped her jaws together to keep her scream from escaping. She couldn't stop the tiny stream of tears that ran down her face.

Fire burned from her hip to the tips of her toes. Her body seized at the pain. He jerked the knife up under her shorts and cut them off of her with a Viking yell. Crimson dripped from the end of the knife. A tiny splatter landed on her tank and she was glad she couldn't see her legs.

It's now or never. She used the fear and anger to fuel her courage. "You are such a fucking coward! Ohhh, what a big strong man you are, having to tie women up and beat them. Nobody loves you. Is that it?"

His anger broke through the devil's facade and spewed out his mouth in a snarl. "Shut your mouth before I cut it off!"

"Nobody wants to fuck you so you tie them up and take what you want."

"Shut the fuck up," he screamed, slamming the knifepoint into the wood of the table two feet from her head.

A laugh slipped between her lips. She must be crazy. But her joyous chorus filled the poor room.

"Shut up! Shut up! Shut up!" His face flushed bright red.

"You're falling apart."

He focused all his demons on her. "Shut up!" His hands flew to her neck. He squeezed hard.

Madelyn tried to keep her neck muscles tight. She had to stay conscious, but there was nothing she could do. Her hands and feet were bound. She could not speak. She could not breathe. Her brilliant plan had backfired.

No chance at salvation. No goodbyes to the man she loved. No childhood scenes or major milestones ran through her thoughts. Nathan's beautiful face filled her mind. Clinging to the truth in his eyes, she surrendered.

Chapter Forty-eight

Nathan picked the rusted lock on the back door. Opening it without Tau hearing was the hard part. It took too much time Madelyn didn't have. A millimeter at a time he whispered the door open enough to squeeze through.

His upper lip furled at the wooden floor that ran the length of the hallway. Half the boards bowed like funky pasta. If he stepped on one, it'd be over. He played musical floorboards until he made it to the kitchenette.

At the sight of Madelyn bound to the table, he was a child again. The helplessness crippled him for the briefest of instances. And then he firmed his grip on the Glock in his hand.

Not so helpless.

He wavered over the next step to take.

Nathan squared the vicious killer in his sights, but wouldn't take the shot with the long blade in Tau's hand. The threat was too close to Madelyn's delicate skin.

He was a good shot. But with the slightest deviation Tau could kill her before he got another round off. What if he shot Tau and the monster didn't go down? The man was the size of a grizzly and it took larger guns than his to take those down. Panic toyed with Nathan's once unshakable resolve.

This was going to have to be a headshot with perfect accuracy.

Nathan could hardly believe his ears. Madelyn was goading the killer. The woman tied to the table with her life hanging in the balance antagonized the man with the knife.

Good girl, keep it up.

Tau's arm arched into the air. Nathan readied to empty the magazine in Tau's head, but hesitated. The man's aim was off. He wasn't going for Madelyn's head. He waited.

The knife impaled the table. Tau's hands wrapped around Madelyn's neck. Nathan exhaled, calculated, and fired.

The crack rang out. A hint of red developed on Tau's forehead. It splattered back like a Jackson Pollock masterpiece. His grip slipped from her neck. He hit the floor with a resounding thud.

Chapter Forty-nine

"The rumors are true." Nathan's crooked smile gave the sterile hospital room enough warmth to make her two-day stint bearable.

"The night nurse and doctor were gettin' it on in the supply closet last night?" Madelyn asked, surprised he'd been able to ferret out the information in such a short time.

"Nope. I think everyone is in the dark on that. We're the only ones who got a front row seat to the concert. You're getting discharged."

"Might as well. Listening was brutal when we couldn't give them a run for their money."

"Two weeks. Doctor's orders," he commanded in a scruffy whisper. "That little cut of yours is in a delicate spot."

"You can be gentle," she winked.

"Yeah, but that wouldn't have won us the gold with the competition."

"No, but it would have been nice to be a contestant."

His deep chuckle filled the room. "You're going to be the death of me, stubborn woman." He rounded the side of the bed and brushed a kiss across her forehead. Madelyn expected each one to be the last. The case, after all, was closed.

The techs uncovered a mass grave of animal bones and one set of human remains at Tau's family home. They also found the ropes, tools, and drugs he used to dispatch his victims, along with evidence that he'd set up Inman to take the fall.

Adrian Tau was dead. And Nathan's job was complete.

Madelyn grabbed the front of his shirt and pulled him down to her mouth. If any kiss could be the last, she might as well make them memorable.

"Oh, ah, excuse me." Madelyn's doctor stuttered in the doorway. The dark fingers of his free hand brushed at the grey gathered at his sideburn. Reluctantly, she released Nathan. Dr. Minna shuffled into the room. "I want to see you back here in five days to remove your stitches. If you have any complications, my number will be in your paperwork. As soon as the nurse finds a wheelchair, you and your fiancé are free to go."

Madelyn's jaw hit the hospital bed and she had to rehinge it to speak. "He isn't my fiancé."

"Sorry. I just thought, well, boyfriends usually just pop in for a while during the day. He's been by your side the entire time."

She didn't dare look at Nathan. "This is Special Agent Nathan Brewer with the FBI. He was guarding me and now he's just making sure I'm okay. It's his job."

She sounded like she was trying to convince herself. If the doctor or Nathan noticed neither mentioned it. Thank goodness.

"Well, now, I didn't see a ring or a badge." The doctor smiled sheepishly. "I just saw what I see before me. Two people who obviously, well...never mind." He must have seen the horror on her face. "I'll be going now. You call me if you need anything."

When the doctor's white lab coat disappeared around the corner Nathan turned to her. "Just a job?"

"Well, he took me by surprise. I didn't know what to say, but I didn't want him to get the wrong idea. And I am your job. Or rather, I *was* your job."

"You think I give all my cases this kind of special treatment?" Nathan grinned and shook his head.

"Well...I..."

He took her face in his hands and kissed her full on the lips. He pulled back too soon. "Let's get you home."

****

Home sounded like heaven to Madelyn. She longed for her dog, her shower, her clothes, her food, and her bed, with Nathan in it. When he stopped the Jeep in front of the villa she knew all her longings would have to wait. Except for Deacon. He didn't wait for anything. He barreled through the crowd, and jumped into the back of the Jeep.

When Nathan caught him he was on his way into her lap. "Easy, bud. I know you're excited, but she's still hurt a little." Deacon pushed his head past Nathan. "Sometimes he plays dumb. I know it."

"I'm so happy to see you too, brilliant man." She nuzzled against his face. "I'm glad Amadi used his ninja skill to sneak you into the hospital. But don't worry, we won't be going back there any time soon."

A group of twenty or more people crowded her front door. Some carried flowers, others food, and they all had huge smiles on their faces.

"What's going on?"

"Looks like a homecoming." Nathan brushed the back of her hand with his knuckles and she met his gaze. "You up to this?"

She nodded. "Come on, bud. It's now or never." Nathan helped her out of the car and tried to gather her into his arms. "Not in front of all these people," she whispered.

"Chicken."

"Maybe."

His body stuck to the left side of hers, bearing a large portion of her weight. When her right calf cramped halfway to the door she realized she was too stubborn for her own good sometimes.

Nathan and Deacon hung in the background as wave after wave of locals offered their gifts and well wishes. Madelyn and Nichole's students made up a great deal of the human mass. They were happy to know that justice had been given to the killer and that she would be football ready in only two weeks.

Ekene and Amadi showed, but after greeting Madelyn talked with Nathan until Nichole's mother and father walked into the living room. Most of the crowd left, giving her time to speak with them in privacy. They were grateful she'd been spared. They also thanked Nathan for his efforts. Nichole's mother kissed his hands repeatedly in praise. Her husband practically hauled her off him.

Some people wanted a blow-by-blow account of her heroic encounter, but she wasn't ready to share the terrifying details. It made them too real. If she kept them quiet inside and brushed them to the dark corner of her mind, she could sum it all up as a horrible nightmare.

Most visitors were pacified with the brush over of the main events. Only her trouble making students Sauda and Zuberi flocked to Nathan's side attempting to milk him for details. When he pulled out handcuffs they scattered.

The last of the crowd had finally sifted through when Jim's large frame entered the doorway. Nathan moved to the center of the kitchen, blocking him from Madelyn.

Jim looked a hundred years old. The polo he wore bagged around his large frame. His shoulders sloped forward and the muscles in his face drooped as though he would never smile again.

"Nathan, it's okay."

Nathan's gaze cut back to her and he stepped to the side, giving Jim just enough room to pass. She motioned for Jim to enter.

"Jim?"

He said nothing in reply. His head hung as he moved through the room toward her. The bundle of wild flowers he carried scraped against Nathan's arm, but he didn't seem to notice. His stare fixed on the framed photo in his other hand. He stopped several feet from the chair she'd been given in the middle of the crowd.

"I know I'm the last person you want to see right now, but I..." His blue eyes finally lifted. "Look, I don't expect you to forgive me. I don't think I'll ever forgive myself because what I did to Nichole—to the only person who ever really loved me, and the only person I ever loved—was unforgivable."

He swiped at his nose with the back of his hand. "Blame it on the parent, right? My father and mother were both functioning alcoholics. Still are. When he drank my dad used a 'heavy hand' as he called it. When I finally grew big enough to defend myself the abuse stopped—or rather changed hands. I never instigated the assaults, but I ended them, since I finally could. The physical abuse stopped when I reached high school. I don't know whether my father grew too tired or too drunk to carry on."

"From a young age, I swore I would never be like my father. The crazy thing is I also swore that I would make him proud of me. So..." His grip tightened on the flowers and his teeth gritted. Moisture gathered in his eyes.

Madelyn could see it was hard for him to talk about. Hell, she'd only told two people in her entire life and those people liked her. She couldn't image telling someone who'd built up a wall of hate for the last two years.

"Please continue," she whispered.

"I worked hard in high school and in college and graduated at the top of my class. When Nichole and I met I was working at the largest bank on Tortola. I was up for a promotion. We hadn't dated long when I asked her to marry me. I made sure she knew about my upbringing. Amazingly, she was okay with it."

He dropped his chin and his blond hair brushed against his forehead. "You see, we made a pact never to have children. I was terrified I'd hurt them like my father had hurt me. She agreed, but never thought I could do that to a child. I know she always hoped I would change my mind and we'd start a family. She always saw the best in me, even when it wasn't there."

"On my wedding night my father requested I take over the family business, his bank on Grand Cayman. It was a bank job like my first, I thought. The pay was better, way better, and we took it. When he showed me how to launder money I'd been there for two weeks. He funneled billions every year. I walked out and haven't talked to him since."

"My father cut me out of his life, told me I was a disappointment to the family. He also made some calls and made it impossible for me to get a job in the banking industry. And as sick as it sounds, I wish that I had broken the law for him. Not for the money, but for the approval I'll never get."

Behind Jim, Nathan tapped out a text on his phone. Knowing Jim's father had Nathan and the FBI on his heels, Madelyn breathed a little easier.

"I spiraled after that. Became everything that I hated. I hurt the woman I love. I ruined the life we'd built. Try as I might, there seemed to be nothing I could do to get back on track."

"I don't remember anything about that night. I woke up the next morning and there was blood everywhere... I wished I'd killed myself." His gaze hit the picture again. "I don't know how she ever found it in her heart to forgive me."

"But she did," Madelyn croaked the reminder for them both.

"Nichole was the best part of me, the only good part of me. And I miss her every second of every day." He stepped forward and extended the picture frame. "She would've wanted you to have this." He placed the frame in Madelyn's trembling hand.

The sun hanging low in the background didn't shine as brightly as the three gaping smiles. She, Deacon, and Nichole huddled together on the beach. Their feet disappeared in the sand and their arms—hers and Nichole's—made a tight circle.

Madelyn clutched the offering to her heart. Tears flowed over her cheeks. "Thank you."

Jim nodded, and then headed for the door. He placed the flowers on the kitchen table and turned back to Madelyn. "Thanks for listening." Then he left.

Chapter Fifty

Madelyn went to sleep that night cuddled in Nathan's arms. She thought the worst was behind her. Tau was dead and Jim had started the healing process. Instinctively, she stretched out in search of Nathan. They usually woke entwined in one another's arms. When her fingers didn't find the treasure they sought her eyes flew open.

The house was quiet. No sizzling noises came from the kitchen. The shower wasn't running. The smell of him faded from the sheets and the air. She jumped out of the bed, forgetting about her injury until the throbbing ensued. Ignoring it, she hobbled through the bedroom.

She peeked around her bedroom door, but didn't find him in the kitchen or living area. He wasn't in the bathroom or on the patio. His papers were not strewn across the kitchen table like the days before. Madelyn stood in front of the wardrobe and clutched to hope. She yanked the door back.

An empty space yawned where his bag had been.

It looked just like the one in the center of her chest.

Her knees gave out and she crumpled to the floor, staring at the vacant space. Numbness settled over her like a comforting blanket. Losing your heart should hurt more. She should scream and cry from the agony.

But if she cried she suspected she'd never stop. Madelyn resigned herself to the numbness, unable to think of all that she had lost in the span of a few weeks.

After a while she peeled herself off the floor and limped into the kitchen. She couldn't eat anything, but maybe Deacon was hungry. A small pile cluttered the island's counter top. Her chest expanded.

Immediately she recognized the Glock, but she moved closer to inspect the rest. The pile consisted of the gun, a cell phone, and a note. Madelyn braced herself on the counter's edge before she began.

The boss called and I had to fly to Miami. I couldn't bring myself to wake you. Keep these close. If you need anything, call me. - Nathan

Numbness shattered and anger pulled ahead. He didn't even say goodbye. Not even a parting kiss. Madelyn screamed like a wild animal. She ripped the note into shreds. Limp-running she hurried into the bedroom with the gun and her phone.

Call him? He hadn't even given her his number.

Madelyn thrust the two devices into the drawer of her nightstand and slammed it shut. How had she thought she'd be fine when he left? Maybe because she'd thought she'd have earned a proper goodbye.

She turned her attention to the bed. The pillow he used hung halfway over the edge. Madelyn snatched it and ripped the pillowcase off. Next came the sheets. She hurled them into the dirty clothes basket, and then replaced them with fresh linens. Pleased that the reminders of him were out of sight, she retreated to the shower to wash the scent of him away.

****

The next week flew by, despite her sterile attitude. She threw herself into work out of fear for idle time and her wondering mind. She'd actually contemplated flying to Miami, only she had no idea where he lived. She'd even looked up the FBI field office in Miami, but chickened out when she thought about how pathetic it would sound when she tried to explain why she needed to talk to him.

Since school was still out, she decided to work on the philanthropy that had been so dear to her and Nichole. She labored long hours each day to raise money for the new football field.

Each day she forced herself out of bed and into the shower. Dressed in her best professional outfits, she spent her days scouring the island for supporters. She used her cunning mind and good looks to wrangle two island hotels and three restaurants into pledging substantial donations to the cause. She also worked several local high rollers at the country club into donations.

Amadi came by every night to check on her. And after every visit Madelyn told him she was fine and he didn't have to trouble himself. But each night he showed up at her doorstep.

His visits were never long or intrusive. He talked to her about his business, his troubled students, or his man whore of a cousin. Madelyn liked to listen to his troubles. They made her forget hers for a time. And when she was being honest with herself she could admit that Amadi's company was comforting. It made her feel like she and Deacon weren't completely alone.

The night before Madelyn was due to have her stitches out she sat on her bed. Her hand rubbed over the puckered skin of her thigh. The cut made her think about the nightmare. Her mind drifted from one facet of it to another.

Soon, she began to think about Jim Gallow. She replayed his life story in her mind, lingering over the good parts and trying to understand the bad ones.

Suddenly, she realized it hurt her less to forgive Jim than to hold on to her hate for him. Jim wasn't innocent in the story of his life. He had free will to do with what he chose. He had repeatedly chosen wrong, but he was, in a sense, a scarred man. The wounds of a broken child had festered into his adulthood and continued to torment him.

Quickly, her mind jumped from Jim to Adrian Tau. She wondered what events in his life, if any, had led him astray. She wondered if he had been born a killer due to some cross wiring of the brain or made one by his universe. Had he been abused in childhood? Neglected?

She would never know the answers to her questions and yet she wanted to do something to make her world right again. Maybe she could help children overcome their scars. She could help them deal with their demons. And just maybe, they would not lose their way.

Then and there, Madelyn decided she was going to go back to school, get her Ph.D. in child psychology, and become a therapist. That was her way of making good come from this horrible situation. It could bring honor to the dead and hope for the living.

A new day dawned for Madelyn. She had some direction for her jumbled life and she was having her stitches removed. The stitches gone would be a sign of healing from the madness.

Chapter Fifty-one

Madelyn washed the day off of her body, and then toweled off. The soreness in her leg was bearable and the swelling had dissipated. But here in the quiet of her home she could finally admit her heart was broken. Life direction or not.

She wrapped in the fluffy white terry cloth and sat on the edge of the tub.

"Where's your phone?" A husky voice boomed from across the room.

Madelyn's heart jumped into her throat, blocking her scream. His burly frame towered in the bedroom doorway. And she was immediately more terrified than she'd been during her encounter with Adrain Tau.

She feared if she blinked the man she loved would disappear. She was afraid that her sanity had snapped and her mind was giving her exactly what she wanted.

"Where's your phone?" he barked.

"In the night stand." She squeaked the words through a constricted throat.

Nathan turned his back on her, stalked to the bedside, and yanked open the drawer. He pulled it from the depths and stomped back to the doorway. His finger depressed the on button so hard she thought it might break. The screen lit his scowl.

"Would you look at that? Fifty-seven missed calls." He held the phone out to her...like she could see it from across the room.

She finally found her voice. "What are you doing?" Well, kind of. The force she'd been going for fell flat. But considering the circumstances...

Nathan took a step into the doorway and dropped his duffle bag. Two day's growth hid his dimple and gave him an air of danger. Or was that his narrowed eyes?

He shoved a hand through his hair. "I get that you're mad. I should've woken you, but you could've at least answered one of my calls. You could've tried to hear me out. You could've called me."

"Call you?" she shouted and surged to her feet. "I didn't even have your number."

His lips pursed.

At least the scowl was gone.

"Any one of these seven-five-three numbers would've done the trick. Or you could've used my cell number, which I saved into your contacts before I left."

"My what?"

"Your contacts. Your phone book inside your phone."

"They have those?"

"Seriously?" His eyebrows grazed the ceiling.

"I've never had a cell phone." She threw up her hands.

"Never?"

"No. My grandmother never had one and my mom wouldn't let me have one. When I was finally out on my own I didn't have anyone to call."

"Well, if you'd known how to use the damn thing, would you have called me?"

"No," she lied.

"Why not?"

"Because I'm mad at you."

"Why?"

"Because you broke my heart, you big jerk."

He crossed the room in two strides and knelt in front of her barely covered body. "I'm mad at you, too."

"Me? Why?"

"Every time I called it went straight to voicemail. I had to get Amadi to come check on you, so I knew you were okay. You stubborn pain in my ass."

His scent filled her lungs and her heart raced. With his face only inches from hers she longed to kiss him, to touch him, to slap the crap out of him for hurting her. The confusion of emotions ordered her to remain still, motionless and quiet, while her brain worked overtime. There were so many things that she wanted to know. So many things she needed to know.

Nathan was quick. Before she knew it he had her hand in his grip. She tried to wiggle it free, but he held tight.

"Madelyn, ask me why I left?"

"No," she said...stubbornly.

"Please."

"Fine. Why did you leave me?"

"I left you because I had to go to Miami. I had to review and sign off on the final case report."

Madelyn narrowed her eyes at the lame excuse. She inhaled to let him have it, but he continued.

"I also had to talk to my mother."

"Your mother. Why? I mean, of course you'd talk to her, but why are you telling me—"

"I had to talk to her to get something."

She was still no clearer on his justification for leaving her heartbroken and alone without so much as a goodbye.

Nathan pulled a small, antique box from his pocket and held it out to her. Breath caught in her throat. He opened the lid. A delicate white-gold band scrawled with intricate loops and vines to the base of a solitary round diamond against black satin. Its clear shimmer flecked wildly in the low light of her room.

"This ring belonged to my great-grandmother. She and my great-grandfather lived sixty-seven years of marriage dedicated to one another... through good times and bad." He pulled her chin up to meet his gaze.

"Madelyn Garrett, I am in love with you. I'd like to spend the rest of my life with you, through the bad and the good to come. Marry me?"

She could not hold still any longer. She flew into his arms as the tears streamed down her face. She clutched him so tight and so fast that they both sailed back. They sprawled over the tile floor. Madelyn buried her face in his chest and never wanted to let him go. When he peeled her up from his warmth she tried to fight him.

"Are you going to answer me?" he asked in a gruff voice.

She nodded, clawing her way back to him. "Yes!"

He didn't let her pass. "Was that a yes you'll answer me or a yes you'll marry me?"

She shut him up with a kiss so hot and passionate it left them both panting. Her hands cupped his face. "Yes, I'll marry you. But you should know as of the end of the school year, I'll be an unemployed PHD student. And—"

His lips cut her off, and she fell into his safe arms. He pulled back, breathless. "I think I can handle a saucy co-ed in my bed." He placed the ring on her third finger, scooped her up, and then laid her on the bed. "Or yours."

Epilogue

"I, Nathan Reed Brewer, take you, Madelyn Haines Garrett, to be my wife, to have and to hold from this day forward, for better, for worse, for richer, for poorer, in sickness and in health, to love and to cherish, until we are parted by death. This is my solemn vow."

Madelyn remembered looking onto the rolling azure water and cotton candy sunsets when she'd lived on Tortola and thinking she'd never seen or heard anything more beautiful.

How wrong she'd been.

The sky faded from yellow to fluffy pink. The waves washed onto the shore. And yet, she couldn't spare them a single glance. She could have married Nathan in a white washed courthouse or here in paradise. The setting didn't matter after all.

Planning a wedding tested every one of her student-hardened nerves. Added to the endeavors of doctorate level schooling, house hunting—since Deacon didn't get along with the front doorman—and planning from a distance, it had been quite a bit harder than she had ever imagined.

And for what?

The ring he slid onto her finger didn't matter. Nor did the ring she slid on his, though she did like the look of it.

Taken, ladies.

His attentive dark eyes. His sturdy shoulders. His dimple and square jaw. His love. He was all that mattered.

The preacher announced them husband and wife. The crowd of their friends and family applauded.

Oh, but wait, the kiss...

Nathan stepped forward. His hand cupped her nape while his other hooked around her waist. He pulled her to his mouth and kissed the breath right out of her. The man of God coughed. So, of course, he dipped her low and deepened the mating of their mouths.

When the whoops and hollers of the crowd grew to record highs Nathan straightened, but kept her close.

The crowd dispersed into Harvey Thompson's beach-front mansion for the reception. When she'd found out Harvey's home was the one on the beach where Nathan had first attacked her she'd overcome her embarrassment about their first meeting—with Nichole's angel for support—and had booked his restaurant for the catering too.

"I love you," she whispered.

"I love you."

His smile... She sighed like a sap.

Blooming ginger plants and lobster claws lined the path leading into the mansion's reception area. Loud cheers and music boomed through the massive carved wood doors.

Nathan tugged her into his arms and smoothed a kiss over her lips. "Well, Mrs. Brewer, it sounds like we're missing a good party."

Madelyn tried to hide her blush against his stunning suit. It was her first time to hear her new name and it startled her. He wouldn't let Madelyn shroud herself in his chest. He grabbed her chin and tilted it up. His gaze kept dropping to her mouth. "Are you ready for this?"

"Not if you keep looking at me like that."

He pinched her bottom and she squealed. "Do we have to go in?"

A burly voice from behind answered her before Nathan could. "Yes! If I have to be here, so do you two." Keen Hunt laid his huge hand out for his partner.

Nathan shook his hand. "Good to see you."

Keen turned his clear blue eyes on her. He extended her his hand, and when she grabbed it he tugged her from Nathan's arms, and spun her around. The ivory silk organza of the Monique Lhuillier gown whirled like a rich dessert. The pleated bodice of the strapless masterpiece moved with her, while the rose embroidered A-line skirt swayed past her and coiled back again.

"Madelyn," Keen bowed his head. "You are the most beautiful bride I have ever seen."

"She is," Nathan agreed. "But she is also the only bride you have ever seen."

"True. I don't make a habit of attending *these* kinds of functions." Keen nodded.

Madelyn hugged the athletic man around the waist. "Hey, good lookin, I didn't think you were going to make it. Wasn't the treatment center supposed to keep you busy with rehab for a couple more weeks?"

Keen gave Madelyn a sly smile she recognized from her short time in Miami. "They decided to let me go early." He half-shrugged his good shoulder.

"He's a fugitive," Nathan chimed.

"Look, they were lucky to have kept me as long as they did." Keen shoved his hands in his pockets.

"So," Nathan began. "What's next?"

"After the festivities here, I'll hop on a plane and take off for a few weeks. I need to leave it all behind for a while." Situating his suit jacket over his tender and broad shoulder, Keen continued. "But don't worry. I'll be back at work making your life hell about the time you get back from your honeymoon."

He put emphasis on the word honeymoon. He arched his eyebrow and gave Madelyn a grin that made her blush. Boy, she was an easy target for these two boys.

Keen turned to the door. "Now enough about me. Let's go celebrate!" He threw open the doors and the small crowd erupted in cheers.

The band announced, "Mrs. Madelyn Brewer and Mr. Nathan Brewer."

For the next hour they were passed around from hug to hug through the small, yet imposing legion of well-wishers.

Madelyn's former students gathered around, thrilled to see her again. They all made a painstaking effort to impress her with their fancy attire and manners. She missed them so much and spent time catching up.

Amadi and Ekene had been to Miami to visit her and Nathan's new digs, but it had been nearly a month since she had seen them. So, they enjoyed their time together, dancing and laughing.

Nathan's mother, April, showed up with her man friend, Howard. Her poor husband—*wow, she had a husband*—referred to him as her "boy toy" when his mom wasn't around. The hottie was young enough to be Nathan's brother. It didn't matter to him that the man was a psychologist with a highly reputable practice in Miami. But, with some prodding from her and the permanent smile on April's face, he took it in his stride.

Madelyn and April were well on their way to a truly great mother and daughter-in-law relationship. They'd grown close in the short time she'd been in the States. From Nathan, to helping victims of trauma, their interest aligned. And they were both pretty darn stubborn.

Nathan's family from Georgia even made the trip to attend. Madelyn watched now-you-just-call-me-Uncle-Preston twirl his wife, Sarah, across the dance floor.

"Don't look too long, or else they'll have you out there dancing until your feet fall off."

Madelyn turned to find the most vibrant red hair she'd ever seen. It cascaded down the fine-boned features of a woman very near her age. "Thanks for the tip. My dance card is about full, especially in these heels. Barefoot on the beach was the way to go."

"It was a lovely ceremony. I can't believe you lived here and gave it up for my smelly cousin." She smiled and Madelyn noticed the sprinkling of freckles on the apples of her cheeks. "I'm Ava Shepherd."

"Madelyn Gar...Brewer. Well, that's going to take some getting used to."

"I can't even imagine."

"It's so nice to meet you. I'm glad you were able to make it."

Ava placed her hand over her chest. "I'm just sorry we missed the rehearsal dinner. It's Ford's fault. I swear, I don't know how my brother is so good at his job when he can't get anywhere on time."

"It's because I'm so good at my job I can't get anywhere on time." Ford, Madelyn guessed, bumped shoulders with Ava.

"Always so humble." His sister rolled her eyes.

"Wife, I see you've meet the hell raisers of my youth." Nathan stepped behind her and wrapped his arms around her middle.

"I think they're still perfectly capable of raising hell," Madelyn corrected.

"I like her already." Ford winked and held out his hand. "Welcome to the family." He patted the back of her hand.

"What kept you from free steak and lobster?" Nathan asked.

"A loony with a pipe bomb and four hostages." Ford crossed his arms as casually as if he were talking about a shot off the back nine.

"You're in law enforcement too?" Madelyn awed.

"I can't believe they let him in either, Madelyn." Keen stepped into the circle. He held his hand flat at about crotch level. "Yeah, they lowered the bar the day they let this kid join."

The two men exchanged ultra-slow-mo punches to the kidney and jaw.

"Wow, the mean age just dropped a few decades." Ava looked down her nose at them.

"Oh, come on," Keen scoffed.

"Don't make me make you squawk like a chicken in front of all these people," Ford warned.

"What was that?" Keen put his hand to his ear. "The sun's rising? The roosters are crowing."

Madelyn had no idea what they were talking about, but already her sides cramped with laughter at the look of horror on Ava's face.

They both stalked toward her one step.

"I swear, I deal with psychopaths all day." Ava's stark green eyes narrowed. "I don't need crazies while I'm on vacation."

They took another step toward her.

"I'll hold her. You tickle her," Ford said.

"No way. Last time I held her and got clobbered in the goods, while you ran away like a sissy." Keen put up his hands.

Nathan's laugher filled her ear and his heaving chest rocked her back and forth. He wiped tears of laugher from his cheeks. "He ran," Nathan wheezed out the words, "because Ava...threatened to tell Aunt Sarah...where he kept his girlie mags."

"How old were y'all?" Madelyn asked.

"College." Ava clamped her lips together fighting back a laugh.

Then Keen and Ford both doubled over in laughter.

"So, Ava, what do you do that you deal with psychopaths all day?" Madelyn wanted to know.

"The Bureau." The porcelain-skinned beauty smiled sweetly.

"Seriously? Did y'all make a pact as kids or something?" Madelyn put her hands on her hips and looked at them one at a time.

Nathan wove his fingers in between hers. "We all have our own reasons for joining."

"Okay, I know why Nathan joined the Bureau. And I'm ninety-eight percent certain you two boys joined so you could shoot bad guys. But Ava, what made you join the FBI?"

Ava's green eyes widened in surprise. "I assumed you knew."

"It's your story to tell, Av, not mine," Nathan told her.

Nathan's big hand settled on her shoulders and turned her to face him. "Love, it's not exactly wedding appropriate conversation." When she narrowed her eyes at him, Nathan leaned down and kissed her. "It's a long story. There'll be plenty of time to tell it, since we're at the beginning of our forever."

PAINTED WALLS
A BUREAU NOVEL

Deadly daddy-issues.

The Blood-Red Killer, America's most notorious serial killer, tucked Supervisory Special Agent Ava Shepherd into bed every night with a bedtime story and a kiss on the cheek.

Thirty years after his apprehension, Ava—still running from his memory—becomes the prime suspect for a murder eerily similar to the ones her father committed all those years ago. Shattered by the accusation, Ava reluctantly accepts former flame Special Agent Kenneth Hunt's assistance in clearing her name.

Kenneth is on the mend, and though their fling is ancient history, the bruises Ava left on his heart throb in her presence. He'll help her, but she'll have to play by his rules.

When the body count and undeniable heat rise, Ava must face the demons of her past and present—or be consumed by them.

ENEMY MINE
A BASE BRANCH NOVEL

When friends become enemies and enemies become lovers.

Born in the blood of Sierra Leone's Civil War, enslaved, then sold to the US as an orphan, Base Branch operative Sloan Harris is emotionally dead and driven by vengeance. With no soul to give, her body becomes the bargaining chip to infiltrate a warlord's inner circle. The man called The Devil killed her family and helped destroy a region.

As son of the warlord, Baine Kendrick will happily use Sloan's body if it expedites his father's demise. Yet, he is wholly unprepared for the possessive and protective emotions she provokes. Maybe it's the flashes of memory ... two forgotten children drawing in the dirt beneath the boabab tree... But he fears there is more at stake than his life.

In the Devil's den with Baine by her side, Sloan braves certain death and discovers a spirit for living.

Megan Mitcham was born and raised among the live oaks and shrimp boats of the Mississippi Gulf Coast, where her enormous family still calls home. She attended college at the University of Southern Mississippi where she received a bachelor's degree in curriculum, instruction, and special education. For several years Megan worked as a teacher in Mississippi. She married and moved to South Carolina and began working for an international non-profit organization as an instructor and co-director.

In 2009 Megan fell in love with books. Until then, books had been a source for research or the topic of tests. But one day she read *Mercy* by Julie Garwood. And oh, Mercy, she was hooked!

Megan lives in Southern Arkansas where she pens heart pounding romantic thriller novels and window-steaming erotic romance. For information on releases and giveaways subscribe at meganmitcham.com!

Facebook: MeganMitchamAuthor
Twitter: @MeganMMMitcham
Pinterest: MeganMitcham5
Goodreads: Megan_Mitcham
Website: www.meganmitcham.com

FOR INFORMATION ON NEW RELEASES & GIVEAWAYS, SIGN UP FOR MEGAN'S NEWSLETTER AT WWW.MEGANMITCHAM.COM.

www.ingramcontent.com/pod-product-compliance
Lightning Source LLC
Chambersburg PA
CBHW070648180626
46817CB00006B/2281